MW00850230

Sinfully Daring

The Daring Daughters Book 12

By Emma V. Leech

Published by Emma V. Leech.

Copyright (c) Emma V. Leech 2022

Editing Services Magpie Literary Services

Cover Art: Victoria Cooper

ASIN No:

ISBN No: 978-2-492133-48-0

About Me!

I started this incredible journey way back in 2010 with The Key to Erebus but didn't summon the courage to hit publish until October 2012. For anyone who's done it, you'll know publishing your first title is a terribly scary thing! I still get butterflies on the morning a new title releases, but the terror has subsided at least. Now I just live in dread of the day my daughters are old enough to read them.

The horror! (On both sides, I suspect.)

2017 marked the year that I made my first foray into Historical Romance and the world of the Regency Romance, and my word what a year! I was delighted by the response to this series and can't wait to add more titles. Paranormal Romance readers need not despair, however, as there is much more to come there too. Writing has become an addiction and as soon as one book is over, I'm hugely excited to start the next so you can expect plenty more in the future.

As many of my works reflect, I am greatly influenced by the beautiful French countryside in which I live. I've been here in the Southwest since 1998, though I was born and raised in England. My three gorgeous girls are all bilingual and my husband Pat, myself, and our four cats consider ourselves very fortunate to have made such a lovely place our home.

KEEP READING TO DISCOVER MY OTHER BOOKS!

Other Works by Emma V. Leech

Daring Daughters

Daring Daughters Series

Girls Who Dare

Girls Who Dare Series

Rogues & Gentlemen

Rogues & Gentlemen Series

The Regency Romance Mysteries

The Regency Romance Mysteries Series

The French Vampire Legend

The French Vampire Legend Series

The French Fae Legend

The French Fae Legend Series

Stand Alone
The Book Lover (a paranormal novella)
The Girl is Not for Christmas (Regency Romance)

Audio Books

Don't have time to read but still need your romance fix? The wait is over…

By popular demand, get many of your favourite Emma V Leech Regency Romance books on audio as performed by the incomparable Philip Battley and Gerard Marzilli. Several titles available and more added each month!

Find them at your favourite audiobook retailer!

Acknowledgements

Thanks, of course, to my wonderful editor Kezia Cole with Magpie Literary Services

To Victoria Cooper for all your hard work, amazing artwork and above all your unending patience!!! Thank you so much. You are amazing!

To my BFF, PA, personal cheerleader and bringer of chocolate, Varsi Appel, for moral support, confidence boosting and for reading my work more times than I have. I love you loads!

A huge thank you to all of Emma's Book Club members! You guys are the best!

I am always so happy to hear from you so do email or message me :)

emmavleech@orange.fr

To my husband Pat and my family … For always being proud of me.

Table of Contents

Family Trees

House of Bedwin
To Dare a Duke

Robert Adolphus Duke of Bedwin *m.* Prunella Adolphus nee Chuffington-Smythe

Lady Elisabeth b.1815

Jules Marquess of Blackstone b.1819

Lady Victoria b.1825

Lord Harry b.1833

Lady Charlotte b.1817

Lady Rosamund b.1823

Lord Frederick b.1827

Lady Octavia b.1838

m.

Cassius Cadogan Viscount Oakley b.1815

???

Nicolas Alexandre Demarteau

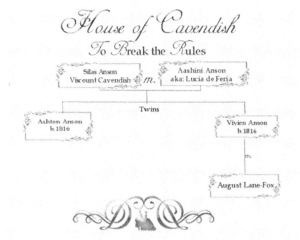

House of Cavendish
To Break the Rules

Silas Anson Viscount Cavendish *m.* Aashini Anson aka: Lucia de Feria

Twins

Ashton Anson b.1816

Vivien Anson b.1816

m.

August Lane-Fox

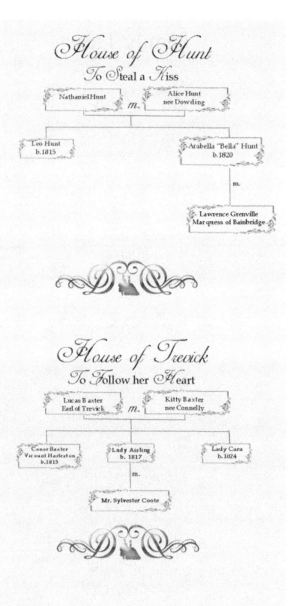

House of Hunt
To Steal a Kiss

Nathaniel Hunt *m.* Alice Hunt nee Dowding

Leo Hunt b.1815

Arabella "Bella" Hunt b.1820

m.

Lawrence Grenville Marquess of Bainbridge

House of Trevick
To Follow her Heart

Lucas Baxter Earl of Trevick *m.* Kitty Baxter nee Connelly

Conor Baxter Viscount Harleston b.1815

Lady Aisling b. 1817

Lady Cara b.1824

m.

Mr. Sylvester Coote

House of St Clair
To Wager with Love

Jasper Cadogan
Earl of St Clair

m.

Harriet Cadogan
nee Stanhope

Cassius Cadogan
Viscount Oakley
b. 1815

m.

Lady Charlotte Adolphus
b. 1817

House of Cadogan
To Dance with a Devil

Jerome Cadogan

m.

Bonnie Cadogan
nee Campbell

Twins

Greer Cadogan
b. 1817

Elspeth Cadogan
b. 1817

Alana Cadogan
b. 1825

m.

Daire "Dare" Kelburn
Viscount Roxborough

m.

Raphe Coote
Baron de Ligne
b. 1811

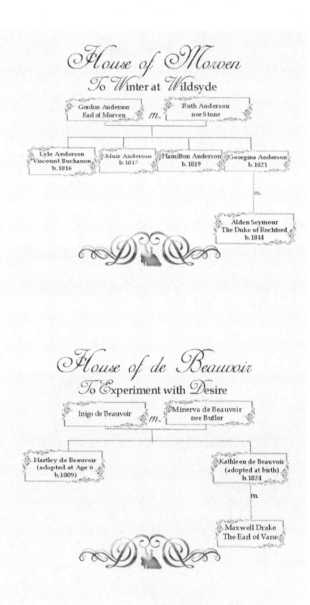

House of Morven
To Winter at Wildsyde

Gordon Anderson
Earl of Morven

m.

Ruth Anderson
nee Stone

Lyle Anderson
Viscount Buchanon
b. 1816

Muir Anderson
b. 1817

Hamilton Anderson
b. 1819

Georgina Anderson
b. 1821

m.

Alden Seymour
The Duke of Rochford
b. 1814

House of de Beauvoir
To Experiment with Desire

Inigo de Beauvoir

m.

Minerva de Beauvoir
nee Butler

Hartley de Beauvoir
(adopted at Age 6
b. 1809)

Kathleen de Beauvoir
(adopted at birth)
b. 1824

m.

Maxwell Drake
The Earl of Vane

House of Rothborn
To Bed the Baron

Solo Weston
Baron of Rothborn

m.

Jemima Weston
nee Fernside

Laskin Weston
b.1816

Grace Weston
b.1821

m.

Mr Sterling Oak
b. 1813

House of Knight
To Ride with the Knight

Gabriel Knight

m.

Lady Helena Knight
nee Adolphus

Florence Knight
b.1817

Evie Knight
b.1822

Felix Knight
b.1824

Emmaline Knight
b.1826

m.

Henry Stanhope
b.1799

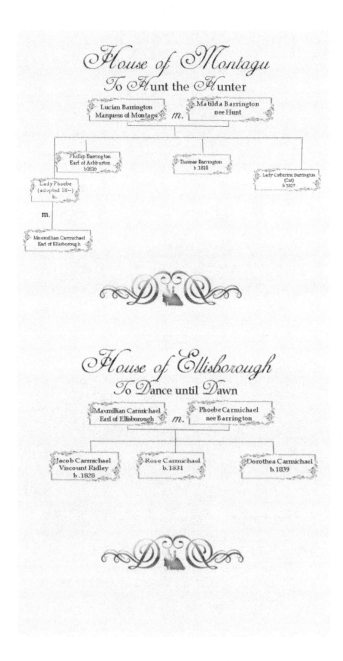

House of Montagu
To Hunt the Hunter

Lucian Barrington
Marquess of Montagu

m.

Matilda Barrington
nee Hunt

Phillip Barrington
Earl of Ashburton
b.1816

Thomas Barrington
b.1818

Lady Catherine Barrington
(Cat)
b.1827

Lady Phoebe
(adopted 18--)
b.

m.

Maximillian Carmichael
Earl of Ellisborough

House of Ellisborough
To Dance until Dawn

Maximillian Carmichael
Earl of Ellisborough

m.

Phoebe Carmichael
nee Barrington

Jacob Carmichael
Viscount Ridley
b.1828

Rose Carmichael
b.1831

Dorothea Carmichael
b.1839

Chapter 1

Dearest Aggie,

Papa has agreed we may host a grand garden party this summer, here at Dern. He hardly ever likes to entertain here, so this is a remarkable occurrence. Even better, I have secured invitations for you and your guardian! I can't wait.

I am so excited for you to be here, for it is to be a lavish affair with everyone invited, even Lord Kilbane! Papa refused to let him come but Mama insists we cannot be so rude as to cut him for it will cause a stir. Papa says he's perfectly content to cause a stir, but Mama told him he must not. He scowled an awful lot until mother promised to make it up to him. I suggested she have the kitchens make his favourite biscuits, but she just smiled and said to leave Papa to her.

—Excerpt of a letter from Lady Catherine 'Cat' Barrington (daughter of Lucian and Matilda Barrington, The Most Hon'ble Marquess and Marchioness of Montagu) to her friend, Miss Agatha Smith.

4th June 1842, The Fashionable Hour, Hyde Park, London.

Rosamund reached down and patted her mare's smooth neck. Melody preened under her touch and shook her glossy head. She had every right to look smug, however, for she was a beautiful creature, jet black save for a white star on her forehead, and she was behaving impeccably, which was more than could be said for some.

"If people do not have the decency to learn to ride properly and pick a mount that suits their abilities, they ought not be allowed out," her father grumbled beside her as they walked their mounts down Rotten Row.

On a fine June afternoon during the Fashionable Hour, the entire *ton* seemed to have come out to enjoy the sunshine, to chatter and pose and feel well pleased with themselves.

Rosamund followed his gaze to where a slender young man was struggling to control a large bay gelding. The beast was sweating and prancing about, clearly unused to the crowds and the man on his back was not helping the situation by shouting at the poor creature.

"Look at that blasted fool. He ought never to have brought that poor animal out in this throng."

"He or the horse are going to get hurt," Rosamund fretted, noticing how the animal's anxiety was upsetting others around it

"Sir. I say, you there!" her father bellowed, until the young man stopped berating his horse long enough to look up. He paled dramatically upon seeing who had addressed him. Well, a duke had that effect on people, even when he wasn't looking irritated. "Take that poor animal back home. He's too much for you and you're going to get yourself killed, or some other poor blighter. Go on. Off with you!"

Rosamund kept her eyes firmly on the path ahead of her, mortified on behalf of the foolish young man. He hardly needed to be humiliated further by seeing her watching him too.

"Papa," she admonished as they rode on. "Could you not have been a little more discreet?"

"No," he said shortly. "The fellow needs to know he can't act in such a reckless fashion without consequences. Perhaps next time he'll think twice."

"Well said, your grace," said an amused voice from beside them. "Lady Rosamund, a pleasure."

Rosamund turned, pleased to see Viscount Hargreaves on a handsome chestnut gelding.

"Good day to you, my lord."

Hargreaves smiled, tipping his hat to her before turning back to her father. "I am grateful you stepped in, for you saved me the trouble. The fool is my cousin and a great favourite of my wife's. It would not have gone down well if I had been the one to tear him off a strip yet again."

"Well met, Hargreaves," her father said with a nod. "And I am happy to be of assistance. Can you not find a more suitable mount for the idiot?"

Lord Hargreaves grimaced. "I have provided several more suitable mounts, to no avail. Sadly, he insists on pretending he can handle a highly strung devil like Baron there. I have intervened frequently but my most diplomatic attempts at good advice only seem to make matters worse."

"Hmph," Papa replied, disgruntled. "Ah, there's St Clair. Excuse me, Hargreaves, I must have a word."

Papa cantered ahead to catch up with the earl, leaving Rosamund with Lord Hargreaves.

"Well, this is fortuitous," he said, his brown eyes twinkling. "I despaired of ever finding you in this melee."

Rosamund looked at him in surprise. "You were looking for me?"

Hargreaves nodded, his eyes twinkling. "Your quarry is here, my lady."

"My…?" Rosamund's mouth dropped open, and she felt herself turn pink.

He was speaking of the Marquess of Montagu's eldest son, Lord Ashburton.

His lordship chuckled. "Oh, come, come. I'm only teasing you. The object of every well-bred young lady is to find a suitable husband. I'm quite certain you would rather be off doing something more interesting, but there's no denying the truth. Your father brought you here to be seen and admired by all the eligible young men, did he not?"

"He did," Rosamund admitted. "Begrudgingly, I might tell you, for he does not want me to marry yet, but must you be so blunt? It quite puts one to the blush."

Hargreaves shrugged, though he looked a little sheepish. "I beg your pardon. I have fallen into the habit of plain speaking, for I discover I prize the truth above all things, but you are quite correct. I shall endeavour to be a little less forthright."

Rosamund stared at him for a long moment, frowning.

"Now what have I said?" he asked, laughing at her consternation.

"Well, I was just thinking that it might be nice to speak to someone who always says exactly what they think. Instead of wrapping everything up in polite nonsense," she said frankly.

He grinned at her. "Careful, my lady. You do not realise what a monster you'll unleash with such permission to speak my mind."

"I never said I gave you permission," she countered, putting her nose in the air, before slanting him a sideways look to discover him laughing. He had a good laugh, warm and deep and it made her smile.

"Then I shall bombard you with compliments and prattle on about the latest *on dits*, like every other fellow here. Did you see the scandal sheets' reports of last night's ball? We can discuss that, or shall I recite poetry for you, my lady? Something to soothe your spirits after my terrible behaviour?"

"Certainly not," she said in disgust. "I think I prefer your plain speaking."

"Even if I ruffle your pretty feathers?"

"Even then."

"Marvellous," he said. "Now then, where… Ah, yes, there he is, with his father. Shall we?"

Rosamund looked ahead of them to where Montagu was riding with his two sons. She hesitated, feeling silly.

"Lady Rosamund."

Hargreaves' voice was softer now, his expression kind. "He's a decent fellow and you are a lovely young woman. We are only going to say good day."

Rosamund narrowed her eyes at him. "That's not what you said at last night's ball. You said you intended to make Pip believe you had… had…."

"Unspeakable designs upon your innocence to spark his protective instincts?" he suggested as her courage failed her, preventing her from speaking so bluntly as he.

She gave a taut nod. "Yes. *That*. Is it still what you plan?"

He shrugged. "I'm not suggesting I twirl my moustache and threaten to carry you off to my lair in his hearing, no. Forthright I may be, but I'm not a fool. And I certainly don't want any but Ashburton to believe such a thing of me. Let us see how the land lies first, hmmm?"

Rosamund studied him for a long moment, seeing only a sincere desire to help her in his expression, despite the amused glint in his eyes.

"Very well."

She followed him as he trotted ahead.

"Lady Rosamund, how do you do?" Montagu said greeting her warmly, as they drew alongside. "I didn't get the chance to speak to you last night."

"No, you were too busy dancing with your lovely wife," Hargreaves replied with a grin, tipping his hat at the marquess. "I can't say I blame you."

"I shouldn't, considering you danced with her too," Montagu replied dryly.

"Afternoon, Hargreaves, Rosamund," Thomas Barrington called, lifting his hat to them and smiling.

"Pip," Montagu said sharply, rousing the attention of his eldest son, Lord Ashburton, who was riding farthest from them and appeared somewhat distracted.

"What?" Pip demanded impatiently, before realising who had spoken to him and paling a degree. "I beg your pardon, sir. Hargreaves, Lady Rosamund, good day to you both. Forgive me, I was wool-gathering."

"It's of no matter," Hargreaves said easily. "Did you enjoy last night's ball? I think I saw you dance once," he offered, sending Pip a mischievous grin.

Pip glowered at him, glancing at his father, whose face was impassive. "I was not in the mood for dancing."

"A pity," Rosamund said, quirking an eyebrow. "When so many of us ladies were languishing for partners of less than six decades. If you will attend a ball, you might remember why you are there now and then."

"I do qualify for that list, I might remind you," Hargreaves told her sternly.

Rosamund bit back a smile, endeavouring to reply with equal gravity. "Ah, yes, though you did not ask me either, but I am remembering now that you are not quite ancient, my lord, only *almost*."

"Almost *thirty*, my lady, and not until next year," he said, shaking his head sadly. "And I was too terrified to ask for a dance from such a dazzling vision for fear of rejection. A fellow's confidence is easily wounded, especially when the lady makes no demur about telling him he is an old nincompoop."

"I never said you were a nincompoop," Rosamund pointed out, her expression grave.

Lord Hargreaves spluttered with feigned indignation. "Pip, this creature is dreadfully cruel to me. Take her away, will you?"

Pip frowned at them both. "He's only nine and twenty, Ozzie. Hardly in his dotage. Why didn't you dance with him if you were lacking for partners? Thorn would have danced with you, too. Why didn't you ask?"

"I wasn't …. He never—" she began, exasperated, before giving up. "Oh, never mind."

She bade Montagu and Thomas a good day and cantered down the row until she was by herself, then slowed to a walk. A moment later, Hargreaves appeared beside her.

"You see how it is," she said, shaking her head and laughing, for what else was there to do? "He's oblivious."

"I do see… *Ozzie*?" he added, grinning.

Rosamund blushed. "My family calls me that, and close friends."

He chuckled, clearly enjoying her embarrassment, the wretch. "Well, your father is there with St Clair. You catch up with him and I'll go back and work on young Pip."

"Work on him how?" she asked, a little suspicious of what he might say.

"Leave it with me," he said airily, before tipping his hat to her and riding off again.

5th June 1842, Mrs Digby-Jones' Ball, London.

Sebastian walked up the steps and into the lavish foyer of yet another grand house. He greeted his hostess politely, his wife's hand resting lightly upon his arm. In a moment they would go their separate ways, her to spend the evening bathing in the attention of whatever hapless fool she could enslave with her beautiful face and figure, and him to the far end of whatever godforsaken ballroom he was doomed to inhabit for the evening. Anywhere he didn't have to look at her. Once upon a time, a single glance at Adelia's face would have made him tremble with longing too, but that was the effect she had in the first weeks and months of knowing her. It took far longer to discover that what lay beneath the lovely exterior was cold and hard. It was still difficult to believe she'd had an affair with another man, for she found the physical aspects of love distasteful. Most of the *ton* thought she cuckolded him regularly, but the truth was rather different.

Adelia thrived on adoration. She wanted to be loved unconditionally, beyond reason and sanity, until that love became too real, too human and messy. Then it was unpleasant and tedious, and she could not get free of you quickly enough. She had been all too happy to give up on her lover, the poor devil. A romantically inclined artist of some repute, he'd been heartbroken, and Adelia only too relieved when Sebastian took her to France until the scandal died down.

It suited her to be married, for it placed a barrier around her that meant she could flirt and behave outrageously and then back off, apparently for fear of her husband's wrath. To begin with, there might have been truth in that. In the early years of their marriage, she had driven him close to madness, causing him heartache and jealousy and inspiring fights and scenes enough to fill a hundred scandal sheets, but no longer. He was weary of her games and could only pity the unfortunate men who got entangled with her. She had broken too many hearts for him to count, and his interference only ended with more scandalous headlines that he could well do without.

He sometimes wondered if things might have been different if fate had blessed them with children, but he could not force his attentions on a woman who made no secret that she found his touch repellent. Sebastian had been patient and as kind as he knew how to be, but she would not allow him near her. He'd considered an annulment, but the humiliation and the scandal would be appalling, and then the realisation of what would become of Adelia if he carried such an act through stayed his hand. Their relationship deteriorated as Adelia's behaviour became increasingly scandalous and Sebastian resigned himself to the fact he had made a mesalliance. So, there was no heir. The title would go to his foolish cousin when Sebastian died. Though the title itself didn't bother him so much, the fact he would never have sons or daughters of his own was a source of private sorrow Sebastian tried to assuage with social activity and friends. That strategy would work a deal better if propriety and society's wagging tongues didn't force him to escort his wife occasionally for the sake of appearances.

So, he did his best to ignore her, to live his life and to find as much pleasure in it as he could. He enjoyed convivial company and whatever amusements were on offer and, whilst many people might believe him a fool, he had friends who understood his predicament and hid their pity well enough to salve what remained of his pride. When loneliness became too much to bear, he retreated to the lavish Orchid House for an evening, to spend the night in the embrace of some lovely courtesan, but whilst the encounters might help to ease his physical longing for female company, they left him empty and unsatisfied, and lonelier than ever.

Even if Adelia had welcomed his touch, which she certainly did not, he could not have borne the thought of bedding her. He'd discovered to his chagrin that he had a romantic soul, and the physical act of lovemaking was hollow when there was no emotion involved. The Orchid House was one thing, and only an act of desperation when he could no longer be easy in his own skin, but to bed a woman he positively disliked and resented, and who could not abide his hands on her, was utterly beyond him.

Once free of Adelia, he strolled around the ballroom, nodding greetings and snagging a glass of champagne from a passing servant. His mood immediately lifted upon seeing the Duke of Bedwin's lovely daughter, Lady Rosamund, standing speaking with her mother, the duchess. Another young lady stood with them: a Miss Morcombe, if he wasn't mistaken. Miss Morcombe was a pretty young woman, but with no dowry to speak of and no connections. That Rosamund had taken her under her wing made him smile. It was very like her. From what he had heard, she always troubled herself to include those unmarried ladies who might otherwise be overlooked.

"Ladies, good evening, I hope you are all in good spirits and ready to dance?"

"Are you inviting us all, Lord Hargreaves?" the duchess asked with amusement, giving him her hand.

Sebastian bowed over it and looked up at her with a smile. "I am. I have been raked over the coals for not doing so at the last ball and would not dare be so remiss again."

The duchess sent an enquiring look towards her daughter, who huffed.

"I did no such thing," she protested. "Mama! He's only teasing, I swear. As if I would complain that he hadn't asked me to dance."

"Hmm," her mother replied, giving Sebastian her haughtiest 'duchess' look.

Not that he was intimidated. Her grace was notoriously tender-hearted and had a lively sense of humour, which he appreciated. She was only playing with him. It was clear her daughter had inherited the same qualities, for she was hiding her mouth behind her fan and Sebastian was certain she was laughing.

"Well, as it happens, there is a quadrille about to begin and I don't have a partner. You may escort me," the duchess said imperiously, holding out her hand.

"You do me great honour, your grace," Sebastian replied, bowing low, before winking at the young ladies and leading the duchess out onto the floor.

He turned and grinned at Rosamund as he went.

"Save me a dance," he said from behind his hand with a mock whisper quite audible to her mother.

Rosamund laughed, her eyes sparkling, and it gave Sebastian an unexpected little jolt of happiness.

5ᵗʰ June 1842, Mrs Digby-Jones' Ball, London.

"He might do better to dance with his wife," muttered a familiar dry voice from beside her.

Rosamund looked away from Lord Hargreaves to discover her older brother, Jules, and his friend, Leo Hunt, had appeared at her elbow.

"I don't think dancing with her is what's required," Leo replied in an undertone, making Jules snort with laughter.

"It's not Lord Hargreaves' fault if his wife is rather… lively," Rosamund said in protest, though of course she knew as well as anyone else did that Lady Hargreaves was rumoured to have had many lovers. Even Rosamund had observed that she was an outrageous flirt, even with men she knew to be her husband's friends.

"Humphrey Price would tell you she's neglected," Jules said, considering the lady with interest.

"Whatever the truth, it's none of our business," Rosamund hissed, appalled that they were discussing the Hargreaves' marriage.

"It's Lord Hargreaves' business. If I were a man, I'd do something about it and not let her make a fool of me at every opportunity," Miss Morcombe said, shaking her head, surprising Rosamund with the comment because she was a sweet-natured girl.

No doubt Miss Morcombe was another victim of Lady Hargreaves' spiteful tongue, for she was not averse to making sport of the wallflowers and enjoying their discomfort and humiliation.

Miss Morcombe was staring at Lady Hargreaves with a troubled expression. She was not the only one. Many an envious girl had turned their heads towards the glamorous woman and her followers. A small knot of eager young bucks stood in the lady's orbit, each of them hanging off her every word.

"She is exquisite, though, isn't she?" Rosamund admitted, because she was inherently fair-minded, and it *was* undeniable. "One can hardly wonder at them falling in love with her."

"Is that what they've done?" Miss Morcombe replied tartly, shaking her head. "It looks like slavish devotion from this angle. Mama says it's an excess of animal spirits."

"Come, Miss Morcombe, let me take you away from all this and fetch you some refreshment," Leo offered hastily, noting Rosamund's frown at the sharp words.

Miss Morcombe's smile was dazzling, transforming her from merely pretty to quite lovely. "Oh, thank you, Mr Hunt. You are very kind."

Leo led Miss Morcombe away in search of lemonade, and Rosamund watched her brother contemplate the lovely Lady Hargreaves.

"Don't you dare, Jules," she hissed.

Jules turned back to look at her, eyebrows raised. "Dare what?" he demanded, all innocence.

"Oh, don't give me that. I'm not so naïve that I don't understand the gossip about you."

"Gossip? About *me*?" Jules laid a hand over his heart and regarded her with a wounded expression. "Whatever do you mean?"

"I mean that you've a reputation for being a…." She pressed her lips together, unwilling to say the word out loud.

"A what, sister, dear?" Jules asked, his eyes twinkling with amusement.

"A, *you know what,*" she retorted crossly.

Jules chuckled, and Rosamund glowered at him. She supposed she could understand why women fell at his feet so easily. He was devilishly handsome, and of course being heir to a dukedom hardly hurt. He shrugged and glanced back at Lady Hargreaves. "Don't worry so, Ozzie. I wouldn't touch the lady with a ten-foot pole."

Rosamund stared at him with interest, intrigued to hear him say such a thing. "Why not? She's so beautiful."

"Now you're complaining?" he exclaimed, smirking when she rolled her eyes. "Because, my sweet little innocent, there is something about her I can't quite like."

"Because she's had lots of lovers?" Rosamund asked curiously.

Jules laughed and shook his head. "No. I don't see why a woman can't enjoy her lovers if she wishes to, though only if her husband agrees with the arrangement. As Hargreaves has still not produced an heir, I cannot think he likes the situation, though, and I dislike that. I dislike deception and causing trouble in a marriage. She does not seem to care for propriety or discretion, but then again Hargreaves appears not to give a damn about what she does either. It's just all a little... odd and... oh, I don't know. It's none of my business, but I wouldn't trust her as far as I could throw her, not enough to take her as a lover anyway. Good luck to her, I say, but she'll not enslave me, that's for certain."

Rosamund nodded, relieved Jules meant to keep away from her.

"Ah, the next dance is imminent. I promised it to Kathy de Beauvoir. Have you seen her?" he asked, looking about the ballroom. "I thought she seemed a bit out of sorts."

"She was with Hart in the refreshments room earlier," Rosamund offered, as he headed off in search of her.

She was glad her brother was dancing with Kathy. He was right, she had seemed out of sorts. Rosamund wondered if it had anything to do with Lord Vane. She'd seemed very taken with him at the St Clairs' ball, but he was not here tonight. Perhaps that was the reason for her distraction?

Rosamund looked up to discover Lord Hargreaves heading towards her.

"Back so soon, my lord, and what have you done with my mama?" she asked, quirking an eyebrow at him.

"Heavens, you make me sound positively villainous. I have returned her safely to the duke," he replied indignantly. "What did you imagine?"

"Oh, I don't know. My imagination is a terrible distraction when I'm bored. I'm sure it comes from having a writer for a mother."

"Bored, are you? Well, I must do my best to be diverting, then. Did you remember to save me a dance?"

"Of course I did. I do not suffer from such problems as plague the aged, like memory loss, my lord." She bit her lip, struggling to keep her expression placid.

Hargreaves tsked at her, shaking his head. "Oh, for shame, my lady. You would mock a man of my advanced years?"

"I would, I'm afraid," she replied with a sigh. "It's very bad of me, I know, but the temptation is irresistible."

"Wicked creature," he exclaimed. "And what dance have you deigned to give this decrepit article? I hope it is coming soon or I may expire before I have the chance to take it."

She laughed at that, too entertained to maintain her grave expression. "My lord, you are too much. I saved you the next waltz. Now do behave, such a lack of decorum is unbecoming in the elderly."

He narrowed his eyes at her as she muffled a snort of laughter and escorted her on a turn about the room.

Chapter 2

Louis,

Time passes, and I have heard nothing more from you. I assume you are married by now? I cannot conceive of a woman who would not throw herself at your feet at the possibility of becoming your countess. Tell me the deed is done and I shall announce it to all of Paris and watch the hysteria the news brings to the female population. There are many neglected ladies languishing in your absence, I doubt the addition of a wife will deter them for long. Come, tell me the news. I tire of repeating that I do not know when you will return, though I have done my best to keep them company, naturally. So where are you? Why have I still had no word? You promised me a visit, old friend, or shall I come and see you, after all?

I have in my possession a quantity of exceedingly fine cognac and the best champagne I ever tasted. I sent some over to Rouge et Noir. You may set it against the outstanding debt your brother owes me.

I think Jacques passed on the information, but you must know by now that someone has been digging up the past here. From Paris they travelled southwest. I suspect I know where they went, don't you? Who knows what they'll uncover. Watch your back.

—*Excerpt of a letter from Wulfric 'Wolf' De Vere to Louis César de Montluc, Comte de Villen.*

10th June 1842, Adelphi Theatre, London.

Rosamund fanned herself as the curtain fell for the interval. The theatre was hot and stuffy, the overpowering scent of too many bodies, some with questionable hygiene, filled the space to the brim, adding to her discomfort.

"A good production," Jules said, which was high praise, as he was prone to be critical if the stage did not do justice to one of his favourite books. The Pickwick Papers had been up against it, but seemed to have pleased him.

"You mean to say it meets with your approval?" Rosamund replied, arching an eyebrow. "Astonishing."

Jules shrugged and made a show of preening and adjusting his cravat. "What can I say? I have high standards, and it is a rare event when the book is not better. However, it was a splendid effort."

Rosamund rolled her eyes. "I shall send word to the theatre manager, I'm certain he will be in alt."

"Ha! You may mock, but I shall tell him myself," Jules replied with a smirk, getting to his feet and hurrying from their private box.

"What he means is, he wishes to flirt with all the actresses," Mama said, shaking her head and making Rosamund laugh. "Come, let us stretch our legs. It's too stuffy for words in here."

They walked arm-in-arm, greeting friends and chatting as everyone mingled during the interval. Mama fell into conversation with Mrs Bonnie Cadogan, and Rosamund, who did not know the people they were discussing, looked about her to see who else was here. A tall man with broad shoulders and dark hair caught her eye, and she smiled, realising it was Lord Hargreaves. He turned and Rosamund raised her hand in greeting. She wondered if it was only her imagination that made his eyes light with pleasure at the sight of her. Either way, he extricated himself from the conversation he'd been having and made his way over.

"My lady, good evening. How are you enjoying the production?"

Rosamund looked up at him with a smile, admiring how well he looked in his evening blacks. His coat and trousers were tightly fitted to his athletic form, as was the fashion, and he cut a splendid figure. "Oh, it's marvellous. I love the theatre, especially when Jules holds his tongue and stops criticising them for changing or cutting bits from the book."

He laughed, the sound making women's heads turn his way, and Rosamund noticed tiny lines crinkled about his eyes. She bit back a smile, wondering if he was truly sensitive about his age as he pretended to be, but the lines only added to his appeal.

"Ah, a critic. I always pity them, for they do not seem to gain half so much enjoyment from the theatre as I do. I, for one, am happy to be transported for an hour or two, even if it isn't quite what I expected."

"Yes, exactly!" Rosamund replied, pleased he felt the same way.

He was such a lovely man, and such good company, Rosamund could not understand why his wife treated him as she did. She immediately scolded herself for the thought, for she had promised herself not to think about or pass judgement on either of them, or their marital strife. It was hard, though, for as she had come to know him better, she had learned how kind and funny Lord Hargreaves was, and the gossip about his wife and the state of their marriage made Rosamund want to weep for him. They had bumped into each other almost daily since the Digby-Jones' ball and he always stopped to speak with her for a few moments. Her mama liked him very much, as did her father, and Jules had even invited Hargreaves to attend his club with him.

"By the by, I spoke to Ashburton yesterday," he said, lowering his voice.

Rosamund's stomach did an odd little flip at the idea he'd been discussing her with Lord Ashburton. "You did?"

He nodded, frowning down at the carpet as he spoke. "Yes, I made a great show of admiring you, made some rather too pertinent comments about your lovely figure, and wondered why some lucky fellow hadn't snapped you up yet."

"Oh." Rosamund stared at the floor too, so he wouldn't see her blush. "And what did he say?"

Hargreaves hesitated. Rosamund looked up, narrowing her eyes at him. "What did he say?" she repeated with a heavy sense of inevitability.

He winced, speaking as though the words pained him. "He said you'd only just come out and couldn't be much over sixteen, so you had plenty of time."

"He said *what*?" Rosamund shrieked, before remembering herself as heads swivelled in their direction.

Hargreaves cleared his throat and glared at anyone who didn't turn away before he spoke again.

"He also said anyone with half a brain would stay clear for a few years or the duke would disembowel them, which seemed a fair point to me, I must say."

"The rat," Rosamund seethed. "I'm nineteen! Oh, how could he?"

Well, didn't that just prove what she had always suspected? Pip thought her a silly child. Perhaps she was, for she'd wasted her time pining for him when he never spared her a thought. Annoyance warred with hurt feelings, but Rosamund was relieved to discover exasperation won out. Well, fine. She was done trying to catch his eye. There were plenty more fish in the sea and she'd jolly well find one that desired her company. It wasn't as if there were not plenty of candidates.

Suddenly aware she'd been fuming silently for some time, Rosamund glanced up to discover Lord Hargreaves watching her with a mixture of sympathy and amusement.

"I beg your pardon," she said, a little mortified by her behaviour.

"There's no need. He's a young fool, I'm afraid, but most of us are at that age. Men take a lot longer to gain good sense in their preferences for women."

There was a wry tone to his words, but Rosamund was too cross to pay it much mind.

"He's only about four years younger than you are," she grumbled.

"Ah, but what a four years that is," he replied with a crooked smile. "At my advanced age, I have gained the benefit of great wisdom, which I disperse with enormous generosity, naturally."

Rosamund gave a huff of laughter. "So you do."

He smiled, but the concern in his expression remained. "You're not too disappointed?" he asked. "I will persevere if you wish me to, though I must be honest and say that Ashburton seems to have other matters on his mind at present. He is only in society at all because his father demands it, I think."

Rosamund nodded. "He seems distracted, I agree. But no, I am not heartbroken, only… Oh, I am disappointed, I suppose. Did he not care that a married man had taken an interest in me?"

Hargreaves rubbed the back of his neck, frowning over the question. "I am uncertain he took me seriously. Sadly, my reputation for good behaviour precedes me. You'd have been better served had the Comte de Villen taken an interest. Now, *that* would cause a stir."

"I don't wish to cause a stir," Rosamund replied, shaking her head. "I just thought it would be a good match. We've been friends all our lives, our families are close, and——"

"And he looks likes Adonis," Hargreaves added dryly.

"Well, it didn't hurt," Rosamund admitted, before catching his eye and bursting out laughing. "Oh, you! You make me say the most outrageous things. Stop it at once."

He smirked at her, looking pleased by her outburst. "I have no intention of stopping you from saying outrageous things. I think it does one good when in safe company, to say just what one pleases."

"Well then, I thank you for providing the safe company," she said, meaning it. "It is a relief to have someone to speak frankly with, and I appreciate the effort on my behalf as well. It was kind of you to try. You don't think me foolish?"

He frowned at that and shook his head. "Finding someone to spend your life with is hardly foolish, but I think you ought to have some fun whilst you are about it, and don't be in too much of a rush. Perhaps Ashburton will come around, but for now, enjoy your freedom, my lady, and take your time. Choose wisely," he added, his tone soft, and Rosamund's heart broke a little as she saw the regret in his eyes.

15th June 1842, The Queen's Levee, Drawing Rooms, St James's Palace, London

Rosamund handed her card to the queen's page in the Presence-Chamber as instructed. A second card she held onto, for that must be presented to the Lord in Waiting, who would announce her name to the queen. She really did not want to be here again, for it was deadly dull and always seemed to be a great deal of waiting about for no good reason. But at least once a year since she had first been presented, she returned to the opulent palace to make her curtsey. The enormous court dress she wore was beautiful, but unwieldy, with huge skirts that meant she had to go sideways through doors. On a heavy, sullen day that was threatening thunder, hefting around so many petticoats and yards of fabric felt akin to being smothered in an itchy wool blanket.

"Once we've paid our respects, we can go if you like," Mama promised her, giving her a sympathetic smile. "I have a chapter I simply must finish. I left the hero on his knees mid declaration, poor thing. He must be most uncomfortable."

She sighed and Rosamund stifled a giggle. Mama often seemed to consider her creations as real people.

To her profound relief, the presentation was mercifully short, and it was not long before Rosamund and her mama were free.

"Oh, darling, I must just have a word with Matilda," Mama said, spying her friend on the far side of a room full to the brim of splendidly dressed noblemen and women. "I won't be above a moment."

Rosamund smothered a snort of amusement, knowing full well that when Mama and Matilda got together, they would chatter for hours given the opportunity. Resigning herself to a long wait, she accepted a glass of orgeat, waving her fan in her free hand, and made her way to an open window, hoping to find something of a breeze to cool her down. She got to the window at the same moment as Lord Hargreaves, resplendent in his court dress of black velvet coat with cut steel buttons, black velvet waistcoat, black pantaloons, black silk stockings, shoes with glittering buckles, a Brussels lace cravat, lace ruffles, and a sword with a black scabbard and cut steel hilt. To finish the ensemble, a cocked hat of the *chapeau bras* variety was tucked under his arm.

"It's my window, I got here first," he said gravely. "I have a sword," he added, narrowing his eyes at her.

Rosamund arched an imperious eyebrow. "I warn you, I will fight to death for the merest suggestion of fresh air. If there is anything resembling a breeze, you are a dead man."

"My, you're fierce," he grumbled, and then grinned at her. "I don't blame you, though. It's stifling in here."

"Too many people," she said with a sigh.

"Many a potential husband," he suggested.

Rosamund pulled a face. "I don't have the energy to make polite conversation," she said glumly, fanning herself.

"I see. Am I to be the recipient of an impolite conversation then?" he asked with a bland expression.

Lips quirking, Rosamund shrugged. "It's entirely possible."

His eyes twinkled with amusement, but he said nothing, turning to examine the rest of the room.

"You look very impressive," Rosamund observed. He did, too.

The old-fashioned court dress everyone was bound to adhere to made many men look ridiculous with all its lace and flounces, but he wore it well. His figure was masculine and powerful enough for the extravagancies of his costume to underline his physique, rather than detract from it.

"I feel a prize twit, like every other gentleman here," he admitted. "Have you *seen* these shoes?" He made a leg, as if to give her a flourishing bow, pointing his toe daintily so the buckle glittered in the light.

Rosamund smothered a snort from behind her fan.

"La! You are quite the macaroni," she teased.

He made a harrumphing sound and returned to observing the room. "What about Mr Weston?" he asked suddenly, gesturing to a handsome young man who was talking to the Marquess of Montagu.

Rosamund frowned. "What about him?"

"He's surely excellent husband material. I don't know him well, but his father, Baron Rothborn, is a good fellow, a war hero, and you do love Gothic novels, I believe."

"What have Gothic novels to do with Mr Weston?" she asked in bewilderment.

Hargreaves shrugged. "Well, one day he will inherit Mitcham Priory. Think of all those ghosts wandering about. Mad monks and the like. That's got to be an incentive, surely?"

Rosamund rolled her eyes at him. "I grew up with Larkin Weston. He's like one of my brothers, *and* he once put a frog down my back," she added with a scowl. "Certainly not."

"Not even with a mad monk thrown in? He's said to be a clever fellow. He's wealthy too, and *very* handsome," Hargreaves added, studying the man with a critical expression.

"Well, you marry him, then!" she retorted, pretending to be affronted, but thoroughly enjoying herself.

"I don't think so," Hargreaves replied seriously.

Rosamund, who knew they were being silly now and did not care a bit, demanded, "Why not?"

"I'm scared of ghosts," he said with a heavy sigh.

Rosamund gave a most unladylike bark of laughter, causing many of the ladies and gentlemen around them to turn their heads and murmur with disapproval.

Hargreaves' eyes glittered with mirth, the devil, and Rosamund bit her lip, trying to contain herself before she got hysterical.

"You are a bit of hoyden, my lady. I'm not sure who we'll find to marry you if you keep behaving so badly." He gave her a tut of disapproval.

"That was entirely your fault," she complained, glaring at him and turning her attention back to the assembled company. "What about him?" she asked, gesturing with her fan to a hulking Scotsman in full regalia. Her gaze quite naturally drifted to his legs, visible beneath the hem of his kilt, his powerful calves encased in white hose.

Hargreaves cleared his throat, and Rosamund jumped, blushing as she realised she'd been staring.

"Well, his appeal is obvious enough," he said dryly.

Rosamund shot him a warning look. "Who is he?"

"Viscount Balmore, I believe. Though I am afraid I cannot offer an introduction, for I don't know him at all."

"Do you know of him?"

Hargreaves shook his head. "Apologies, my lady. If I hear anything, I shall let you know."

"He's rather intimidating," Rosamund mused, though she could only see his back from where they stood, but he was built upon mountainous proportions and towered over the ladies he was speaking with who were craning their necks to look up at him.

"Well, that's nice, I must say," Hargreaves grumbled.

"What?" Rosamund tore her eyes from the impressive Scot to look back at him.

"You threaten me with bodily harm if I dare get between you and a bit of a breeze, and him you find intimidating. I'm crushed."

Rosamund bit back a grin and reached out, patting his arm soothingly. "There, there, Hargreaves. You're just not cut out to be a Highlander."

Finally, seeing her mama waving at her to come along, Rosamund turned back to him with a grin. "We're leaving, but thank you for keeping me company. It would have been very dull without you."

"Without me to mock and insult, you mean?" he replied, smiling at her.

"Precisely," she said with a snooty little sniff, before curtseying to him and taking her leave, hearing his soft chuckle follow her across the room.

24th June 1842, The Royal Academy Exhibition, Trafalgar Square, London

Sebastian could not help the smile that curved his lips as he admired the portrait of Lady Rosamund on display in the Academy exhibition. There were many such paintings of fashionable young women and noble ladies of the *ton*. To him, though, this one outshone everything else in the room. He did not think this was only because she had become such a dear friend. Though they seemed to trip over each other daily, which perhaps was not surprising, as they knew many of the same people and moved in the same circles, but seeing her had become the highlight of his day. She never failed to make him laugh and lighten his spirits. They had the most fascinating conversations, for she was interested in everyone and everything, and his only complaint was that the time passed too quickly. He did not dare spend too long with her, or monopolise her time, aware of how the gossips would view his friendship with an unmarried lady. So, by tacit agreement, they were scrupulously careful, limiting their conversations and ensuring they were always in full view of the room, or better yet in company with friends.

Sebastian studied the painting with a keen eye. It was the promise of a smile at her lips, almost but not quite curving her lovely mouth, that kept you staring, almost certain you would see it blossom into life. The artist had captured her well, her beauty, her innate grace, and that little sparkle of something mischievous in her eyes that suggested she'd surprise you. She surprised him constantly, with her humour above all things, but her humility too.

Young women in her position were rarely as down to earth as she was, as he knew to his cost. A young woman blessed with a fine face and figure, wealth, and title had little chance to gain the depth of character and understanding of humanity that Rosamund had. How could they, when they were sheltered from reality and cosseted and spoiled at every turn? But the Duke and Duchess of Bedwin were unlike many of their ilk, though Sebastian suspected the duchess was most to thank for this. She had a ready wit, as proven by her many published novels, but was not shy about confronting the darker side of life either. Indeed, she had courted scandal herself with her refusal to bow to society's whims and her dedication to her own agenda: most of all, what she considered the proper education of her daughters. The family were becoming rather notorious. The second eldest daughter was rumoured to have stolen her sister Eliza's husband, and Lady Eliza had married an illegitimate Frenchman. Then there was the young marquess who was fast on his way to gaining a reputation as a rake. Under the watchful eye of the powerful Duke of Bedwin, however, no one dared to criticise them.

"She's certainly a beauty," murmured a cultured voice from beside him.

Sebastian turned to see the Marquess of Kilbane standing beside him, staring at the portrait with interest. Some protective instinct in Sebastian reacted to Kilbane's presence, making him want to shield Rosamund from the man's gaze. Foolishness, he told himself; it was only a painting, and yet the sensation lingered.

Kilbane smiled, amused by Sebastian's obvious discomfort. "Good day, Hargreaves."

"Kilbane." Sebastian nodded, knowing he ought to move away from the portrait, people were already murmuring about how often he sought Rosamund's company, but some force beyond his control made him turn back for another look.

"She's a friend of yours, I believe?" Kilbane asked politely.

"I have that honour."

A wicked glint flickered in Kilbane's unusual violet eyes, as if he knew Sebastian was praying he'd not ask him for an introduction, for it would force him to refuse. No gentleman would introduce Kilbane to an innocent young lady if they could help it. Refusing a marquess was never an easy task, however.

"You've heard the latest gossip, I take it?" Kilbane spoke with his usual lazy tone, as if he could barely muster the energy to endure the conversation, though his piercing gaze told another story. This man missed nothing.

"Have I?" Sebastian's instincts prickled. One never knew with the marquess where the exchange was going to go. It was often the conversational equivalent of walking a moor in the dark, one never knew when one risked plunging into a deep dark hole until it was too late.

"The fellow who tried to murder Lord Vane struck again."

"What?" he exclaimed in shock. He did not know Vane well, as a young man he'd been an absolute viper and Sebastian had given him a wide berth, but he seemed to have changed in the past few years and become a tolerable human being.

"Another failed attempt, happily," Kilbane remarked. "I should hate to lose a friend, for there are few men who consider me—ah, but I forget—he reminded me I no longer have the honour. *C'est la vie.* Still, it seems he was heroic, saving the life of Mrs Oak, no less, though one wonders what she was doing at Vane Hall with her husband. Miss de Beauvoir was there too. They're to be married, you know... Miss de Beauvoir and Vane, that is."

"Are they?" Well, that was a union Sebastian would not have predicted.

"Yes. All the old tabby cats are up in arms about the match, naturally," Kilbane said, inspecting his nails. "The girl was born in the workhouse, which is tantamount to being Satan's spawn, apparently."

"You disagree?" Sebastian could not help but ask.

Kilbane's family were hardly famous for kindness to others and the old marquess had been a stickler for lineage. Such snobbery seemed ill placed as Kilbane's family lineage was Irish, which made him the source of disdain to some among the *ton*. Any such distinctions seemed petty to Hargreaves. Nonetheless it was an old and revered title going back many generations and the man's attitude was surprising.

Kilbane chuckled, a low wicked sound. "My dear, my family have always prided themselves on the purity of their bloodline, and just look at us." He made a sweeping gesture towards his own elegant figure, one dark eyebrow quirked. "Are we not the very model of everything the best of the nobility ought to be?"

His tone was mocking, clearly alluding to the reputation he and his family had for revelling in vice. The man's father had been a disgusting old satyr and had raised his sons in his image. The older son had died young but had been well on his way to following in his father's footsteps. Kilbane was young and beautiful yet, but if rumour was to be believed, his heart was black as pitch and his tastes were wide and insatiable. Not that Sebastian believed all rumours to be true. He knew better.

"Well, I hope they'll be very happy," Sebastian said, meaning it, and uncomfortable with the scrutiny he felt himself to be under in this man's company.

"Ah, we all wish for happiness, but so few of us get it," Kilbane said with a heavy sigh. "One poor decision and our fates are forever changed. It seems damned unfair to me."

It seemed damned unfair to Sebastian too, but he held his tongue, unwilling to get drawn in.

Kilbane's gaze slid over the crowd.

"Lady Hargreaves is with you?" he said in surprise.

Sebastian felt a shock of disappointment and turned to discover Kilbane was correct. He'd thought Adelia was not attending until later in the day.

"No," he replied shortly, dismayed to discover his wife had her entourage in tow.

He turned his back on her, realising too late whose portrait he was before, and pivoted away again. Adelia met his eyes across the room, her lively expression cooling when she saw him, and becoming positively frosty when she saw the portrait he stood before. Hargreaves experienced a chill of foreboding.

"Oh dear, that augurs ill," Kilbane murmured. "Have a care, my dear."

The comment rankled but Sebastian could not dismiss it.

"Good day, Kilbane," he managed, giving a taut nod and walking away.

He had been enjoying the exhibition, but his pleasure in it evaporated like mist before the sun, knowing that Adelia was there, flirting and making a spectacle of herself with her admirers. He dared not even speak to his friends when she was with him, too mortified when she turned her beautiful eyes towards them and batted her lashes, trying to snare their attention as she had once done with him. He had tried to speak to her about it, to negotiate a life where she could do as she pleased if she only left his friends out of it, but she seemed to take pleasure in taunting him. Her eyes would glitter with excitement when she knew he was caught between making a scene or letting her get away with humiliating him. Sebastian had never considered himself an especially proud man, but his pride had taken such a battering over the past ten years he was uncertain how much more it could stand before he snapped and did or said something terrible.

He hurried towards the entrance, which was still thronged with people. Suddenly desperate to get outside and breathe fresh air, he picked up his pace, needing to get away from the prying eyes of society, forever judging him and the state of his marriage. As if most of them had managed any better; they just had wives who were discreet.

He was barely ten feet from the door when a familiar voice called to him.

"My lord."

Sebastian turned, letting out a breath as he saw Rosamund. Better than fresh air, better than an escape from the crowd, was the smile she gave him. The tension thrumming through him eased under the sincerity of that simple happiness. Was she *truly* so pleased to see him? *Don't be a fool, Hargreaves.* She was simply a lovely, vivacious young woman who took pleasure in all things and welcomed her friends with warmth and grace.

"You're leaving?" she asked. Was that disappointment in her eyes?

"Yes, I'm afraid so," he said, wishing he did not have to, but Kilbane was right.

Adelia might not want him, but she was not above petty jealousy. It was why he'd never taken a mistress, despite his loneliness. He could not abide Adelia's retaliation and the constant sniping whenever she felt he was enjoying someone's company too much. So far, she had not cared about his friendship with Rosamund, not considering an unmarried lady a rival. She knew Hargreaves too well to believe he would ever dishonour an innocent. If she believed he had become fond of the girl, however, that might change. He needed to be more careful.

"Oh. Can I not persuade you to stay a little longer?" Rosamund asked, and then blushed. "Forgive me. That was dreadfully presumptuous."

He smiled, shaking his head. "Not at all. I am flattered that my company pleases you, though you must avoid giving me such compliments, it will go to my head."

"No, it won't," she said, laughing. "You're the most modest man I've ever met."

"Now you're just being silly," he said, ridiculously pleased by her words. "I'm a conceited ass and you know it. But you have made my day all the same, just as your beautiful portrait has made the exhibition… though, as exquisite as it is, it cannot compare to reality."

"Oh, now who is being silly?" she replied, eyes alight with humour. "There's no need to pour the butter boat over me."

He ought to have replied in kind, he knew, ought to have made a joke out of it as their bantering was always teasing and light-hearted, but his words remained sincere. "For once, I'm not the least bit silly, or ridiculous. It's a magnificent portrait and yet it does not do you justice, not even close."

Her breath caught at his words, her cheeks flushing, and Sebastian knew it was time to leave before he said something he ought not—something *else* he ought not. So instead, he injected a teasing note to his voice. "You'll have every man in London in love with you by the end of the exhibition, mark my words."

"Oh, surely every man in the country," she said, laughing, but there was a forced air about her comment, about the laugh, something uncertain in the way she looked at him, and Sebastian cursed himself.

They were friends, nothing more. He had no business offering her such compliments. Young women were too easily led into believing their hearts attached and he did her no kindness in confusing her emotions, or his own. It would not be kind to either of them.

"Every man in Europe," he countered, smiling as jovially as he could manage before giving her a polite bow. "Must dash. Enjoy the exhibition. It really is very good."

With that, he escaped, hurrying out of the front door and promising himself he would keep away from Lady Rosamund for a while until he was feeling more himself.

Chapter 3

Dear Kathy,

I am so happy for you. Though I admit, I was never more surprised when I heard you had married! I am very cross with you for not telling me. How romantic to be swept off your feet as you were, though. And now you are Lady Vane! I cannot wait to see you and hear all about it.

I send you all my best wishes and much love.

—Excerpt of a letter from Lady Rosamund Adolphus (daughter of Their Graces, Robert and Prunella Adolphus, the Duke and Duchess of Bedwin) to Katherine Drake, Countess of Vane (daughter of Mrs Minerva and Mr Inigo de Beauvoir).

30ᵗʰ June 1842, Mrs Hallewell's Rout Party, Chelsea, London.

Rosamund sighed inwardly as Lady Balderston bore her off towards the card room. She would much rather be mingling with the crowd of chattering guests in pursuit of her friends, but she had promised Papa she would keep the old lady company. This was not such a hardship, though, as Lady Balderston had a sharp wit and a sharper tongue, and some of her comments made Rosamund snort with laughter. She had hoped to catch up with Cara Baxter, however, who was here this evening. Her parents had allowed her to come out this year but only to a few of the more modest events, to give her time to grow used to the cutthroat world of society. Rosamund was keen to see how she was faring.

She also hoped to see Lord Hargreaves, whom she had not seen all week.

He had attended Herr Thalberg's concert at the Hanover Square rooms but had not sought her out, nor had he spoken to her except in passing, at any of the balls and soirees she had attended. Hargreaves had greeted her briefly when they had almost literally bumped into each other on Bond Street, but he had seemed intent on keeping his distance. Though she too had heard stirrings of gossip about the two of them, Rosamund regretted that he would take it so very much to heart. She missed his irreverent company and was determined to speak to him tonight.

Lady Balderston wished to play whist, however, and had already commandeered her nephew, a Mr Barnaby Godwin. The three of them sat down at the card table as Lady Balderston fidgeted with impatience.

"Well, this won't do, we need a fourth. Where is the comte?" she demanded of Mr Godwin.

"Ah, no. We're not playing with Louis," Barnaby said, his voice firm. "Sorry, Aunt Hester. He dislikes whist in any case. Never plays."

The old lady tsked. "Is he here, at least?"

"Yes, I think so. I'm sure he'll come and see you soon," Barnaby soothed. "We'll find someone else for a fourth." Looking around, he caught the attention of someone behind Rosamund's back.

"My lord, good evening. Care to play? We need a fourth to partner Lady Rosamund," he said, smiling with relief as they agreed to come over.

Rosamund waited until their fourth appeared and looked up to discover Lord Hargreaves smiling down at her. Her heart did an odd little flutter in her chest, making her feel suddenly shy, which was most peculiar.

"Lady Rosamund, a pleasure to see you again," he said, nodding to her.

"Never mind all the chitchat, sit down, young man. Barnaby, deal the cards," Lady Balderston instructed.

Hargreaves inclined his head politely and did as he was told, though his gingerbread eyes danced with amusement. He leaned towards Rosamund, whispering.

"Young man," under his breath.

Rosamund stifled a giggle.

"Hargreaves, meet my great Aunt Hester Henley, Lady Balderston," Barnaby said, looking somewhat apologetic. "Aunt, Viscount Hargreaves."

"Yes, yes, pleased to meet you, let's play," the lady said, and made a sharp gesture for Barnaby to get on with it.

Hargreaves slid an amused look at Rosamund but said nothing as they settled down to their game.

"You lost on purpose," Rosamund accused him some forty minutes later as he escorted her from the card room towards the refreshments.

Lord Hargreaves frowned down at her. "You are assuming I have any skill with the game? I might be a hopeless player."

Rosamund considered this. "No. You did in on purpose, you wretch. I suppose someone told you I hate to lose, and so you thought to have some fun at my expense?"

He laughed at that, his expression curious. "Do you really? How fascinating. Well, no, Lady Suspicious. No one told me, though admittedly, that is a bonus."

"Why, then?" she demanded.

"Because Lady Balderston has not been in society for many years and winning pleased her far more than it would you."

"Oh. That was well done of you, then," Rosamund allowed, having to agree that the old woman was looking very pleased with herself. She had begun another game with some old friends, though her nephew had been forced to remain to make the four.

"Besides which, if we'd played well, she would have wanted to play another round, and I need a drink," he added candidly.

"Fair enough," Rosamund replied with a smile. "I should like another glass of champagne, but I suppose I had better not. The lemonade is always too sweet or too tart, though."

"I'll let you drink my champagne in secret if you like," he offered. "If you're certain it won't go to your head?"

Rosamund rolled her eyes at him. "I am not a child. Two glasses of champagne will not make me silly, I assure you."

"Then why did you say you'd better not?" he asked, curiosity in his gaze.

"Because," Rosamund began, and then stopped. She'd been about to give a glib answer, but she knew Hargreaves would understand. "Because I'm the daughter of a duke, and people are always watching me, waiting for me to put a foot wrong. Happily, Mama and Papa do not expect or desire perfection in their children, but society is always so quick to criticise. I shall not give them an excuse to find fault, with... with *either* of us," she added quietly.

"Ah." His expression darkened, and beneath the hand that lay upon his arm, she felt the tension singing through him. "Then you too have heard the whispers."

"Yes, and I know that's why you've stayed away, but it's nothing but nasty minded gossips," Rosamund said, wondering if she ought not have spoken, but it was too late now. *"I* shan't avoid someone I consider a dear friend because of their idle tongues."

43

"Perhaps you should," he said softly, glancing at her.

"No! Oh, you can't mean to say you would turn your back on me entirely?" she said, too horrified to disguise the hurt in her voice.

"Hush," he said, covering her hand with his own. "I could never do that."

Rosamund looked up at him, unsettled that their friendship might be spoiled or lost entirely.

"Then what do you mean by that?"

Hargreaves shrugged. "We should have a care, that's all. Perhaps we should only speak when in company with other people. It is only sensible. Your reputation is too important, my lady. I would not damage it for the world."

"I'm a duke's daughter with a large dowry. It would need to be shocking indeed for any actual damage to be done," she said irritably, her expression dark.

"A liaison with a married man *would* be shocking indeed."

Rosamund jolted, startled by his words and unable to halt the blush that surged over her. It began at her toes and seemed to swallow her up… which was silly, obviously. She had no intention of having a liaison with anyone, certainly not a married man.

"I beg your pardon, my lady. That was an unforgiveable thing to say. I've frightened you," he added, his expression wretched with remorse.

"What?" Rosamund replied, distracted by her reaction to his shocking words. She turned to look up at him, caught at once in the warmth and affection she saw in his eyes. Gingerbread and spice, she thought at once, and wondered if his skin would smell deliciously spicy too. She stiffened, horrified she had even considered such a thing. Forcing her attention back to the conversation she nodded.

"Oh. *Oh,* yes. That is sensible. To only speak in company, and no—not frightened. I could never be afraid of you," she added, her voice faint as she stared up at him.

His gaze fell to her mouth before he looked away.

"It's for the best," he said, his tone adamant.

Rosamund did not feel she could disagree. Perhaps, after all, one glass of champagne had been too much.

1ˢᵗ July 1842, Beverwyck, London

"Finally," Aunt Hester said, casting her embroidery aside the moment the door opened, and Barnaby stepped through. With wry amusement, he acknowledged his company was not what the old woman was so eager for. "I thought I would take root, waiting for you two to show your faces today."

"Forgive us for neglecting you, my lady," Louis César said smoothly, crossing the room to where Lady Balderston sat and taking the hand she held out to him. He bowed over it and even pressed a kiss to her knuckles, the devil. To Barnaby's astonishment, colour rose in his aunt's cheeks. Good Lord, she was blushing!

"Hmph. Think you can get around me with that pretty face of yours, do you?" Aunt Hester blustered as Louis released her hand.

Louis' eyes twinkled at her and Barnaby watched in amusement as she let out a sigh. "Well, you're not wrong. Diabolical, that's what I call it."

"You would not be the first to say so," Louis said, his tone dry. "But I cannot help myself. I seek only to please you."

The lady snorted. "If you'd have said that to me ten years ago, you might have found yourself in a deal of trouble, young man. Lucky for you, I'm not so quick as I once was."

Louis laughed, the first genuine laugh Barnaby had heard from him since they'd left Fort William. Whilst it pleased him to see his friend's spirits lighten, it was still disconcerting to see his formidable aunt turn girlish before his eyes.

"Louis, stop flirting with my aunt. It's unnerving."

"Barnaby, hush. There are certain things a lady of my age can still enjoy, and making outrageous remarks to handsome men young enough to be our sons is one of them. Don't spoil it."

"Fine," Barnaby grumbled. "Is there any tea?"

"Of course there's tea. It will be here presently," she said, tsking at him. "Now sit down, you're giving me a crick in my neck. No, *monsieur*, you will sit there, where I can keep an eye on you." She patted the seat closest to her.

They obeyed her, for there was no point in doing anything else, and once the tea had arrived, waited for her to pour.

"How is Bedwin?" Barnaby asked, taking his cup from her. "As terrifying as ever?"

"Not a bit of it. He's perfectly charming, just as his uncle was, and the duchess is such a sweet creature. Beverwyck is a glorious place to stay, and she's made me feel perfectly at home."

"She is a remarkable woman," Louis offered with a smile as Aunt Hester held out his tea.

"She is," Aunt Hester replied, fixing him with a steely gaze. "And one who laments your refusal to become a part of the family, I might add. How many of her dinner invitations have you accepted this year, might I ask?"

Barnaby watched with interest as Louis frowned and looked a little uncomfortable. "She is too kind, but just because my brother has married into the family does not mean—"

"Stuff!" Aunt Hester announced before Louis could say another word. "I never saw a fellow more in need of a family, and

"Jolly well, thank you, and you're looking in prime twig today, if I might say so."

Lady Rosamund laughed, her green eyes dancing. "You might, I thank you. Can I help you? You seem lost, not that it's any wonder in this cavernous place."

"If you would direct me to the library, I should be grateful. Aunt Hester has left her shawl and demands I fetch it for her."

"I'd be happy to escort you," she offered.

"That's very good of you, if it's no trouble."

It wasn't, she assured him, and led Barnaby through rooms of such grandeur that it was all he could do not to gape. The life of a duke differed significantly from that of a baron's younger son, and no mistake.

"Lady Millicent asked after you," she said, nearly making Barnaby trip over his own feet.

"Did she, by Jove?" he exclaimed, with such obvious surprise that Lady Rosamund laughed.

"Yes, she did. She was sorry to have missed you last night. They got delayed at another event and you'd left to escort your aunt home by the time she arrived."

"Well," Barnaby said, flabbergasted. "Well."

Rosamund smiled at him and patted his arm. "Perhaps you should call upon her. Take some flowers."

Barnaby grinned. "Perhaps I shall."

1st July 1842, Beverwyck, London

Unlike Barnaby, Louis did not believe for one moment that Lady Balderston had left her shawl in the library. She had been trying to get him alone ever since Fort William, to no avail. Not that Louis had helped her in that endeavour, too aware of her sharp mind and penchant for overly personal questions to invite any further intimacy. He liked the lady a good deal and respected her more, but that did not mean he wanted her digging up his past or interfering in his future.

"Well then," she said, fixing him with a look that boded ill. "What happened at Fort William? Hmmm?"

Louis sat back, knowing he looked entirely at ease even if he did not feel it. He studied the tea in his cup and wished fervently that it was cognac. "'Appened?" he replied, deliberately dropping the *h* as ladies found his accent charming and, the more charmed she was, the less likely to pursue this topic.

"You heard me. When you finally returned to the dress shop, you looked like a tomcat who'd found a deal more than a cream pot to indulge in."

"You paint a vivid and not terribly flattering picture, my lady," Louis murmured, sipping his tea.

Lady Balderston snorted. "Barnaby has finally grown a backbone—your influence, I collect—and refuses to breathe a word about you to anyone. Even me!" she added, as though this was inconceivable. "You found her, didn't you? Your young lady."

Louis held her gaze and his tongue while she studied him as though she could pry the information from his brain if she tried hard enough. She wagged a bony, bejewelled finger at him.

"I will discover who the gel is, you mark my words."

"And what then?" Louis demanded, too aware she could do it.

"Oh, keep your hair on. I won't interfere," she said, setting her cup and saucer down.

Louis returned an incredulous expression.

The lady bristled. "Well, I *might* help if I approve the match," she added with a sniff.

"And if you do not?"

"Do you think I would not?" she asked him, her voice softer now.

Louis shrugged, struggling to keep his relaxed pose and indifferent mask in place. He couldn't honestly imagine anyone *approving* of him marrying Evie. Not if they had any sense, or care for her.

"Tell me she's not some pretty little ninny with nothing in her head but jewels and frivolous nonsense," she demanded, fierce now.

"Certainly, she is not!" Louis retorted, and then cursed himself for the slip, for he had just dismissed many of the unmarried females on offer amongst the *ton* and the lady knew it.

She sat back, her smile smug and Louis prayed Barnaby would be back soon.

Chapter 4

Wolf,

I am not married. Not yet. Though I am determined to change this soon. Believe me when I tell you, not all women throw themselves at my feet. Some have more sense. You will not come here, my friend. Not yet. If you had the slightest bit of sense, not at all, but you will insist on kicking the hornet's nest. Just don't complain when the wretched things sting you to death. You might be the unofficial king of Paris' darker world, but your kind of power cannot fight the ton. Society will eat you alive.

Thank you for the champagne, though one wonders how you think we might forget the debt when you remind us of it with such frequency. Nic has more honour in his little finger than the two of us put together, but you know this. You try only to bait me, and I shall not play your games.

Yes, damn you, I know where they went. I also know who it was. Find out what they discovered, and for this I owe you nothing. For if I fall, you do too.

—Excerpt of a letter from Louis César de Montluc, Comte de Villen to Wulfric 'Wolf' De Vere.

1ˢᵗ July 1842, Connaught Place, Bayswater, London.

Ciarán St Just, Marquess of Kilbane, turned the elegant invitation around and around between his long fingers, considering it with a frown. Usually, such an event would not interest him, but an invitation from Lady Montagu was another matter. It was too delicious to refuse.

The lady intrigued him almost as much as her husband did. She certainly had more backbone than most. He admired her greatly for the way she'd stood up to him, batting away his lewd comments as though he were nothing more than a snot-nosed boy. Most women of her ilk would clutch at their pearls and run in the opposite direction the moment he entered a room. Which was fine. He'd no need of the matronly sort. There were men with a taste for being mothered, but he was not one of them. Christ, he wasn't certain he'd recognise the quality, never having experienced it firsthand. He assumed it would be a lot of fuss and cosseting, which struck him as nonsensical when one could just get on and tup without enduring a lot of silly sentimentality neither of you meant, anyway.

He wondered if the marquess knew his beautiful wife had invited him. That would be interesting. But no, Lady Montagu was not devious, and would never be so foolish as to surprise her husband by playing silly games. For a moment Ciarán was diverted by imagining the games they could play, the three of them together. He gave a wistful sigh. Such a pity they were so damned devoted to each other. He simply could not understand it. Ciarán had an endless variety of bed partners to choose from and they still bored him to tears. So little diverted him. Nothing relieved his ennui, and it drove him to behave worse than ever, to gamble greater sums, take bigger risks, and to live increasingly dangerously. Just to feel… *something*. Anything. How a powerful, complicated man like Montagu could find satisfaction with only his wife for all these years was a mystery to him. Love, he supposed, with a sneer of disgust. Not that he believed in such things. One might as well believe in unicorns and faeries, but people told themselves the lie so often that something resembling constancy seemed to evolve from it. For some, anyway.

Very well, then. He would go to the garden party. If nothing else, it would be amusing to see the horror on everyone's faces at discovering the satanic Marquess of Kilbane out in daylight hours at a garden party, of all things. Oh, the horror. Perhaps someone would faint. He snorted, entertained at the thought. He might even get to speak to Montagu himself, and that alone would make it worth enduring an entire afternoon's tedium.

Montagu disliked him, he knew. He did not mind. Perversely—for what else was he if not that?—the knowledge was quite delicious. Perhaps, if Ciarán was *very* bad, the man would lose his temper, which he never did. He smiled and made a note of the date in his diary.

1st July 1842, Beverwyck, London

"I'm sorry," Rosamund's father said, looking wretched. He stood beside Mama's desk as she set down her pen, watching her reaction to the news, before rubbing a weary hand over his face. "Montagu's in the same boat. We'll be there for the garden party and perhaps a few days after that, but I am afraid we cannot quit London entirely for the summer, not for a while, at least. We will be back and forth for some time. It's unavoidable."

Mama nodded her understanding and squeezed Papa's hand. "You're tired, darling. Take a nap. You need not accompany us tonight if you would rather not. Jules will escort us."

"Are you sure?" he asked, frowning. "I hate to disappoint you, but I don't mind telling you this year has been a damned bear bait."

Unlike many of her friends and contemporaries of the *ton*, Rosamund understood why that was. Her parents refused to shelter her from the reality of how some people lived. She had learned from an early age that she was incredibly privileged, and that such privilege came with responsibilities. Britain was in the grips of a devastating economic depression. For four years in a row, the price of wheat had averaged over sixty shillings a bushel. Manufacturers and minors alike were suffering the consequences. Wages were declining rapidly, along with employment. The pressure of economic distress naturally had the Chartist movement rallying but their timing was off. The movement had struggled to gain momentum, and what could have been their grand moment of triumph was happening too late to bear fruit. Yet again, it seemed as if the government would only pay lip service to the corn laws, reducing duty and making a great hue and cry as if this would be enough to allow the poor to feed themselves. There were more voices making themselves heard, Lord Vane having recently thrown his weight behind the campaign as well, but it was too late to drive through the abolition of the unfair law that saw those most in need starving. The country was in crisis and the prorogation of parliament would not happen in July this year as they'd hoped.

Her mother stood and slid her arms about Papa's waist, kissing his cheek.

"I will mind very much that you are not with me, but only because I shall miss you. You need some peace and quiet. If you are still awake when I return, I shall regale you with all the latest gossip, but do not feel the need to wait up. Now, up you go, and get some rest."

"The very best of wives," he murmured, smiling adoringly at his wife.

Rosamund looked away and concentrated on her book, trying not to listen to their low murmurings, which were clearly not meant for her ears. With a sigh, she wondered if she would ever find a man she could have that kind of relationship with. Mama and Papa discussed everything, even argued about things, but Papa never told Mama to hold her tongue, or to stop interfering in the affairs of men. Indeed, he sought her opinion out and listened to her advice. He even took it! But not only that, they were so obviously still besotted with each other, even after years of marriage and eight children. What must that be like, that amount of love and trust and shared history? She wanted that for herself, wanted a strong, decent, fiercely devoted man like her father to stand beside her.

Lord Hargreaves' face came to mind, and Rosamund wondered if his wife understood the value of the gift she had thrown back in his face. For a man like that was a gift, surely? He was strong and decent, loyal. Despite everything, he had never said a word against his wife. Belatedly, Rosamund remembered she was not supposed to sit in judgement upon either of them, and tried to banish the thought from her mind. No one understood what went on in someone else's marriage, besides the people involved. For all she knew, Hargreaves was cruel in private, or had betrayed his wife or… or… No. She simply could not believe that. But she did not *know*, insisted the voice of her conscience. Lady Hargreaves might act in a way that drove people to believe her fast and wicked, but perhaps….

Oh, stop thinking about them!

Rosamund sank her hands into her hair and groaned.

"Is something wrong, darling?" Looking up with a start, she realised Papa had left the room and Mama was gathering up her writing materials and putting them away.

"Oh, no. Not at all," she said in a rush. "Is it time to get ready?"

"It is," Mama agreed, watching her with concern. "You're certain nothing is amiss? Are you worrying about Lord Hargreaves?"

Rosamund almost gasped. Her mama was usually far too prescient for her children's comfort, but even for her, that was startling.

The duchess gave a little snort. "I hear the gossip too, darling, and if I did not trust your very good sense, I might be worried. I don't *need* to be worried, do I?"

"Of course not," Rosamund said, automatically and with utter sincerity. It was only after the words had left her mouth that she wondered if she were being honest with herself. But Mama had heard the truth in her reply and nodded.

"Well good. Naturally you must be extra careful, and do not spend too much time with him, but you're the daughter of a duke, and other people ought to mind their own business. Hargreaves is such a decent man, too. Papa likes him very much and feels so sorry for him. Of course, he understands the poor man's predicament more than most." Rosamund nodded, knowing her father's first marriage had been a deeply unhappy one, despite his best efforts.

Rosamund knew she ought not, but could not help but ask. "Is it true, then, what they say about her? That she's unfaithful?"

Mama shrugged and closed the lid on her writing desk. "As to that, I do not know, but she is the most dreadful flirt, that I have seen firsthand. She seems to go out of her way to goad the poor man. When they were first married, she nearly got him killed, starting fights wherever she went. She seemed to revel in the attention." Mama shook her head, thoughtful now. "I've often wondered if it was because of her father's lack of interest in her. It makes her seek attention from other men."

Mama tapped her finger against her lips, as she often did when wrestling with her work. Figuring out the vagaries of human nature was her greatest fascination. She sighed, shaking her head.

"She too is the daughter of a duke, of course, though her papa was more consequence than substance. He was a cold fish, and I dread to think what manner of father. And as for her mother, a hard woman who believed children should be seen and not heard, and not seen too often at that. The poor girl likely never stood a chance."

Rosamund discovered she was not feeling charitable enough to pity the lady as she ought to and scolded herself for her lack of empathy. Just because she'd been lucky in her parents did not mean she did not appreciate that other people had very different experiences. Her mama was a perfect example, for her father had been a violent man.

"Anyway, enough gossip and tittle-tattle. We must go and dress or Jules will throw a fit. You know how he cannot abide tardiness in anyone but himself."

Rosamund laughed, relieved to change the subject, and hurried after her mama to ready herself for the ball. As she climbed the stairs, she could not help but reflect that Lord Hargreaves was right, they ought not seek each other's company out so often, and only ever with others present. She saw too late that she was more than a little fond of the man, and that would not do. To interfere in another's marriage, no matter the circumstances, was beyond the pale. To harbour feelings for someone else's husband—oh, no. That was an appalling situation that could only make her miserable, and if anyone else knew—if Hargreaves knew— Rosamund went hot and cold at the idea.

Hurrying to her room, Rosamund greeted her maid and readied herself for the evening, with the determination that she would act precisely as she ought to do. She would dance and converse with her friends, and keep an eye out for a man who might be everything to her that her father was to her mother.

A good, strong, decent, kind, loyal, *unmarried* man who would never let her down.

1st July 1842, Peregrine House, Grosvenor Square, London.

"Papa?"

Evie's father looked up from his desk as she spoke. A nervous sense of foreboding skittered down her spine as she stood in the open doorway, the sense that she was in trouble looming over her like the villain in a Gothic novel.

"You wanted to see me?" she managed, aware her voice quavered somewhat.

"I did, yes, love. Come in and close the door."

Evie did as he asked and walked into the room, her heart thudding unpleasantly. *Don't let this be about Louis*, she prayed silently, though somehow she'd known this day would come, eventually.

"Sit down," her father said as he got up and moved around to the front of his desk.

He leaned back upon it, looking down on her. Love and warmth shone in his eyes as always and Evie told herself she was silly to be so anxious. He was her darling Papa and would never hurt her. Yet the sensation remained.

"We must talk, I think."

"Oh?" she said, her voice unnaturally high, betraying her nerves.

He nodded, his expression grave. "I never explained why we left so suddenly, did I? Yet I believe you know. I very nearly dismissed Neil when I discovered he had been your messenger to the Comte de Villen."

Evie felt the blush steal up over her chest, her throat, her cheeks burning. "Papa, no," she said, as her stomach roiled with misery. "It was not his fault. I—"

"I know. You should never have put him in such a position," her father said firmly. "If anyone had found out, you'd be ruined. You understand that?"

"Lo—" Evie began before snapping her mouth shut. "He would have married me."

"We shall get to that," her father said, his voice dark. "I will not ask you to explain yourself, or demand for how long this ill-advised friendship has been going on. That your mother has seen fit to allow it at all has been a source of contention between us these past weeks. She naturally has a romantic streak and sees in Villen a likeness to me and our situation."

Evie dared a glance at him, hope flickering in her heart that this might not be so bad as she'd feared.

"It's not the same, Evie, love," he whispered. "Bedwin didn't want me to marry your mother, partly because of the inequality of our positions. There is no denying your mother's status in society was damaged by marrying me. That is not the case here. It's true that I was a devil with women and hard living, but the comte goes far beyond anything I ever did. My biggest crime was being born in the workhouse. I was a gambler and libertine, yes, but I worked hard for what I have. Honest work."

"What do you mean?" she asked, breathing hard. Her fingers gripped the edges of the chair so tightly it was painful.

"I have done some investigating these past months. I sent men to France to see what they could discover about the comte, which, to begin with, was very little apart from the obvious. Though I must tell you now, I have known for some time that Villen and his brother made the money to finance their club as jewel thieves, breaking into people's houses to relieve them of their valuables. They told me that themselves some years ago."

Evie's eyes grew wide, and she remembered then how easily Louis had climbed into her bedroom to deliver her birthday present. *Oh.*

"Rouge et Noir is an exclusive club where dukes and princes may mingle freely with artists and bohemian types—if they can afford it. There is a deal of mystery about what else goes on there, however. So much so that it cannot be anything good, but that is a minor point. If it were only the club and the stealing, perhaps I could turn a blind eye, but it is not."

He paused, watching her reaction and Evie forced herself to wait when she wanted to demand what more he had found out that was so very damning.

"The Comte de Villen has a half-brother, as we all know, but there is another man closely associated with him. They are not of the same blood, but consider themselves family from what we could gather." He paused, his expression one of sympathy. "Why do you think it was so hard to gain this information, Evie?"

"Because there is nothing to discover, perhaps?" Evie countered, knowing that was not it but feeling the need to defend Louis, even though she suspected that everything she had feared about a future with him was true, and far worse than she'd imagined.

"Because everyone is too damned terrified to speak about him, because Wulfric de Vere is the king of the Parisian underworld and the comte's protégé. So who do you think put him there?"

Evie swallowed, hearing the words but not making sense of them. "Underworld?" she repeated, imagining Hades and pomegranate seeds before scolding herself for being fanciful. Except she could too easily imagine Louis as Hades, a wickedly beautiful god, tempting her, daring her to live in the darkness with him.

"Yes, the underworld. Criminals, love. Every vice, every wicked thing that happens in that city happens under the watchful gaze of *Le Loup Noir de Paris*. The Black Wolf, they call him, and he answers only to the comte."

The room felt hazy and unreal, her painful grip on the chair the only thing anchoring Evie to reality. "So this Wolf person is a criminal, that does not mean—"

"Yes. It does," her father said, his voice implacable. "And God knows I did some things in my time, love, but I was never a criminal, and I certainly never took a man's life."

Evie gasped, looking up. No. No, not Louis. Not gentle, kind, Louis. She would not believe it. Evie shook her head, her throat too tight to deny the words, to defend Louis as she wanted to.

Her father crouched down before her and carefully released her hands from the chair, rubbing them gently between his own.

"I'm so sorry, my darling girl. I would never willingly hurt you, or cause you a moment's distress, but I must protect you from making a mistake you might regret for the rest of your days. He is beautiful, and he has been kind to you. Believe me, I understand all too well why he is drawn to you, too. Your sweetness and innocence fascinates him. When one has led a life in the darkness, one does long for the light, and that is you, love. Understand me when I tell you, I do not believe he is evil or malicious, but I do believe his life is one of darkness and danger. He will drag you into that world, Evie, even if he does not mean to, and that is not what you want. That will not make you happy."

Evie could only swallow, too numb with shock to react at all.

"We all know what kind of life you have dreamed of, for you've told us often enough. You want a quiet life surrounded by people who love you, your friends and family. A loving home and a large family and everything safe and familiar. It *is* what you have always wanted, is it not?"

Evie nodded, unable to deny it. She did not wish to deny it, for that was exactly the life she had dreamed of.

Her father held her gaze. "He cannot give you that. Perhaps he wishes to, perhaps he even believes he can, but he has blood on his hands, love, and that leaves a stain a man cannot wash away."

"B-Blood?" Evie repeated, wondering if she might be sick.

Her father nodded. "I do not tell you this to frighten you, love. You know you are safe here, that I will always protect you no matter what?"

Jerkily, Evie nodded.

"From what I can discover, he has been implicated in the deaths of three men, one of them de Vere's father. Perhaps he had good reason, Evie, but it does not change the fact that he has killed, more than once. Any witnesses to these crimes were too afraid to speak out against them, but there seems little doubt Villen was responsible. Certainly my men discovered enough to convince them the Comte de Villen is a very dangerous man."

Evie's breath came in odd little gasps as she tried to reconcile the man he described with her Louis. She ought to be appalled, she told herself. She ought to be terrified, yet the voice in her head only told her that if Louis had truly killed someone, he *would* have had a reason. Perhaps he'd had no choice, perhaps he'd been defending himself, but even if that were not the case, she knew she would not condemn him. Evie knew him, she knew his heart. Whilst she had always known there was darkness lurking there, for she had sensed it from the start, she knew too that he would protect her from it. She was safe with him. Perhaps others were not, but she was. Not that she would ever say those words to her father, no matter how she wished to defend Louis.

Evie could see the fear and worry in her papa's eyes, the desperate desire to keep her safe, and she understood why he did what he did. She knew he would never understand that she was safe with Louis, no matter what. Though it broke her heart, she knew too that he would never let her marry Louis, even if she decided she wished to, and she could not marry without her parents' approval, for that would hurt them so badly. Tears swam in her eyes.

"I'm so sorry, my love," her father said, and his voice was unsteady now. "Truly, I would cut my own heart out before I would cause you pain, but a little pain now is surely better than living a life that would not only make you unhappy, but might even put you in danger? Evie?"

He looked so wretched and full of regret for having hurt her that she could not be angry with him. He was only doing his best to keep her safe, even if the results were going to be unbearable.

She nodded again, for what else could she do? She had no words to explain the truth, even if the tightness in her throat would let her speak them. If she tried, she would weep and that would only break Papa's heart a little further and he was carrying guilt enough as it was. He would never see Louis as she saw him, and she would certainly never convince Papa they were only friends after what had happened at Fort William. It would be a lie, and Evie had never been able to lie successfully, not that she'd ever needed or wanted to before. But if she could not get away with a little fib about how much she'd spent on books, a lie about Louis being only a friend was quite beyond her, because it was no longer true.

"You will not speak to him anymore, Evie. I am not asking you to cut him in public. You will, of course, be polite if he approaches you, but you will not seek him out, you will not converse with him, or dance with him. You will not encourage this friendship. For his sake, as much as your own, you must do everything to put an end to any further interaction, or I will do so myself. If I must take you away again, I *will* do it. Please, don't make me do that, love."

Evie's mind raced. She had no talent for deception or intrigue, but she understood if she argued the point, Papa would have cause to distrust her. That she could not have, for she had no intention of losing Louis' friendship entirely. What that meant, she did not know, but she could not simply cut him from her life any more than she could cut him out of her heart. She loved him. Irrespective of whether she wished to marry him, he had been her dearest friend and confidant for years, and now… and now she was going to break down if she did not get out of this room. Belatedly, she realised she still had not answered.

"I understand," she said carefully, for she would not agree to her father's commands and then break her promise, but she did understand them, even if she had every intention of disregarding them. "May I go now?"

Thankfully, Papa could see she was on the verge of tears and nodded, so Evie got to her feet and was immediately enfolded in his strong arms. It was impossible not to cry then, and she sobbed into his waistcoat.

"Forgive me, my darling Evie. I swear I am sorry for it."

She nodded without looking up and then pushed out of his arms and ran for the door, needing nothing but to escape, so that she might break her heart in private.

Chapter 5

Monsieur Boucher,

*What you ask is impossible. My likeness is
plastered over walls and windows the length
and breadth of the city. I hardly dare leave my
rat-infested rooms. I have lost everything, and
you think to blackmail me into giving more?
What more have I left? If I must be your
damned puppet, then so be it, but not for
nothing. You'll pay me as agreed, or perhaps
the pretty comte you are so fascinated with
will do better with the information I have
about you?*

**—Excerpt of a letter from Mr Graham
Franklin to Monsieur Etienne Boucher.**

3rd July 1842, Mrs Palmer's Summer Ball, Piccadilly, London.

"Stop fretting, Cara, you look positively glorious," Rosamund
said, slipping her arm through the girl's as Cara stared about her
with wide eyes. It was true: Lady Cara looked like the goddess of
the harvest, everything about her ripe and abundant. Her red hair
shimmered in the candlelight and her pale green gown hugged her
splendid figure, setting off her fiery colouring to perfection.

"Are you sure?" Cara asked, casting Rosamund a doubtful glance. "Everyone is staring at me."

"That's why they're staring, you silly goose," Rosamund replied with a smile, though the way some men were looking at her friend made her want to hurry her away.

Her parents had been right to give her a few small tastes of her first season, though, or next year would be thoroughly overwhelming. At least at a relatively minor affair like this one, she could dip her toe in the water without getting out of her depth. Some of the grandest balls could have seven hundred people in attendance and in your first season, it felt like being swallowed alive. One could only hope to emerge on the other side intact and with one's sanity, and—more importantly to the *ton*—one's reputation unblemished.

"Who is your first dance with?" Rosamund asked.

Cara fumbled with her dance card and Rosamund stopped her, taking both her hands and holding on.

"Look at me," she instructed.

Cara did as she asked, her blue eyes the colour of a summer sky at dusk and full of anxiety.

"Now, take a deep breath and let it out again. You have nothing to worry about. You'll only dance with people you already know. Jules has promised to stand up with you, remember, and Leo Hunt. There's no need to be nervous with them, is there now?"

"No," Cara said, the tension in her shoulders easing slightly. "No, thank you, Rosamund. I'm being silly, I know. I've wanted this for an age and now...."

Rosamund laughed, shaking her head. "Not the least bit silly, or at least no sillier than I was, and likely every other girl who has ever come out to society. It's thrilling and wonderful and awful and terrifying at the same time. Now, who is your first dance partner?"

Cara glanced down at her card and smiled. "I cannot think how I could have forgotten. It's Mr Anson."

"Lucky Mr Anson," Rosamund said with approval.

"Lucky me," Cara corrected. "He's a marvellous dancer, and so very funny. He makes me laugh."

As if they had conjured him, the man himself appeared before them and gave a deep bow. "Lady Rosamund, Lady Cara. Good evening, and may I say how beautiful you both look?"

"You may say it as many times as you like," Cara said, her nerves apparently melting away under Ashton Anson's admiring gaze.

"In that case, I shall. Now, I hope you remembered to put me down for your first dance, for I claimed it well before this evening to be certain all the other gentlemen did not elbow me out."

"Indeed, I did," Cara said, beaming at him.

Her gaze drifted down to his waistcoat, which for Ash was quite subdued. Men's fashion was becoming increasingly sombre, with an emphasis on black and dark colours, something which Ash was quite vociferous in lamenting. At an affair like this, the men were all dressed in identical outfits, with black coats and trousers and pristine white waistcoats. Ash, too, wore a white waistcoat, though his was lavishly embroidered with silver thread.

Ash held out his hand to Cara, his dark eyes alight with merriment. "Then shall we?"

Cara glanced back at Rosamund, who nodded. "Have fun, dear."

"She's with me, of course she'll have fun," Ash retorted, winking at Rosamund as he placed Cara's hand on his arm. "Don't worry, I shall return her safely to her mama when the dance is over."

With that, they disappeared into the crowd.

Emma V Leech

"Lady Rosamund?"

Rosamund turned, blinking in surprise as it took her a moment to place the man before her. He was tall and strong, with powerful shoulders and laughing tawny eyes. Rosamund frowned.

"Do ye nae remember me? It's only been a year and a half since we last met."

"Muir!" Rosamund exclaimed in shock. "But… But you look…."

Words failed her. The last time she had seen Muir Anderson he had been romping through the fields around his home with dogs barking at his heels, his hair wild and shaggy and looking thoroughly disreputable. Now, though….

Muir pulled a face and rubbed the back of his neck, the picture of embarrassment. "Aye, well, Ma said I had better not let her down in front of all her cronies. I feel a right numpty."

"You look splendid," Rosamund said on a breath, meaning it. His hair, for once, was neatly trimmed, and his coat and trousers hugged an impressively muscular figure that was already drawing many admiring gazes from the females in their corner of the ballroom.

"Ach, I don't know about that, but Da said I scrub up well enough, so I guess it's fine. Am I too late to secure a dance with ye?"

"Oh, no. I only arrived a moment ago so you may have the next if you like?" Rosamund found the space upon her card and took up the small pencil attached. "Does this mean Evie is back?"

"Ah dinnae ken," he said, watching as she wrote his name in for the galop, an exuberant dance that ought to suit him nicely. "I was hoping you might know. Her family left Scotland before I did but they were visiting friends on their way home. Is she nae here tonight?"

Rosamund studied him, noting with interest that he looked disappointed. Ah, so that was how the wind was blowing.

"I don't know. Shall we see if we can find out before the dance begins? I see Lady Balderston there and she has been busy gathering the latest gossip ever since she came to town."

Muir agreed with this plan and so they made their way towards where Rosamund had glimpsed Lady Balderston's shock of thick white hair, which had been elegantly arranged with diamond hair clips and deep purple feathers which matched perfectly the stunning evening gown she wore. As they drew closer, Rosamund smiled to see her nephew Mr Godwin was there too with his friend, the Comte de Villen. As ever, the Frenchman looked like a fallen angel, almost too beautiful to be the same breed as the other mere mortals about him. His dark hair glinted in the candlelight, and though he wore the same outfit of fitted black coat, black trousers, and white waistcoat as every other man in the room, somehow he made everyone else look as though they had either slept in their clothes or were trying far too hard.

"Good evening, my lady," Rosamund said, giving her a curtsey before greeting the two men. She turned back to Lady Balderston "How wonderful you look tonight. That gown is simply divine."

"Thank you, my dear, but divinity certainly had nothing to do with it," she said with a twinkle in her eye. Her mouth quirked, and she glanced at the comte, who met her gaze and inclined his head slightly. Not understanding the exchange, Rosamund carried on.

"Might I introduce my friend to you, my lady?"

The lady snorted and extended her hand to Muir. "No need. Barnaby and I know this scoundrel. Good evening, you young scamp. My, you look almost civilised this evening."

"Thank ye kindly, my lady. Good evening, Mr Godwin. It is good to see ye both again, and almost civilised is exactly what I was aiming for. There's nae need to get overexcited, aye?"

"Hmmm," the lady said, considering this. "That rather depends on your point of view, I fear, but you look very well, very much like your father. Is he here?"

"Na, Da can't abide London, ye ken. Ma's here, though, catching up with all her old friends."

"Excellent. Tell her to call on me when she has the time. I'm at Beverwyck for now and I should be pleased to catch up with her."

"I will do."

"I suppose I ought to introduce you," Lady Balderston said, and it was only now that Rosamund noticed the slightly odd atmosphere as Muir and the comte faced each other. Mr Godwin was obviously aware of it too, as his gaze darted nervously from one man to the other.

"Monsieur Le Comte, would you allow me to introduce Mr Muir Anderson? Mr Anderson, Louis César de Montluc, the Comte de Villen."

The two men faced each other, and Rosamund shivered as she saw the look in the comte's brilliant blue eyes. They seemed to burn, as though lit by an azure flame under the bright light of the ballroom.

"Monsieur," Muir said, and bowed, interest flickering in his tawny eyes.

The comte inclined his head very slightly, saying nothing. To say the atmosphere had plummeted to arctic temperatures was an understatement.

Mr Godwin cleared his throat, looking ill at ease and like he was desperately racking his brain for something to say. Whilst he was floundering, Rosamund did her best to step into the breach.

"We were wondering if Miss Knight was here this evening, my lady. Have you heard if she has returned from Scotland yet?

She was a guest of Mr Anderson's family, and he was hoping to speak to her this evening."

Rosamund wondered if she imagined the temperature plunging another several degrees, or the way the comte appeared to seethe with repressed energy. She had always found him a very calming and relaxing presence in the past, so this seemed most peculiar. Lady Balderston was obviously aware of it also, her eyes alight with interest as she gave Muir another contemplative once over before glancing back at the comte. Whatever the issue was, he seemed to have himself back under control now, his expression as bland as his beautiful countenance could allow.

"I believe they are back in town, yes. I noticed the knocker back on the door this morning as it happens. As to whether Miss Knight is attending tonight, I'm afraid I cannot say."

With some relief, Rosamund realised people were taking their places for the next dance and looked expectantly at Muir.

"My dance, I think, my lady," he said with a warm smile, before offering her his arm.

"If you would excuse us," Rosamund said, and allowed Muir to escort her onto the dance floor.

3rd July 1842, Mrs Palmer's Summer Ball, Piccadilly London.

Sebastian watched Rosamund and the handsome young man she was dancing with as the energetic galop had everyone flying about the ballroom at speed. Full of life and energy, her complexion pink with exertion, her mouth curved in a smile, she was a delight to watch. He smothered the niggle of jealousy that made him wish he might be the one dancing with her. Sebastian knew the Earl of Morven and his sons were decent men. Certainly, he'd heard they got into the usual scrapes and difficulties all young men experienced but that was only to be expected, welcomed even, for a few humbling mistakes at that age saved you from making larger ones later on. It would not be a brilliant match. In terms of wealth and status, she could do better, but he felt certain that was not what Rosamund wanted or cared about.

The dance ended, and he watched with amusement as Rosamund struggled to leave the dance floor, accosted at every turn by young men demanding she write their names upon her dance card. A pity he could not do likewise, but he was not so foolish as he once was. Admiring her from a distance was one thing, a pleasant conversation unexceptionable, but dancing with her, holding her in his arms …. A strange sensation coiled about his heart, as though it were being squeezed within his chest. *Stop it, damned fool*, he told himself severely. *No. You will not think of it.*

Forcing his gaze away from the dance floor, he turned back to the group of men he stood with and concentrated on the conversation.

For the rest of the evening, Sebastian only caught glimpses of Lady Rosamund and did not seek her out. As the evening wore on, he had to admit he was bored to tears. The idea of making polite conversation over supper was too much. He would leave now instead, rude of him but he was tired of being well behaved all the time when everyone else seemed to get away with murder. The heat of the ballroom receded as he walked away. There were fewer people in this part of the house, most on their way to or from the refreshments, or taking a moment of quiet.

"La, all alone, my lord? Surely your little debutante is eager for your company? She'll cry herself to sleep tonight if you insist on ignoring her so."

Sebastian stopped, schooling his features into the impassive mask that always served best with Adelia. If she could not rile him, she would grow bored and leave him be. It had taken him a long time to learn that lesson, but he'd learned it well. He turned to face her, very aware that they were not alone, and the *ton* would delight in yet another scandal to satisfy their desire for an interesting piece of gossip.

"Good evening, Adelia. You look very well tonight."

As ever, flattery diverted her for a moment and she smiled, smoothing a hand over the wine-coloured silk of her gown. He wondered if she had ever touched her lover with such affection and suspected not. Certainly she had never touched him so, even when she had professed herself madly in love with him. He'd been as gentle and patient with her as he knew how, reassuring her and giving her time, but his touch had never been welcomed.

Before they had married he had misread the signs, believing her lack of physical passion towards him only maidenly reticence, for she had flirted and given every sign of desiring him, and so he had never pressed her for more than a kiss. Once they had married and he discovered the truth, he'd done everything he could think of to please her. He had spoken to her at length during the early months and years of their marriage, needing to discover if anyone had hurt her in the past and made her afraid, or if she had heard stories about what happened between men and women that had twisted her view of lovemaking. He had discovered nothing. Adelia had given him nothing, shutting him out at every turn. When they retired at night, he had suggested they simply lay side by side, holding hands, hoping if they began with something small, she might come to trust him. He had never understood why she would not even try, why the moment they had married she lost all interest in him.

When he had taken her away to France, after the mess she'd made with her artist, she had seemed to regret her actions and he'd offered her another chance to try again, but that too had been thrown back in his face. Within two days of leaving England, she was using her beauty and wit on one bedazzled Frenchman after another. Short of locking her up, he could do nothing to stop her. If he divorced her, she would be ruined, and he was not so cruel as to do that to her, to cut her off from the society she lived for, but he'd sworn then that she would not hurt him that way again. They would lead separate lives and he would find what happiness he could among the wreckage of his life.

"Well, are you not going to dance with the poor child, at least?"

Sebastian sighed inwardly. "I think Mr Price is looking for you," he said. "You'd best ask him to take you into supper."

"Why, where are you going?" she demanded, irritation making her usually melodious voice snappy and sharp.

"Home. I'm rather tired."

Adelia snorted, looking at him in disgust. "How did I come to marry such a dull old man?"

For a moment, Sebastian felt a pang of regret as he imagined hearing those words spoken by another woman, but with gentle humour, teasing him about his great age. Too late, he realised his face must have betrayed him, his lips curving in a wistful smile, for Adelia's expression grew thunderous. Sebastian cursed himself.

"Go then," she said, her beautiful eyes cold. "I don't need you or want you."

Despite knowing better, Sebastian gave a mirthless laugh. "You have made that abundantly clear, Adelia, but thank you for clarifying. I shall leave with a clear conscience."

He turned to leave, but she was not yet done with him.

"Will you indeed? Or perhaps you are arranging a tryst in my absence? Will I see Lady Rosamund feign a headache and slip away too?"

She did not modify her tone or lower her voice, and Sebastian experienced a chill of terror at the idea she might harm Rosamund on purpose.

Sebastian whirled about to face her, his face cold and hard.

"Do. Not," he said, his voice very low.

"Or what?" she sneered, contorting her lovely features into something hard and ugly. "Or you'll call me out? Will you confront a delicate little female on the field of honour? Oh, no, I forgot. You don't have the nerve."

"Stop, Adelia. Or I swear, you will not like my repost," he said, struggling to keep his temper. Why was it so much harder tonight to ignore her?

She snorted, looking him up and down like he was beneath her notice. "How terrifying you are, my lord. Or you might be, but I know that Lord Hargreaves is too much of a coward to fight, even to defend his wife's honour."

"Honour? You truly believe me shooting some poor bastard who's done nothing but be foolish enough to fall in love with you is honourable? Do you truly believe you have any honour left to you after the hearts you have broken and the damage you have done?" he demanded, so shocked by her wilful blindness to reality that he did not guard his tongue as he ought.

He knew better, but he was all sharp edges these days.

Adelia flushed scarlet, her eyes glittering with the desire for retribution. If he was not careful, there would be the most dreadful scene. Sebastian took a breath. People were already taking note and that would not do.

"Forgive me, Adelia. I believe I am feeling rather out of sorts," he said, forcing the words out, though they almost choked him. "I hope you enjoy the rest of your evening."

He turned then and experienced a jolt of shock, and then remorse as he found himself facing Rosamund. She had a glass of lemonade in her hand and was obviously returning from the refreshments room. Her beautiful face had blanched alabaster white, and he knew at once she had overheard the exchange. Not daring to leave her in proximity with his wife, he took her arm, guiding her away. He did not speak a word to her until he had returned her to the ballroom. He found her brother talking to some of his friends and when they were a few feet away, he stopped, bowing to her.

"Goodnight, my lady," he said, hoping she could read the regret in his eyes.

"But—"

Sebastian shook his head. He could not do this, could not risk Adelia's retribution hurting her. He must not see her again.

"I shall not speak with you again, for your own sake. Forgive me," he whispered, and turned and walked away.

Chapter 6

Louis,

I am so sorry. I do not know what to do, how I am ever to speak to you again. I do not want to cut you from my life. I <u>will not</u> do so, but I do not know how it can be otherwise. I am trapped.

—Excerpt of a letter from Miss Evie Knight (daughter of Lady Helena and Mr Gabriel Knight) to Louis César de Montluc, Comte de Villen.

3rd July 1842, Lansdown Place, Sloane Square, Chelsea, London.

Sebastian headed directly for his study and rang for his butler. The man arrived a moment later, seemingly unsurprised by his master's premature return. The staff here were used to their odd comings and goings and knew better than to show any interest.

"I will be leaving for an extended voyage, Peterson," he told the man. "Have the carriage ready for me first thing in the morning. I'll instruct Forbes to pack enough for a few days, he can follow on with the rest of my belongings later. I'll forward an itinerary when I have more information, but you may contact me at this address for at least the next ten days."

He handed the address to the butler, who glanced at it.

"You are returning to France, my lord? Will Lady Hargreaves—"

"She will not," he said curtly. "Yes, I shall spend a few months in France before travelling to Italy. It would be in everyone's interest if you did not mention this to *anyone* until after I have left in the morning."

"You expect to be gone for some time?" Peterson ventured, his expression carefully neutral.

"I do," Sebastian replied.

His heart ached with regret and frustration, but there was nothing else to do. Adelia had Rosamund in her sights and all the time she suspected he had anything resembling affection for her, Rosamund would be at risk of being caught up in their miserable lives. He would not risk her happiness, not for anything. She deserved a loving husband, a happy life, and he was not about to let her lose that chance. If it meant exiling himself, then so be it. Perhaps when Rosamund was safely married, he might dare to return, but certainly not before.

"Lady Hargreaves will, of course, remain here until the season ends but I don't doubt she will give you instructions for the coming months."

"Very good, my lord."

Sebastian nodded and dismissed the man and then stood, swiping up the brandy decanter and a glass before heading up the stairs to his bedroom. He intended to get very drunk indeed, and if he suffered the torments of the damned on the journey to France tomorrow, it was only what he deserved. If he was in enough pain, at least he would be too wretched to regret what he was doing, to spare any last maudlin thoughts for what his life might have been, if he'd not been such a damned fool all those years ago.

3rd July 1842, Mrs Palmer's Summer Ball, Piccadilly London.

Louis stalked around the edges of the ballroom, quite unable to hide his restlessness. Over the years, he had become adept at hiding his emotions, at wearing the elegant mask of the refined Comte de Villen, whilst the real man simmered inside. These people did not know that man. If they did, they would think twice about being in his company, and tonight, the mask was in danger of slipping. Muir Anderson was everything he had feared. Handsome, young and thoroughly decent, he exuded an endearing if rough charm and good humour, and in different circumstances, Louis might have liked him. As it was, he had never felt such a rush of resentment and hostility towards a man who did not deserve his enmity.

People moved out of his way, taking one look at him and deciding it was for the best as he cut his way through the crowd, searching for Evie.

Barnaby hurried towards him, his expression one of concern. "Come and have a drink," he suggested. "There's a card game in the library. You could bankrupt a few noblemen, make you feel better," he suggested with a wry smile.

Louis snorted, not deigning to answer.

"Well, at least stop pacing up and down," Barnaby implored, as he kept pace with Louis. "It's like watching a panther prowling about the ballroom, wondering who he's going to pounce on first."

Louis slanted him a glittering look and Barnaby huffed out a laugh.

"Yes, well, *I'm* not in any doubt who's first, admittedly."

"Where is she?" Louis growled, tugging his pocket watch free and scowling at it.

"Ah, as to that. Er… Louis," Barnaby said, tugging at his arm.

Louis stopped pacing, turned to look at Barnaby and then followed his gaze. The entire ballroom fell away. The people, the noise, the chatter all disappeared like mist, his entire being riveted on the woman who had just entered the room.

She wore a gown he had designed for her. A ripe pink, it hugged her voluptuous curves, and his hands itched with the desire to slide them lovingly over the swells of her magnificent breasts, the dramatic line of her waist as it flared out to her hips and lush bottom. Desire and love and longing burned inside him until he was nothing but sensation and need, teetering too precariously on the edge of sanity to behave with any sense. And yet then he saw the stiff set of her shoulders. He saw the bloom in her cheeks had vanished, her complexion pale and wan, the joy he usually sought and found in her eyes entirely gone.

What had happened?

Her green eyes swept over the ballroom, settling unerringly upon him as his heart jolted with concern. Was she ill, or had someone hurt her? He was moving towards her, drawn as inexorably as if pulled by a magnet. Her eyes widened, fear giving her features a sharp edge as she gave a tiny but definite shake of her head. Louis stopped in his tracks, reading her message, the anxiety emanating from her in waves. Though it went against his every instinct to go to her, to comfort and protect her, he did as she asked, but he did not look away. Her eyes glittered, misery in her expression as she turned away from him. Louis' breath caught.

"Something's wrong." Barnaby's soft voice pierced the turmoil of his thoughts as he turned to his friend, realising he too had witnessed it.

"Go to her, *s'il te plait,*" Louis begged, clutching his arm. "Something has happened, and she does not want me to approach her, that much is clear, but I must speak with her, Barnaby. Go to her and find out what has happened. Tell her I'll do anything to make it right. Anything at all. Tell her to trust me."

Barnaby patted the hand that was grasping his arm too tightly. "All right, old man. Don't worry. I'll go."

Louis paced as he watched Barnaby make his way around the ballroom. He clung to the shadows, observing from a distance as Evie looked up and saw Barnaby, hurrying towards him. It was a brief conversation and Barnaby's grim expression made Louis' guts tighten into a knot until he was sick with apprehension.

"Well?" he demanded before Barnaby could speak a word.

"Her father knows about your... friendship," Barnaby said carefully. "He has forbidden her to speak to you, and she is to end any communication between you at once. He has threatened to take her away again if she does not do so."

Louis cursed long and low, a volley of obscene French that did not begin to relieve his feelings.

"She gave me this," Barnaby added, handing him a note.

Louis took it and tore it open, devouring the scant words and taking little comfort from the fact she would not cut him from her life.

"Tell her I will come to her. Tonight," Louis said, ignoring the look of appalled shock on Barnaby's face. "Tell her to dismiss her maid as quickly as she can and to put a candle in the window when she is alone."

Barnaby gaped at him. "You're not serious?"

"You think I would joke about such a thing?" Louis demanded, taking a breath as Barnaby reacted to the fury in his voice. He exhaled, trying to moderate his voice, no simple task when he wanted to tear the damned ballroom down in frustration. Two weeks he had waited to see her again, and now this. Well, just let them try to keep him away. "Forgive me, Barnaby, but just give her the message."

Barnaby shook his head slowly, his expression one of deep regret. "Louis, no. I c-can't tell an innocent young lady such a thing. You can't ask it of me. Quite apart from all the moral reasons, you'll break your blasted neck! Have you *seen* Peregrine

House? It's on Grosvenor Square, the front is completely exposed."

"Which is why I shall go in the back," Louis said, being well aware of the difficulties.

Barnaby gaped at him, momentarily silenced. It did not last. "You'll never get in with no one seeing. Even if you do, that means you need to go through the house to find her room, supposing you can! How many servants will you have to dodge, never mind security? Knight takes his family's safety seriously after what happened to his eldest girl. What if you're caught? My God, there will be the almightiest scandal. Think about what you're saying."

"I've done it before," Louis replied evenly, earning himself a look of such horror he might have laughed had the circumstances been otherwise. "And if you repeat that to another soul...."

Barnaby's expression shuttered and Louis cursed himself. Barnaby would never betray him or Evie. Indeed, he was trying to keep Evie safe and Louis from acting rashly. He raked a hand through his hair and swore under his breath.

"I beg your forgiveness, Barnaby. I had no right to say such a thing to you. I trust you, implicitly. You know I do. I'm just—"

"You're overwrought is what you are," Barnaby said frankly.

Louis let out a shaky breath. "I cannot argue with that observation."

"Did you really?" Barnaby asked him, looking incredulous.

Louis nodded. "Not their London home, but yes. Swan Hall in Sussex, and no, I did not take liberties. I delivered her birthday present and left at once."

Barnaby let out a breath, shaking his head. "It's hardly the same, then," he said darkly.

Louis resisted the urge to howl with frustration before he noticed a young lady at the edge of the ballroom writing a name upon the little booklet that served as the ladies' dance card. He left Barnaby without a word and strode over to her. The young woman, a Miss Glover, gave a squeak of shock as she looked up to see him beside her and then blushed scarlet.

"Bonsoir, Miss Glover, a pleasure to see you this evening, and looking so enchanting, too. Might I ask a great favour of you? I need to write down an address for my friend. The poor fellow has a lamentable memory and will have forgotten it by morning if I do not."

"Oh," the woman said, gaping up at him. "W-Would you like—?"

She held out the tiny booklet and pencil and Louis gave her his most dazzling smile.

"Indeed, I would, and you are kindness itself, Miss Glover. *Milles mercis."*

Miss Glover gave a breathless little laugh and handed over the pencil and booklet. Louis neatly tore out one of the blank pages at the end of the book and scrawled a note to Evie, careful the young lady could not see the words. With a formal bow, he thanked her profusely for her help and hurried back to Barnaby.

"Here," he said. "Give that to Evie. You don't need to say a word or involve yourself further."

Barnaby stared at the note in Louis' hand, his expression taut with apprehension.

"Je t'en prie, s'il te plait," Louis said, his voice betraying his emotions. "Please, Barnaby. I need your help. I love her. You know that I love her. I would never hurt her, but we must speak. How am I to resolve this if I can never see her again?"

Barnaby sighed and took the note from his hand. "What will you do?"

"That all depends on Evie," Louis said, and hoped to God he could depend on her too.

Chapter 7

Mon amour,

I will come to you tonight. Dismiss your maid as soon as you are able and put a candle in the window once you are alone.

Je t'aime, Evie. I will let no one keep us apart.

LC x

—Excerpt of a letter from Louis César de Montluc, Comte de Villen to Miss Evie Knight (daughter of Lady Helena and Mr Gabriel Knight).

3rd July 1842, Mrs Palmer's Summer Ball, Piccadilly London.

Rosamund went through the motions for the rest of the evening, though she felt oddly numb and out of sorts. She danced and smiled and made polite small talk until she felt like she might scream. Needing to escape for a moment, she sought a little peace by walking the corridors where it was quieter, though whether she was hoping to escape the ballroom and all its guests or herself, she was uncertain.

"Ozzie?"

Rosamund turned to see Evie sat in an alcove. Mrs Palmer had supplied chairs in several secluded corners for the guests to take a moment to rest quietly, or for lovers to indulge in a little tête-àtête. Seeing her friend gave Rosamund a moment of relief until she realised Evie looked as wretched as she did.

"Not enjoying yourself?" Rosamund guessed with a wry smile.

Evie shook her head. "You?"

"No," she replied, her voice flat. "I hate everyone and everything."

"I know just how you feel," Evie said with a heavy sigh.

They looked at each other and both gave a despondent laugh.

"You go first," Evie said, reaching out and taking Rosamund's hand. "I saw Lord Hargreaves leave earlier. Is that why—"

Out of nowhere, tears pricked at Rosamund's eyes and her throat grew tight. She swallowed hard, trying to tell herself she was being a great ninny, but it didn't help. A fat tear rolled down her cheek.

"Oh, Ozzie, love," Evie said, her voice aching with sympathy. "Come with me. We can't have anyone see you like this."

Evie tugged her to her feet and checked the corridor was clear before hurrying her along to the first door they found. They went inside, discovering a small, comfortable parlour. Evie guided her to a settee, and they sat down, side by side, as close as their voluminous skirts would allow. Tugging a pretty lace-edged handkerchief from her sleeve, Evie handed it to Rosamund.

"Here, don't worry, I brought extras. I had a feeling I might need them tonight," she added, giving Rosamund a sad smile.

Rosamund took the handkerchief and wiped her eyes, watching Evie with concern. "Why, what's wrong?"

Evie shook her head. "You first."

"Oh, I'm being foolish, only I feel so wretched for the poor man, and for myself. His wife is notorious for her affairs and makes a fool of him whenever possible, yet she will not allow him to be friends with me. He has said he won't speak to me again, and I could tell how upset he was. I know it's for the best but... but it's so awful. If only he wasn't married to that horrid woman."

"You have feelings for him, Ozzie?" Evie said, her voice cautious.

Rosamund shrugged. "I'm not in love with him, Evie. Nothing like that. I do have some sense, honestly. I just liked him so much and he's so unhappy and... and there's not a thing I can do to help him. It's not fair!" she exclaimed, knowing she sounded like a spoiled child and not caring.

Evie would understand. Indeed, she was always a good friend, always listened without judgement and did her best to help.

"Life isn't," Evie replied softly, the words so stark and unlike the usually optimistic girl Rosamund knew that something must be badly wrong.

"It's for the best you don't get too close to him," Evie said. "There's nothing worse than falling in love with a man who is n-not suitable."

Her voice quavered and Rosamund saw the effort Evie took to compose herself.

"Evie?" Rosamund took her hand, squeezing it with encouragement. "You're in love?"

Evie's lip trembled, and she gave a jerky nod. Rosamund stared at her in shock, for Evie had never given her the slightest clue that... *Idiot*. Of course she had.

"The Comte de Villen?"

Evie made a sound of distress and put her head in her hands. Rosamund put her arms about her, holding her tightly as she wept, great racking sobs the pain of which seemed to reach through Rosamund and squeeze her heart. This was why she must stay away from Lord Hargreaves. Evie was right, and so was he. Falling in love with the wrong man was disastrous.

"But he has feelings for you too, I think?" Rosamund offered, wishing she could help her friend, take away this dreadful pain and make it all better.

Evie nodded, wiping her eyes, her breathing still uneven. "I believe he does."

"Your parents?"

"My father, he…." Evie clamped her mouth shut and tears rolled down her cheeks again. "Oh, I can't tell you!"

"Why?"

Evie just shook her head. She took Rosamund's hands and held on tight, her green eyes swimming with tears. "Stay away from Lord Hargreaves, Rosamund. If you care for your own heart, or for his, stay away from him. He's married. There's not a thing either of you can do about that except protect yourselves. You are fond of him, or you'd not be this wretched now. Don't fall in love with someone you can't have. *Don't!*" she added, the command ringing with desperation.

Rosamund nodded, knowing her friend spoke the truth, and her obvious pain was warning enough of what she would face if she was foolish enough to disregard her. "I won't, Evie. I promise, but is there nothing I can do for you?"

Evie shook her head. "No. No, I must figure this out for myself, and I will. It… It just might take some time."

Rosamund could not help but feel daunted by the idea of marrying a man like the comte, who was notorious for his mistresses and remained something of an enigma. Though a popular addition to any guest list, Rosamund did not believe society entirely trusted him. He was too beautiful and held himself too much apart. There was too much about him people did not know, and he did not invite confidences.

"You would marry him then, if your parents approved?" she asked.

Evie's tears erupted once again. "I don't know! I love him, but…."

Rosamund did not need to hear the *but* to understand her concerns.

"But," she agreed, nodding in sympathy.

"Oh, Ozzie," Evie said, her voice so wretched Rosamund's heart broke a little. "Why is this so hard? When people talk about falling in love, it's supposed to be easy, isn't it? This is not easy at all. No matter what I do, I shall hurt someone I love, and myself. How can I make a choice like that?"

"I don't know, Evie," Rosamund replied sadly, and hugged her friend a little tighter.

3rd July 1842, Hans Place, Knightsbridge London.

Despite Louis' best efforts to persuade Barnaby to stay at the ball, he insisted on coming home with him. He sat on Louis' bed, arms folded, glowering, as Louis tugged out a chest from under it and flung it open.

"What's in there?" Barnaby asked.

Louis didn't reply. What would he say? *Well, Barnaby, these are the clothes I used to wear when I was breaking into people's houses to relieve them of their jewels.* He had kept them as a reminder of exactly who and what he was, not that he was ever likely to forget, but now he was glad of it. The clothes were unremitting black, made of fine soft cloth and loose fitting enough to climb in with ease, but not so loose that they'd get caught on things. Then there were the soft leather shoes, again to help him climb, but also to move about in the darkness, stealthy as a cat. No, best he hold his tongue. Barnaby would draw his own conclusions and, knowing him, they'd be far kinder than the truth.

Louis stripped off his clothes, amused when Barnaby turned his back. He was not the least bit modest. There was little room for modesty in the circus, and not much privacy to be had. As a skinny, malnourished boy he'd been mortified, especially when compared to his big, strong brother, but such concerns had quickly vanished when he'd been properly fed and given a punishing routine of physical exercise. Everyone pulled their weight in the circus, and he'd been no exception. He hadn't wanted to be an exception, too desperate for approval, to fit in and find something resembling a family.

"You don't have to be here, *mon ami*, if it troubles you so."

Barnaby shook his head. "I'm your friend. If I can't talk you out of this idiocy, I can at least try to ensure you don't get caught."

"Non," Louis said, his voice firm. "I do this alone. I will have no one believe you had any part in it. You are too decent, Barnaby. You are a loyal friend, but this is my affair, not yours."

Barnaby turned around to protest, discovered Louis stark naked, and went an interesting shade of scarlet. Despite everything, Louis laughed.

"You are so terribly English," he said fondly, shaking his head.

"And you are so very French," Barnaby retorted as Louis reached for the black trousers. "How am I to carry on a conversation with you when you're—" He waved a hand at Louis' person with an air of aggravation.

"I didn't know the sight of me naked bothered you so," Louis said wickedly, glancing up at him from under his lashes as he fastened the trouser buttons.

"Now you're doing it on purpose," Barnaby grumbled. He took the black shirt and stood up, tugging it over Louis' head. "Behave yourself. I'm already cross with you, don't make it worse."

Louis sighed. "I know, I know, and I am sorry, but I intend to marry Evie, and how can I do that if I cannot even speak to her? Being a gentleman will get me nowhere. I have tried, have I not? Well, I am done playing nice. I am not nice, Barnaby, and the sooner you realise that the better."

"Don't say that," Barnaby said, looking awkward.

Louis felt a rush of sympathy for his friend, as well as for himself. It would hurt Barnaby when he discovered the truth and found himself disillusioned by the reality of who and what Louis was. It would hurt Louis too, to lose such a friend, one who was good and decent, untainted by life in the way he and Wolf were. But the past was stalking Louis, and he did not think he could evade it much longer. He could feel it growing closer, breathing down his neck. He had dreamed of his life in that god-awful place again last night. The terrible memories of his past that he'd tried so hard to banish were coming more frequently. The feel of it clung to him still, defiling him. It had been too real, too strong a reminder of how helpless he'd been. He'd woken shivering and wretched, convinced he still slept on the stone floor of the kitchen in that terrible place, at the mercy of an evil man who despised him and everything he stood for. Oh, yes. It would catch up to him soon. Gabriel Knight had been digging, and he'd found enough to condemn Louis. That he did not doubt. Neither did he doubt it would be enough to ruin him in English society if Knight used it against him. So he must act before Gabriel did, before he lost any chance of being with Evie. He could not let that happen. Once Evie was his wife, Gabriel would want those secrets buried too.

If he must play dirty to get what he wanted, then so be it. He was playing to win now, and nothing and no one would stop him.

Louis took the last item he needed from the trunk: a black silk cravat which he tied loosely about his neck and would use to cover his face when the time came. Closing the trunk, he pushed it back under the bed and walked out into the living room, where he poured himself a glass of cognac. Good for the nerves. He offered

Emma V Leech

one to Barnaby, who shook his head. Louis shrugged and carried the drink with him, heading to the study to retrieve a small set of lock picks.

The door to the study swung open with ease, and a waft of cigar scented air billowed out. The vile smell hit him like a punch to the gut and the fine crystal glass dropped from his fingers, shattering as it hit the floor. Louis could do nothing but grasp the doorframe as all the air left the room, left his lungs, and a sensation akin to being plunged into ice water made him shiver.

"Louis!" Barnaby was beside him a moment later, a hand on his arm, his face full of concern. "What is it, old man? My God, you look like you've seen a ghost."

"Un fantôme, oui," he murmured, dazed and horrified, trying to catch his breath. "Elton," he rasped, hardly able to get the word out.

"Elton!" Barnaby shouted, and the valet ran in a moment later.

"Yes, Monsieur, Mr Godwin?" He took one look at the smashed glass and nodded. "Oh, I'll deal with it at once, monsieur."

"Never mind the damned glass," Louis managed, getting himself back under control. "Who was here, in my study?"

"Here, monsieur?" the valet said in confusion. "No one was here."

Louis' temper rose, and he gestured to the room with an angry sweep of his hand. "It reeks of cigar smoke. Someone was here. Tell me the truth, man!"

Elton paled, his expression one of mortification. "I swear it upon my life, monsieur. To my knowledge, no one has been in that room."

"Louis, he's telling the truth, you can see he is," Barnaby said gently. With a quiet word, he dismissed Elton, who was only too happy to leave. Turning back to Louis, he grasped his shoulders and gave him a little shake. "What is this about, Louis?"

Louis could not answer. With legs that did not feel entirely steady, he moved across the room to pick up a lamp. Steeling his nerves, he walked into his study. Nothing was out of place, not so much as a pencil moved from where it ought to be, yet the scent of a French cigar lingered in the room.

"Non, non, non," he moaned, raking his hands through his hair. It wasn't possible. No, it could not be. It could *not* be. Barnaby was looking at him as if he'd run mad, which did not seem as unlikely as it might have a few hours earlier.

"Are you going to tell me what's going on?" Barnaby asked, studying Louis far too closely for comfort. "What makes you think someone was in here?"

"Can't you smell it?" Louis demanded, his stomach churning unpleasantly as memories fought free of the locked box in which he kept them. No. No. He would not think of that.

Diable, mauvais esprit, démon, serpent dans le Jardin d'eden.

"Smell what? I can't smell anything. Are you quite well, Louis? Perhaps you ought not—"

Démon, pécheur

"Tais toi!" he hissed as misery hit him in a wave.

Barnaby stiffened and Louis cursed himself and all the vileness that came with him. Barnaby's French was limited but Louis had been helping him, and he knew what *shut up* sounded like.

"Not you, Barnaby," he said, knowing he must sound utterly unhinged.

He had to see Evie. This only confirmed his suspicions that the past was coming for him. It was not possible, and yet Louis knew with a sickening sense of certainty that it was true. They must be married before everything went to hell or he would lose her, and lose himself, and any hope of happiness. He would not allow his life to be ruined yet again. No one would take this astonishing chance he had been given away from him. He tugged the drawer in his desk open, unlocking the small box inside and taking out the lock picks. Tucking them away in a pocket, he slammed the box shut and headed for the door.

"Louis!" Barnaby called after him, but Louis ignored him.

Barnaby would have him wait, be sensible, behave like a gentleman, but he could not wait any longer. If he were a different man, he would give Evie the time he had promised her, he would prove himself to her parents and marry her with their blessing. But he was Louis César de Montluc, God help him, and he could not change that. He would be whatever Evie wanted him to be once they were married, he would have the rest of his life to prove to her parents that he was what she needed, that he could make her happy, but there was no more time.

3rd July 1842, Lansdown Place, Sloane Square, Chelsea, London.

Sebastian stirred, aware of a gentle hand stroking his hair. He sighed, knowing it must be a dream. No woman ever touched him that way. Adelia despised him and, though his dealings with the courtesans at the Orchid House were mutually acceptable, he never asked them for false displays of affection. It would have given him the guilty feeling that he was demanding too much of them in the circumstances, though he longed for comfort of a kind he could not find in an emotionless joining of bodies. Rosamund's face drifted into his mind and, drunk as he was, he forced it away. He must protect her. His brandy-soaked brain might be full of fog, but that much he remembered.

He blinked, suddenly aware the hand was still playing with his hair. This time, it gave a sharp little tug.

Sebastian jerked awake.

Adelia stood looking down at him, wearing a black silk negligee that clung to her lovely figure. Grimacing, he rubbed a hand over his face. This was the last thing he needed right now. He was under no illusion that she had come to his rooms to give herself to him. Oh, no. He had made that mistake in those early days, believing she had come to make up with him, allowing her back into his heart, to arouse him and get his hopes of a reconciliation bursting back to life, only to find her slamming the door in his face a moment later. He would not be her plaything. Never again would she toy with his emotions. But she knew that, and he admitted it surprised him she had come. It had been many years since she had tried this tactic.

"What do you want?" he demanded, hearing the slur in his words.

"From you?" she asked with a brittle laugh. "Whyever should I want anything from you?"

"I have no idea. Now we've established that, get out of my room." He watched her, wary as hell. Sebastian didn't trust her an inch and, if she was here, it was to make trouble and for no other reason.

"Not yet. I want to know why I heard the servants talking about packing. You're not thinking of going somewhere without telling me?" Her eyes glittered as she bent down, one hand on each arm of the chair, giving him an eyeful of her breasts encased in the scandalous black silk. She pouted and put on a babying voice. "Running away with your tail between your legs like a little puppy dog, are you?"

"Go to hell, Adelia," he growled, his temper rising.

"I mean it, Hargreaves," she said, her voice hard. "Where are you going?"

"Away from you," he said, cursing himself the moment the words left his mouth.

He needed to stay calm. The only way to deal with her was to stay calm, but the brandy was like a fire in his blood, burning away the restraints that kept his anger tethered down.

"Where are you going?"

He recognised the edge to the words, the razor-sharp glint to her features that boded ill. She was going to goad him until he exploded and said things he ought not say.

With a Herculean effort, he tamped down his anger. "Just away for a little while," he said, doing his utmost to sound reasonable. "I'm going to visit some old friends."

"Where?" she asked, daring him to contradict what she obviously already knew. Damn and blast his gossipy bloody servants. One night. They had to keep it to themselves for one bloody night.

"France," he said, his tone curt.

Adelia let out a breath of laughter and crossed her arms. "My God," she sneered, shaking her head at him. "You're taking yourself away from temptation."

Sebastian felt a muscle ticking in his jaw but only clenched it harder, determined not to rise to the bait.

"Do you fancy yourself in love with your sweet little debutante, Hargreaves? Is that it? Is that why you're drinking all by yourself, poor baby, because you're going to be honourable and good, because that's what you do, isn't it? You make yourself miserable doing the right thing and blame everyone else for it."

He surged to his feet, incandescent with rage. "And what the hell else am I to do, Adelia? What choice do I have—have I *ever* had? I am chained to you like you're a goddamned anchor, dragging me down. You don't want me, but you don't want anyone else to have me either! For Christ's sake, just let me go away. You can live as you want, do exactly as you please, and never hear a word about it from me. Just let me go!" he bellowed this last, too desperate to leave to hold on to his temper any longer.

"No!" she shouted back at him.

Sebastian roared with frustration. Grasping hold of her arm, he marched her to the door and opened it, pushing her out into the corridor. "I'm leaving, Adelia, and you can't stop me."

"And have everyone say you went to escape me?" she said, glaring at him with icy contempt. "I think not. You will stay here."

Sebastian saw movement flickering out of the corner of his eye and saw a maid and a footman frozen in an awkward tableau at the far end of the corridor.

"Go away!" he shouted, and they scrambled for cover, melting into the shadows as they hurried down the corridor.

He turned back to Adelia, who stared at him, the determination to get her own way writ large upon her hard, beautiful face. In that moment he felt as though he were a thousand years old. The fury that had energised him abruptly drained away and a sense of hopelessness stole over him.

"We'll talk about it in the morning," he said wearily, knowing he'd lost as he always did. If he went now, she'd do something dreadful: cause a scandal, or even hurt Rosamund. There was no choice but to stay until she cooled down. He just wanted Adelia out of his sight, for this night at the very least, so he did not have to look at her a moment longer.

"There," Adelia crooned, all smiles now she'd got her own way. "That wasn't so hard, was it, Hargreaves?" She leaned in and stood on her toes, kissing his cheek.

Revulsion shivered through him at her touch, and it took every iota of willpower for it not to show on his face.

"Goodnight, my lord," she whispered, blowing him a kiss, and then her voice hardened, her eyes glittering with malice. "Sweet dreams."

Sebastian went back into his room and shut the door. He leaned back against it for a long moment and then forced himself to move, slumping back down into the chair, utterly drained. Putting his head in his hands, he tried to calm himself as desperation settled over him like a smothering pall of black smoke, choking him until he couldn't breathe. Christ, was he to die like this? Trapped in this hell of his own creation? If only *she* would die, he thought as despair clawed at his heart. Instantly, he wished he'd never thought it, horrified at his own wickedness.

"God help me," he said aloud, pressing the heels of his hands against his eyes and breathing hard against a sudden burst of emotion. "God help me."

He didn't want this, didn't want this mess of a marriage, of a life. If only he could escape it. If only she would just leave him be, but she never would. He knew that much. She enjoyed her power over him, over all the other poor sods she held in her grasp. They, at least, were lucky. She might leave them frustrated, or broken-hearted, or angry, but she left them. Sebastian would give anything for that, anything for an end to this misery. He had to get away from her, and this time… this time he would. One way or another.

"Couldn't this have waited until morning? Or at least, a sensible hour of the morning," the Duke of Bedwin demanded tersely, glaring at the clock over the fireplace. It was a reasonable question considering it was barely two o'clock and Sebastian had roused him from his bed.

"I don't think so," Sebastian said, wondering if the man would murder him. He rather hoped he would. It would be one way out of this bloody mess, if a little drastic.

"Well, get on with it then." Bedwin waved a hand at him, tying his silk dressing gown a little tighter before sitting down behind his desk. He gestured impatiently for Sebastian to take a seat, too.

"It's my wife," Sebastian said, his tone grim. "I was going to leave first thing this morning, an extended visit to France, perhaps spend a few months in Italy. But Adelia found out, and she... she does not want me to go."

"What the devil has this to do with me?" Bedwin asked, and then his eyes darkened. "Your friendship with my daughter—"

"Is exactly that," Sebastian cut in. "I hold Lady Rosamund in the highest regard and would never willingly cause her trouble, but Adelia has taken exception to it. She rarely troubles herself about my friendships, but... she suspects... she believes I have feelings for the lady."

Looking at Bedwin was akin to regarding a granite sculpture in that moment and Sebastian was very aware that he addressed a duke, and a man who protected his family at all costs.

"Do you?" he asked, his voice clipped.

"No," Sebastian said at once, before letting out a breath. "She has been a wonderful friend to me, and I will always be grateful for that. If I were not already married, things would be different, yes. I admit it. But I am neither so foolish nor so cruel as to allow such inappropriate feelings to develop and I would certainly never encourage them in an innocent girl. Your grace, I swear it, upon my honour. I made my bed. I was a damned fool and I'll pay for that until the end of my days, but I'm not a cad, Bedwin. You know that. There is nothing between us, and there never will be."

"Knowing that is one thing, but if this is going to cause Rosamund trouble, I give you fair warning, I *will* kill you," the duke growled, his expression thunderous.

Sebastian raked a hand through his hair, feeling like a boy facing his father. Absurdly, he wished that were the case, but his father was dead and had not guided him when he'd wished to marry Adelia, had not warned him to have a care, to be cautious, to take a little time to reflect.

"I don't blame you. Only I don't know what the hell to do with her. She's forcing me to remain in London with the threat of damaging Lady Rosamund's reputation if I don't. Obviously, I'll stay, and keep as far from Lady Rosamund as I can get, but… I don't trust her, Bedwin. She's spiteful."

"So, what are you telling me?"

"Warn your daughter to be on her guard and make certain you take care of her. Adelia is clever and cruel. She enjoys playing with people's emotions, mine most of all."

"Can't you do something with her?" Bedwin demanded in frustration.

Sebastian laughed, staring at him. "Like you managed with your first wife, you mean?"

For a moment, he wondered if he'd gone too far. The duke looked positively murderous, but then his anger drained away as quickly as it had arrived, and he slumped back in his chair with a groan.

"Oh, bloody hell," he muttered, rubbing a weary hand over his face. "Young men ought to be locked up until they've sense enough to go out into the world. When they're about forty might be safe."

"No argument here," Sebastian replied with a huff of bitter laughter. "What should I do, Bedwin, tell me? I could lock her up, keep her prisoner. That's my right as her husband. Or should I beat her, frighten her into not daring to disobey me?"

"I know, Hargreaves," Bedwin said, his distaste for the subject audible. "A worse man would do just that, which is why she isn't married to such a one. You are decent and honourable, and now she can manipulate you with those very qualities."

"I feel like I'm losing my mind," Sebastian admitted, a little astonished that he was confessing such a thing to Rosamund's father of all people, yet the duke was one of the few men who could truly understand. "Like I might do something I'll regret if she keeps pushing me."

"I know," Bedwin said darkly. "I remember the feeling of impotent fury all too clearly, but I promise you, there are worse things than living with such a woman."

Sebastian put his head in his hands. "I keep remembering when we first met and wanting to shake myself for my stupidity. I was so utterly dazzled by Adelia, by her beauty and wit, her sharp mind, that I did not look beneath the surface. My arrogance and lack of experience made me take her at face value. I assumed she loved me as madly as I did her, because why wouldn't she? God, what a lackwit," he said in disgust.

Glancing up, he saw understanding in the duke's eyes, and something that might have been pity. What remained of his pride squirmed uncomfortably.

"She's not *actually* unfaithful to me, you know. At least, not after that one time, which I told her I forgave her for. So even if I wished to divorce her, I would have to lie to prove adultery. It would be easy enough to do, of course, but I don't think I could live with that. I know now that Adelia is in love with the idea of love, but she does not really understand what it is. For her it's a beautiful painting, with everything perfection, a moment frozen in time. But as soon as it becomes messy and real and human, as all real emotions are, she runs away. I've tried to talk to her, to understand why. I've asked her to explain it to me so many times, but I've come to wonder if she even knows herself. Perhaps she is afraid. Too afraid for my reassurances to give her courage enough to face it, anyway. I think she is lonely, but she does not know how to stop it, and that makes her angry and jealous, and she lashes out at me if she thinks I am not lonely too."

"Damnation, Hargreaves," Bedwin said, and this time Sebastian definitely heard the pity in his voice and that was far worse than his anger.

Sebastian shrugged, returning a crooked smile, for what else could he do? Weep?

"I certainly feel damned. Damned to live with my mistake. Until the day one of us dies," he mused, softly. He shook his head. "Well, I've said my piece, and for what it's worth, I am more desperately sorry than you know. I will do whatever I must to protect Lady Rosamund though. You have my word upon that, Bedwin."

"See that you do," Bedwin said, his expression implacable. "Because I have every sympathy for you, Hargreaves, and I know you are a decent man, but if you or your wife harm my daughter's reputation, you will answer for the consequences."

Sebastian nodded, having expected nothing other than that. "I know, your grace, and I understand."

He rose and bowed, then left the room, leaving the duke staring thoughtfully out of the window at the darkness beyond. Sebastian's footsteps rang out as he walked across the elegant marble floor that led back to the grand entrance to Beverwyck, and he was so lost in thought, he almost didn't hear the soft exclamation.

"Lord Hargreaves?"

He turned abruptly, jolting in shock as he saw Rosamund, dressed in her nightclothes, a glass of milk in hand.

"My lady," he said, uncertain of what he ought to do.

"Whatever are you doing here?" she asked him, moving closer. "Is anything amiss?"

The subtle scent of vanilla reached him, and Sebastian wondered if it clung to her from the kitchens, or if it was something she used on her hair or skin. Abruptly, he shook himself with a stern reminder of where he was and why. *Bloody imbecile.*

"I—" he began, racking his brain for some excuse before realising it was pointless. He had asked the duke to warn his daughter, after all. "My wife believes…."

Hesitating, he wondered how to put it.

"She believes there is more than friendship between us," Rosamund said calmly.

He shrugged. "I'm uncertain she truly believes that, but she knows I admire you, that I am… *fond* of you. That is enough. She will do you harm, my lady. You must be on your guard."

Rosamund nodded, her expression full of sorrow. "I feared that might be the case. I will be careful, my lord. I promise you."

Sebastian nodded, utterly wretched. "Please do. I should never forgive myself if—"

She shook her head, her expression fierce as she spoke, interrupting his heartfelt words. "This is not your doing, Lord Hargreaves. Not your fault. I shall never blame you or regret our friendship."

She reached out, laying a hand on his arm and her gentle touch struck him with the force of a lightning bolt. He sucked in a breath, shaken, and withdrew his arm, taking a step back. He stared at Rosamund, committing the sight of her to memory, knowing this was all he could ever have.

"I cannot be your friend any longer, and that pains me more than you will ever know," he said, his heart aching at the sadness in her eyes. For the thousandth time, he cursed himself for rushing into marriage with a woman he did not really know or understand. How different his life might be if… But there were no ifs or buts. He was married. It had been the worst mistake of his life, but he must live with the results.

"I do know, my lord, for I have the same weight of regret," she said softly.

Sebastian steeled himself to bid her farewell, knowing he would never speak to her again.

"Goodnight, Lady Rosamund. I shall miss our talks. I wish you every success in finding a husband worthy of you, though I am not sure such a man can exist," he added with a wry smile. "He will be the luckiest of men."

With that, he gave a low bow, and turned from her, walking away from Lady Rosamund for good

Chapter 8

Dearest Torie,

I am so sorry I shall not see you at Mrs Palmer's ball. What a rotten moment to come down with a cold! I wish you were going to be there to hold my hand. It's all rather daunting, and yet I dare not complain too much as I have nagged and nagged everyone to let me come out this year instead of next. And you may stop laughing at me, for I know you are, you horrid girl.

My gown is glorious, however, and I hope I shall not behave too dreadfully and make a spectacle of myself. I mean, it's bound to happen eventually, but I'd rather put off the inevitable until at least my third season. Assuming I'm not married by then, which seems most unlikely.

I try to imagine it sometimes, finding a man who makes me feel the way Mama described with Papa, but they loved each other from children, so it is not at all the same. I rather wish I could have one of those 'love at first sight' moments people speak of, for I fear missing the man of my dreams because I wasn't paying attention properly. It would be just like me. Oh, what a ninny I am. Do get better soon! I need you!

—Excerpt of a letter from Lady Cara Baxter (daughter of Luke and Kitty Baxter, The Earl and Countess of Trevick) to Lady Victoria Adolphus (daughter of Robert and Prunella Adolphus, Their Graces, The Duke and Duchess of Bedwin).

Early hours of the 4th of July 1842, Peregrine House, Grosvenor Square, London.

Barnaby watched Louis as the carriage crossed Grosvenor Square, though he could see nothing but the glitter of his eyes against the unremitting black. His driver would let Louis down on the far side of the Square, so no one would suspect Barnaby's involvement in this dreadful scheme. He wished to God he could have talked Louis out of it, but he may as well talk to the wall, so he held his tongue, afraid to upset his friend and damage his trust. He suspected trust was something Louis did not give lightly or easily, and he did not wish to risk that. Yet he had a bad feeling about all of this. Knight was not a man one crossed, and he wondered if Louis understood what he was getting into.

Sometimes Barnaby wondered if he was getting into something himself by being Louis' friend, for the man was clearly hiding a great deal. Not that it would have changed a thing. Louis was Barnaby's friend. That was all he needed to know in the end.

The carriage drew to a halt and Louis moved, reaching for the door.

Barnaby reached out a hand and grasped his arm. "It's not too late to change your mind," he said desperately.

Louis smiled, patting Barnaby's hand. *"Ne t'inquiète pas, mon ami.* I will be fine, and so will Evie. I promise."

Barnaby sighed and nodded. "Have it your own way, but if you need me—"

"I know," Louis said softly. "And I am more grateful than you know."

With that, he slipped out of the carriage. Barnaby shifted to the window, looking out at the lamplit street, but Louis had already gone, vanished into the shadows.

Though he had sounded sanguine enough when speaking to Barnaby, Louis had not underestimated the difficulty in getting into the Knight residence. Unlike at Swan Hall, this would not be a simple case of climbing a building. What he had not explained to Barnaby, however, was that he was very used to breaking into large and exclusive houses with too many servants. Having been a servant himself—if you could give such an exulted title to a boy treated like a mangy dog—he also understood how houses like this worked. The easiest way in was the place no one wanted to be, the same route the rubbish took.

He slipped past a night watchman prowling outside the garden walls and climbed the high gates that secured the entrance to the back of the house with ease, running noiselessly down the alley. The door into the basement and the storerooms was easy to locate and though the lock was a secure, modern one, it was child's play for Louis to pick. A moment later and he was inside, careful to relock the door after him so as not to raise suspicion. He could hear voices from the kitchen, as there would still be a few staff on hand in a household like this, even at this ungodly hour, just in case the family needed anything. Louis clung to the shadows, his eyes having adjusted to the dark as he moved down the corridor in search of the servants' staircase. Twice he had to duck out of sight, but luck was on his side tonight and he made the staircase with no problems.

From past conversations with Evie, he knew she was on the third floor, facing the square, information she had dropped innocently, and he had tucked away, out of habit. He'd had no nefarious intentions, nor did he consider his intentions in such a light now. He ought not be here, of course, but he loved her, and he was gambling his all on the fact that she loved him too. Not that she had ever said so, but then neither had he, until the note he'd written that night. Now she had it in black and white. His heart stripped bare.

He paused in the darkness, suddenly breathless. Not from nerves because of what he was doing, but because he would face her shortly. He would stand before her with his heart exposed, as if it beat on the outside of his chest. Louis understood what it was to be vulnerable, to be at another's mercy, as few did. Yet the realisation that he was about to face the possibility of her rejection struck him then and made him more afraid than he'd ever been.

Don't be a fool, he told himself, closing his eyes. *She won't let you down. Not her. Not Evie.* She had put the candle in the window for him. Why do that if she did not want him to come to her?

Steeling himself, he carried on, listening at the bottom of the staircase and discovering the house above him quiet. He ran, slowing towards the top to scan the corridor, pleased by the plush carpets that would muffle his footsteps. The next staircase was just the same and the next, and to his relief reaching the third floor posed no difficulty, but now he must find her room, very aware that her siblings must sleep on the same floor, perhaps her parents too. He froze as a door opened and closed somewhere in the house, listening intently. There was no other sound, so he carried on, and eventually found himself standing before a window on the landing that looked out over the square, judging where he was in the house by what he could see. Then that door to his right was Evie's.

Heart thudding, he tugged the silk scarf from his face and moved towards it, turning the knob silently and easing it open, relieved to discover the hinges well oiled. He slid inside, closing it behind him, and paused as he heard a little gasp of shock.

Evie.

She stood before him in the golden lamplight, dressed all in white, like a virgin sacrifice. Her nightrail was a feminine extravaganza of ruffles and ribbons, putting him in mind of sweet treats and expensive confections, and the desire to unwrap her was tantalising. His immediate instinct was to run to her and take her in his arms, but the look in her eyes made him stop in his tracks.

His heart froze, the first stirrings of panic rising in his gut. He leaned back against the door, watching her warily. She stared at him, studying him as if she had never seen him before, as if he was something other than she had believed him to be. So, her father had spoken to her about what he'd discovered.

"What did he tell you?" he asked, wondering if she could hear the fear in his voice as audibly as he could. There was a long, uncomfortable pause.

"Bad things," she whispered, wrapping her arms about herself as if she were cold. "Terrible things."

They stood that way, a distance of mere feet between them and yet in this moment it felt like an ocean, as if she was being drawn farther away with every passing second.

"Are they t-true?" she asked him, her green eyes full of anxiety.

Louis gritted his teeth, his jaw flexing, but there was little point in lying, and he had sworn to always give her the truth, had he not? He wanted her to know the worst of him and love him anyway, but he had wanted more time than this, wanted her bound to him before she could run from him in fear, cowardly as that was. Louis lowered his lashes, staring at the floor with a frown as he wished he could deny it all, but he could not. He would not.

"Probably," he said bitterly.

She nodded, as if she had known all along.

Louis lifted his eyes to hers again, aware of the tension vibrating from her. "You're afraid of me." He wanted to weep, to howl with misery but did not move an inch, just watched her. She nodded.

"Yes, you know that."

The silence stretched out, taut and sickening.

She swallowed, and he saw the way her throat worked. He thought perhaps she was trembling. Was she truly that frightened of him? His heart clenched.

"Papa... Papa said... he said you've killed three m-men," she stammered.

Louis flinched, the words too stark, too awful. His stomach roiled but he faced her, hiding nothing. "Yes."

She sucked in a breath, and he knew she had hoped her father had been mistaken, that Louis had been maligned. He could not lie to her, would not lie. Only Wolf knew the whole truth, and he would never betray Louis. Her father's men must have been clever indeed to find one of the few people willing to speak against him, to uncover the truth when even his brother did not know everything.

"Why?" There was pleading behind that one word, a wrenching sound that cut at him, but the desire to understand him shone in her eyes and he took comfort from that, clinging to hope.

"Because they deserved to die," he said, meaning it with all his heart. "I'm glad they're dead. Does that horrify you?"

She nodded, her complexion ashen. "Why did they deserve it?"

He shook his head, vehement on that point. He would not sully her with such explanations. "I shan't tell you that. You would have nightmares, but they were evil, cruel, vile excuses for men. I don't regret it."

There was defiance in his words, and he held her gaze, refusing to feel shame for what he'd done.

She nodded again, her eyes glittering with tears now. He wondered how much more she could take before she screamed for her father, for help.

"Do you want me to go?" He felt sick, not wanting to give her the choice, terrified of the answer, for he did not know how to walk away from her.

It was a long time coming as she stared at him, her breathing fast and panicked. Then, slowly, she shook her head.

"No," she whispered, barely audible, and then louder, more decisively. *"No."*

Louis let out a breath of relief, though he knew he had not yet won her over. He swallowed, waiting. She watched him, like a mouse watching a cat prowl a circle around it, waiting for the killing blow.

"You're dangerous," she said softly. "That's what he said."

"And is that what you think?" he asked, wretched now, his voice rough, remembering when she'd trusted him with everything she had and feeling his throat tighten at the trepidation in her eyes now.

"Yes," she said, and the pain of that answer lanced through him, cutting him to the quick. "But… But not to me. Never to me, Louis."

She ran to him then, ran into his embrace and Louis could not help the soft cry of joy that escaped him as he closed his arms about her, holding her to him.

"Mon amour, mon amour, Dieu merci, Dieu merci," he murmured into her hair, tears stinging his eyes as he breathed her

in, the familiar achingly innocent scent of chamomile so intoxicating he was drunk with it, with joy, with the relief of holding her in his arms. "Evie, my love."

He pressed his mouth to her temple, kissing the tender skin, cupping her face within his hands and kissing her eyelids, her nose, her cheeks, engulfed by the tenderness he felt for her. It rose within him, a tide of love and longing and hope, overwhelming him with everything he wanted.

"Did you mean it?" she asked, and he did not pretend to misunderstand.

"Of course, you think I would write such a thing in black and white if I did not?" he said, smiling now, his heart bursting with joy.

"Tell me," she whispered, her hands fisting the fabric of his shirt as she gazed up at him.

"Je t'aime," he said helplessly, the relief of saying that to her out loud so profound his voice trembled. "I love you, my Evie, my heart. I have done for a long time now. You are everything I want, that I dream of. I need you. I need your kindness, the goodness that shines from you. I have had so little that was good in my life before, Evie, but I will cherish you if you give yourself to me."

She stared up at him in wonder, a sheen of unshed tears in her eyes as a single drop trembled on her lashes before spilling over, tracking down her cheek. "I love you too."

Louis' breath snagged in his throat, and he made a harsh sound of exclamation, beyond words. There would never be words enough to express how it felt, to hear her tell him that, the words he had needed to hear for so long now.

Slowly, he lowered his mouth to her cheek and kissed away the tear, tasting salt. He heard her soft intake of breath as his lips trailed across to her mouth and he kissed her, gently, so, so sweetly, as he ought to have kissed her at Fort William when the devil inside him had gained control. He lashed that wicked part of him down now, holding it in check, to give her this as she deserved, infinitely patient, achingly tender. She sighed, sliding her arms about his waist, pressing herself closer.

Louis suppressed a groan, suddenly rivetingly aware she was naked beneath her nightgown and wrap. There were no thick layers of skirts and petticoats, no corset to protect her body from his questing hands. He broke the kiss, putting a little distance between them before things got out of control.

"Evie," he said, grasping her wrists when she went to reach for him, to pull him back to her. "Wait."

He smiled at her and kept hold of one hand, tugging her farther into the room and getting her to sit on the bed. Heart thudding an uncomfortable tattoo, he knelt before her, taking her hands in his.

"Evie, my love. My life. I know I am not the good, decent man you want me to be, I am far from that, but I will give you everything, if would you do me the very great honour of becoming my wife."

She stared at him, eyes wide, her mouth falling open on a gasp of surprise. She had not expected this tonight, he realised, and why should she? Evie had told him many times she was not ready to marry, but he must persuade her now. He must make her see that there was no choice for them. If they were to be together, it was the only way. Louis watched her, a little wary now.

"Evie?"

She still said nothing, but her chest rose and fell too fast. "My father will never allow it, Louis. He's forbidden me to even be your friend," she said, clearly agitated, and then she sprang to her feet, pacing the room. Louis rose too, following her.

"We do not need his permission," Louis retorted, unable to keep the irritation from his voice. "We will elope, we can go to Gretna Green, or to France. I know how to disappear so that even he will not find us."

Louis did not underestimate what he was asking her to do. For Evie, family was everything, the trust and loyalty she had in them, her foundation. He understood that, because he wanted it too, wanted that from her, that sense of solidity, of security, but he would still ask her to betray it, for him.

She turned back to him, regret in her eyes. "Louis, I c-can't, not yet. I'm not ready for this. It's… It's too much. It's all happening too quickly. I did not think to marry for several years yet. You know that. I've told you before now."

"Yet you were ready to give Mr Anderson an answer." Louis regretted the words and his harsh tone the moment they left his mouth, but he could not take them back.

Evie stiffened. "I promised you I would accept no one. I had no intention of marrying anyone at once. Even my parents suggested a long engagement, perhaps two years, and that seemed a good idea. Florence was two and twenty when she married. I'm only nineteen!"

"Twenty in a few days," he said darkly, folding his arms.

She made an exasperated sound. "And what of all my father said about you? What of everything you have not yet explained? For I suspect there is a great deal you've not yet told me." She ran back to him, and her expression softened as she reached up, touching her hand to his cheek, a soothing caress that made him shiver with longing. "I meant what I said, Louis. I love you. *I do.* But you… you frighten me. The things you have done, all the things I do not know about you—"

"You don't trust me."

The words were stark, and he felt suddenly hollow, like he might shatter at the slightest touch.

"It's not that, at least, not precisely that," she said, her voice gentle. "But I don't know what our life would look like, what to expect, and yet you want me to run away from my home, from everything I know and marry you, even after everything you have admitted tonight? That's not fair, Louis."

Louis' jaw clenched and he fought to listen to her words, to understand what she was saying when disappointment at her reaction warred with everything he was so close to having. "And if I said I would wait for you, if you gave me your promise to marry me, would you answer me now? Would you say yes?" he demanded, the hard note in his voice betraying his unease.

Anxiety flickered in her eyes, and she did not need to speak the words aloud for him to hear her answer. She feared the future with him, feared what kind of life he would take her too, and who could blame her? He had just confessed to murder, and that was hardly all of it.

Louis raked a hand through his hair, holding onto his sanity by a thread as the future unravelled before his eyes. "And if I told you everything? If I gave you all of me, Evie? If I held nothing back?"

She slid her arms about his waist. "I want you, Louis. I love you, but I need to believe we have a future together. If I make a mistake, we will both be miserable. Knowing your past would be a good start, I think. I need to know I can trust you."

"You think you can't?" he repeated, unable to hide the hurt in his voice.

She opened her mouth, hesitated, and then took a breath and tried again. "You've never been faithful to anyone, Louis. Mistresses come and go, and you don't even blink. You've never loved anyone of them, never cared for them. You grow bored with them in a few months, weeks sometimes. Perhaps you will grow tired of me?"

He shook his head angrily, words bubbling up so fast he could not grasp at the ones he wanted, too frustrated by this entire conversation.

"I'm not exciting, Louis. Not sophisticated or worldly." She blinked, her eyes shining too bright. "I'm afraid I'll bore you."

His frustration vanished in an instant when he saw the fear in her eyes, the vulnerability. He had been so swamped with his own fears and needs that he had not considered that she might fear holding him. He almost laughed. *Dieu*, if she knew, if she truly understood the power she held over him, she need never worry.

"Evie," he said, pulling her closer to him, but for once, words failed him as desire rose.

He had wanted her too much for too long and she was here, in his arms. Her body was warm and soft beneath the fine fabric of her nightclothes, and it would be so easy, so deliciously easy, to take what he wanted.

"Evie," he said again, but his voice was darker now, the voice of a man set on seduction.

Her breathing hitched, and she stiffened in his arms, aware of the change in him.

"Louis, you should go now, I…. My parents—"

He did not allow her to finish the sentence, stealing the words he had no wish to hear with a searing kiss. Her resistance melted away as if it had never existed and she slid a hand up his neck, into his hair, pressing her lush curves against him as fire blazed in his blood.

He swept her up into his arms, smothering her little exclamation of protest with his mouth as he carried her to the bed and laid her upon it. She gasped, eyes wide as he followed her down.

"Louis, we c—"

He kissed her, stopping her from denying him, reminding her how much she wanted him with a kiss that was slow and deep, and a moment later she was reaching for him, pulling him down to her. Triumph blazed through him. She was his. She wanted him too much to deny him.

Diable.

Louis ignored the hateful voice, concentrating on Evie, on the pleasure he could show her. He tugged at the ribbons holding her wrap closed and pushed the lacy creation aside. Beneath it her nightgown was simple white cotton, but so very fine. It clung to her body, the outline of her nipples just visible beneath the delicate weave of the cloth. Louis swallowed, knowing he had wanted no one, wanted nothing in his life before, like he wanted her. His heart thudded unevenly, as if he were an untried boy touching his girl for the first time. He reached out and cupped her breast, revelling in the soft weight as his thumb teased the nipple.

Unable to resist a moment longer, he bent his head and suckled her breast through the thin cotton, tugging the delicate flesh to a hard little peak. He made a low sound of satisfaction deep in his throat and worried the little bud with his teeth until she gave a moan that shot straight to his groin, making his cock throb with the need to be inside her.

"Je t'aime," he whispered, kissing his way across the slope of her breast, up her slender neck, returning to nuzzle the delightful curve between her shoulder and leaving soft little kisses as his thumb and finger continued to toy with her breast beneath the damp fabric. *"Dieu,* I want you so much, *mon amour.* I want to love you, to kiss you everywhere. I want to take everything you have, to do things you never dreamed of. I want to show you just how wicked I can be, and you will only want more, I promise."

She writhed beneath him, whimpering with desire, her eyes dark and hazy as she stared at him.

"Shall I touch you, *ma petite?*" he asked, holding her gaze.

Her skin was flushed, rosy with wanting him, like sun-kissed peaches on a lazy summer's day, making his mouth water with the desire to taste her.

Evie swallowed, her mouth opening but no sound coming out. Louis lounged beside her, apparently at his ease, though he was all raw need and exposed nerves. He caressed her breasts, cupping first one generous mound and then the other, squeezing gently. She was a lush landscape of lavish contours, and he was aching to explore her. Evie gasped, arching into his touch. Louis laughed softly, delighted by her response to him as his hand coasted lower, over the soft curve of her belly.

"Shall I touch you here, Evie?" he asked, his fingers trailing back and forth over the place where a shadowy dark triangle lay beneath the thin fabric. He wanted to tug the fabric out of the way, to see everything hidden from his gaze but he held back, aware he was pushing her already.

"It's... It's wrong," she managed, so breathless she could hardly speak.

"Who says so?" he asked her, holding her gaze. "Does it feel wrong, little love?"

He let his hand stray lower, the lightest caress between her legs as his fingers trailed over the fine fabric, barely touching her. Her breathing quickened, her green eyes darkening. Louis kept up the delicate torment until her thighs parted, allowing him more. He hid his smile, knowing she was succumbing to desire.

"Do you like that, Evie? Tell me how it feels?"

"So good," she managed, laughing softly. "Sinful!"

He grinned at her then, hardly about to disagree.

"Then I must be doing it right," he replied and reached for the hem of her nightgown, sliding his hand beneath. His breath caught as his palm glided over her satiny thigh to the soft thatch of curls. Louis closed his eyes, groaned, and bent his head to her breast again, rubbing his mouth over her nipple as his fingers sifted through the warm triangle of hair to find her already hot and wet.

"Louis," she sobbed, lifting her hips towards his touch, wanting more. "Oh, please..."

"Easy. I'll give you what you want. *Mon Dieu,* but you are lovely, *si belle, si douce, mon coeur.*"

She made a startled sound as he eased into the damp folds, stroking carefully as he sought the little nub that would bring her pleasure. Evie sighed and widened her thighs further, encouraging him to give her more. Louis watched, his thumb caressing her clitoris as he eased a finger inside her. She moaned and rolled her hips, her intimate muscles working greedily to take him deeper, and Louis admitted himself startled to discover her so responsive, all traces of shyness vanished in the heat of her need for him.

"More," she demanded, her voice agonised, pleading. "Oh, yes. Don't stop."

Louis could not look away, enraptured by her as she writhed beneath his touch. His own body throbbed with arousal as he built her pleasure, astonished by her innocent passion, her fierce desire demanding enough to equal his own. He had been prepared for shyness, for hesitation, to have to soothe her and encourage, but she was all fire and heat and need and he felt as though he stood before an inferno, wanting nothing more than to burn with her.

She sobbed, clutching at him, not knowing what to do with the emotions he was rousing in her. Louis made soft sounds of reassurance, trying to soothe her as she grew wilder, grabbing at his shirt and tugging, reaching for him. He gave her his weight, his neglected cock sending a jolt of exquisite pleasure through him as he pressed against her hip. Evie tugged frantically at his shirt and his heart skipped at her need to touch him. Distantly, he wondered how this was so very different, for he knew what it was to be desired, wanted beyond reason, only he had never felt it in return before. Not until now. There had been countless women who believed themselves in love with him, willing to do anything to be with him, and none of them had ever moved him, nor touched his heart when they touched his body.

Finally, her clumsy tugging freed his shirt from his trousers and his breath hitched as her hands touched his skin, sliding up over his sides to his back. Louis had wanted this so badly, dreamed of this moment so often, that he hardly dared believe it was real.

Evie wanted him. She *loved* him. He had despaired for so long that the realisation overwhelmed him. Shivering under her questing hands, he wondered what she would make of the tattoo beneath her fingers and knew he would not let her see that until they were safely married. She pulled him down, raising her face to his, seeking his mouth and he kissed her, wondering how the hell he would keep control of the situation when his hold on his own desire was fraying rapidly.

Unless he didn't. Unless he gave her everything she wanted from him. He could take her, he knew. She was beyond the reach of common sense, beyond coherent thought, overwhelmed by her body's response to his touch.

Diable, mauvais esprit, démon, serpent dans Le Jardin d'Eden.

He shut the voice out, concentrating on Evie. He wanted to be inside her, now... *now*, with an urgency that threatened to break him. For so long he had dreamed of losing himself inside her, except he would no longer be lost, but found. They would be joined, inextricably. He could go to her father and tell him what he had done, and he would have no choice but to let them marry.

She would hate him for that.

A knock at the door had them both leaping with shock. Louis sat up and covered her mouth with his free hand, smothering her squeak of shock as her eyes grew wide with panic.

"Miss, are you still awake? I'm so sorry to bother you so late, but I forgot to tell you. Lady Victoria won't be coming tomorrow morning. She's poorly, so you can lie in after all. I thought it best to tell you now instead of you getting up before you needed to. Seeing as you're often up before I come in, even when I scold you for it." The maid chuckled and then waited for a response. Louis removed his hand from Evie's mouth, but kept his finger inside her, pressing gently against her sex with his thumb. He raised his eyebrows at her, knowing he was smirking and not caring. *"Miss?"*

"T-That's fine, th-thank you for telling me," Evie managed, clutching at Louis' arms and glaring at him.

Wickedly, knowing he was playing with fire, Louis slid another finger inside her, working deeper, holding her gaze as he touched her so intimately. Evie's mouth opened in a silent cry as she tightened her grip on his arms, so hard he'd have bruises. He hoped so, anyway.

"Are you all right, miss?" the maid said, concern in her voice. "Can I get you anything?"

Evie buried her face against his chest, quivering as Louis continued to pleasure her, his fingers sliding in and out with a steady rhythm designed to drive her to the edge, delighting in the tremors rippling through her body with every caress.

"Miss?"

"No!" Evie bit out, convulsing beneath Louis' hands. "No, thank you. That will be all."

Evie glared at him, her eyes wild and glittering as she reached up, grasping his hair hard and tugging him down, kissing him feverishly.

"Well, if you're sure, then. Goodnight, Miss Evie."

They heard the maid's footsteps retreating, and Louis broke the kiss, gasping for air. He stared down at Evie, shocked and aroused.

"You are a very bad girl," he observed, utterly beguiled by her.

"It w-was you," she protested, shaking her head. "I didn't—"

"Mais, non, Ce n'est pas vrai," Louis whispered, chiding her gently. "You enjoyed that, enjoyed the wickedness of it, my naughty little love. *Putain,* but how wet you are. Do you want more?"

Evie had turned scarlet by now and closed her eyes, avoiding his knowing gaze. Louis chuckled and nipped at her ear.

"Well?"

"Yes, yes, yes," she said desperately. "Yes, I want more. Give me more."

"So greedy, *ma petite*," he murmured approvingly. "And I am so hungry for you, too. Do you want me, my Evie? Is this enough, or do you need me inside you?"

She moaned, lifting her hips to encourage him to give her more, pressing her face against his neck. He shivered as she kissed him there, trailing her tongue over his skin, her hands still exploring beneath his shirt. One hand slid up his chest to toy with his nipple. Louis jerked as she pinched it, struggling to keep control as she laughed with delight at his reaction. She was more than he could have dreamed, possessing a rapacious sensuality that rivalled his own, a beguiling mix of sweet innocence and unfettered physical need that threatened to undo him completely. All this, and she loved him, loved him for the man he was, not for the pretty mask he wore, but the real person so few people saw. His determination to never let her go only grew with each second in her arms.

"Tell me," he rasped, hardly able to speak, his body was so taut with need.

"Yes," she cried softly, desperation in her voice. "I want you, *need* you inside me. Louis, I ache for you, please, just… oh, *please….*"

He let out a breath, triumphant, knowing she would let him have her, take her innocence, let him spend himself inside her so no other man could ever claim her but him. Perhaps his seed would take hold and they would have a child. The knowledge burned through him, a thrill of satisfaction.

Démon, pécheur, destructeur d'innocence!

Louis stilled, not wanting to listen to the vile words that had taunted him for so long. They weren't true. They *weren't* true, he reminded himself. Yet if he did this, if he took advantage of Evie's innocence, of her trust in him, would that not make him everything he had always been told? *The serpent in the garden of Eden, destroyer of innocence, sinner, tempting the righteous from the light into darkness.*

"Louis, please, *please*," Evie begged, her hand skating down his chest, his abdomen, past his waistband and moving lower.

Louis grasped her wrist before she could touch him, for if she put her hands on him there, he did not think he could resist. As it was, he drew in a ragged breath, staring down at the woman he loved, and knew he could not betray her, could never take from her so selfishly.

"*Regardez moi*," he said, commanding her attention. "Look at me, *ma petite*. That's it. I'm going to make it better, I'll make it so good. Yes, *mon ange*, relax now. Just let it happen."

She stilled, staring at him, such trust in her green eyes, green as spring and everything fresh when the world was new again. She made him feel renewed, as if anything were possible, and so he gave instead of taking, watching as he caressed her, circling the swollen little bud between her thighs until she arched off the bed, trembling and shaking as the climax shattered her. Louis gasped, seeking her mouth, taking her cries inside of him as if he could share in her pleasure as she clutched at him, pulling him closer, wanting more, always more. As with every other revelation this evening, she stunned him anew, as one orgasm merged into another, her pleasure so intense it rolled on and on, with such force he almost spent himself, imagining how it might feel to be inside her now as her body convulsed frantically around his fingers.

When finally she subsided, dazed and flushed, her body limp and sated, she cuddled against him, wrapping her arms about him.

Louis pressed kisses to her forehead, her cheek, until her eyes opened, and she blinked up at him, as if emerging from the dark into light.

"Oh, Louis," she whispered sleepily. "You are dreadfully wicked."

"And you love me," he reminded her.

"Mmmm," she said with a heavy sigh. "I do."

"I shall come to you again, little love, and we will talk, and I will love you some more," he promised her, kissing her mouth, not wanting to stop touching her.

"I want you to, Louis, but it's too dangerous," she protested, looking at him with concern. "You'll get caught."

He shook his head and smiled. *"Non.* I won't, and next time—" He leaned close to her ear, murmuring as he crooked his fingers inside her and she shuddered all over again. "Next time I shall use my mouth, and pleasure you with my tongue, but you will need to take care not to scream."

Her cheeks flamed scarlet, and she gasped, squirming with excitement and shock. "Oh. Oh, y-yes, please," she whispered as her intimate muscles clenched around his fingers at his words. She would dream of him doing that to her until he made it a reality. She gave him a guarded look, curiosity glinting in her eyes. "But do you really want to?"

Instead of answering, he put the fingers that had been inside her in his mouth and sucked, giving a low moan of pleasure as the taste of her exploded on his tongue.

"You do want to," she said with a pleased smile.

Louis chuckled. "You doubted it?"

"Not anymore, but I wish you would do it now. I still ache for you," she admitted, touching a finger to his mouth. She stared at him, breathing hard, so obviously aroused that Louis' breath caught. He did not think it possible to love her more, but to find a woman like her, so innocent, so sweet and kind and loving, and whose passion matched his own was more than he had dreamed possible.

"*Mon Dieu,*" he said on a huff of shocked laughter, wanting nothing more but to indulge her every desire, but then they really would risk getting caught. "I wish the same, so badly it hurts, but I cannot. I must leave you now but know this, I cannot wait to make you my wife, *mon amour.* When you are entirely mine, we will break furniture, make the devil blush and burn brighter than the sun."

Evie gave a shaky laugh, and he could do nothing but smile.

He lent down to nip at her ear, whispering to her. "Until then, you must take care of your own needs. Think of me when you touch yourself, *mon amour.* Think of my mouth on you, my tongue inside you, pleasuring you, and touch yourself until you come. I will check if you have obeyed me next time I see you," he warned her, enjoying the scandalised look in her eyes, and knowing the idea excited her. "Don't disobey, *ma petite,* or I might be forced to punish you."

Her breathing hitched, her green eyes dark with desire.

"I must go," he said, regretting the words when he wanted so much to stay with her. "I will return to you as soon as I can. Keep putting the candle in the window once you are alone, yes?"

She nodded, holding his gaze.

"*Je t'aime, amour de ma vie,*" he said, hoping she heard the truth of his words.

Louis bent and kissed her, swift and hard, and climbed off the bed before he could think twice about it. The skies were growing lighter, and the servants would be about their day soon. He must leave now. Cursing, he rearranged his aching cock and tucked his shirt in, watching her all the while.

"Beaux rêves, mon amour," he said softly, shaking his head and chuckling as she gave him a sleepy, quizzical smile. "We must improve your French, *ma petite.* I said, sweet dreams, my love."

She sighed, and he bent to steal one last kiss before leaving her to dream of him, and all they had not yet done.

Chapter 9

He will be away all weekend, at Lady
Montagu's garden party.

—Excerpt of a letter from Mr Graham
Franklin to Monsieur Etienne Boucher.

10th July 1842, The Marchioness of Montagu's Garden Party,
Dern Palace, Sevenoaks, Kent.

"Isn't it splendid?" Cat asked Aggie as they stared at the
glorious vista before them.

The gardens at Dern Palace were always magnificent but now,
on a perfect summer's day with flowers blooming all around them
and the five hundred members of the *ton* arrayed in their finery, it
seemed like something from a fairytale. There were marquees set
up with tables and chairs, each one decorated with silver and
crystal and flowers and fine linen tablecloths. There was boating
on the lake and music from an orchestra, games for all ages to
enjoy and entertainments from jugglers to magicians, to poetry
recitals and readings from famous authors.

"I've never seen anything like it," Aggie admitted, her eyes
wide with wonder.

Cat linked their arms together as they strolled among the
guests. With summer dresses in jewel tones and pastels, the
glamorous society women looked like exotic butterflies, their skirts

rustling like wings as they admired the gardens and each other, not to mention the men. As it was an event meant for families to attend, the place was thronged with children, which was a wonderful thing as it meant Cat and Aggie and their friends got to be a part of the fun for once, instead of watching from a distance before being ushered off to bed.

"Shall we get something to eat? There's such a marvellous amount of food, every delicious thing you could think of," Cat said with a laugh.

"Strawberry scones?" Aggie asked hopefully.

"Yes, of course! I asked especially as I know they're your favourite."

"You did?" Aggie stared at her with delight. "Thank you, Cat. You are a wonderful friend."

"Of course I am. I am the very best of best friends, but only because you are too." Cat grinned at her and then stopped in her tracks with a little gasp, her heart giving an erratic thud in her chest.

"What—?" Aggie began, but Cat clapped a hand over her mouth, smothering her question.

"Hush."

Aggie's eyes widened with surprise, but she turned her head to follow Cat's gaze. Cat's hand fell away, and she gave a wistful sigh.

"Oh, would you just look at him? Isn't he magnificent?"

Aggie frowned, a sceptical expression on her face but Cat didn't care. To her eyes, the Marquess of Kilbane was everything the villain ought to be, before the heroine redeemed him, anyway. Tall and dark and compelling, he moved through the crowd like a predator, all lean grace and danger.

"He's a bad 'un," Aggie observed frankly, folding her arms. "You ought to stay away from him."

"He's a bad one," Cat corrected gently, having promised to help Aggie with her diction. "Though really one ought to say, he's 'no gentleman.'"

"Hmph. Whatever you call him, I should keep well away."

"Oh, don't be a bore, Aggie. Let's follow him!" Cat said, suddenly inspired by the idea.

"What? No!" Aggie shook her head, appalled.

"Oh, please. *Pleeease,*" Cat cajoled, jumping up and down. "I want to see who he talks to and hear what they say. Most respectable people won't give him the time of day, which he probably says is just how he likes it, but I think it must be rather lonely, don't you?"

"Cat," Aggie said, her voice stern. "You're getting romantic notions about the villain again, aren't you?"

"So what if I am?" Cat retorted, a little indignant.

"Ugh! You've got to stop falling in love with the baddies. They always come to a sticky end, you know that! And any heroine who gets tangled with them gets into a dreadful fix."

"Oh, pish. That's just in the stories, and you hardly ever find a heroine with an ounce of pluck. Why they must go swooning five times a day is beyond me. I wouldn't swoon if the villain carried me off."

"No, you'd probably suggest a more efficient way of doing it," Aggie replied darkly.

Cat shrugged. "The only decent heroines are the ones by the Duchess of Bedwin, and the mysterious author of those two books, and I shall discover who that person is, you mark my words."

Aggie sighed.

"Oh, come along, he'll be lost in the crowd if you don't move," Cat pleaded, taking Aggie's hand and towing her behind as she hurried along.

Rosamund sipped at the chilled glass of lemonade, relishing the tart sweetness. It truly was a splendid garden party. Though Lady Montagu's parties were always the highlight of the year, it was rare for her to entertain at Dern. The marquess guarded his privacy fiercely and did not enjoy opening the magnificent place to the public. This, naturally, had made it the most anticipated event of the summer.

Searching the crowd, Rosamund hoped she might glimpse Evie, who ought to be here somewhere, though she despaired of finding anyone on purpose. The guests were simply too many to expect to find a particular person, so one simply strolled about and waited to see who appeared.

Beside her, Rosamund's sister, Eliza, was chatting to her friend, Elspeth, Lady Roxborough, and cooing over her baby son, Samuel. Lord Roxborough, known universally as 'Dare', was trying his best to soothe their two-year-old daughter, Araminta, who was wailing about something and refused to go to her nanny.

"What's all the fuss?" demanded a carrying voice that made everyone in the vicinity turn their heads and gawk. "Minty, do stop that racket, you're giving me the deuce of a headache."

The child looked up, tear spangled eyelashes fixing on the imposing figure of the Marquess of Bainbridge, who was carrying his six-month-old son, Aurelius.

"Want to see Aurey!" Araminta demanded, tears forgotten as she put her hands up in the air, demanding to be picked up.

Bainbridge snorted and crouched down instead so the girl could inspect the baby. He glanced up as his wife looked down at them with a smile. "The boy has inherited my looks and charm, by

Jove. Six months old and the girls are already all over him," he said with a smug grin.

His wife shook her head with an expression of fond bemusement.

"And how is Marie-Anne?" Rosamund asked, walking to the wheeled bassinet the nanny was pushing.

"Far easier than her twin brother, naturally," Arabella said with a laugh. "Boys are so very demanding. I swear, he's always hungry."

"Also like his father," Bainbridge added with a wicked grin, sending Arabella a wink.

Arabella's lips quirked and then she looked around her with a frown, scanning the crowd. "Oh, where has that dreadful man got to now? Oh!" She put her hand up and waved. "Over here, Alfie, dear! Cooee!"

Rosamund watched with astonishment as the belligerent Duke of Axton, the terror of servants everywhere, grinned at the sight of his daughter-in-law and hurried over. He was a large, intimidating man, with steel grey hair and arctic eyes of the same shade. Leaning on a silver-topped ebony cane, he fixed Arabella with a fierce expression.

"Trying to lose me in the crowd, eh? I know your game, harpy."

Rosamund started at hearing her friend spoken to so harshly, but Bella merely rolled her eyes at the duke. "Yes, you old goat. That's why I stood on tiptoes and waved at you, shouting to get your attention like the veriest hoyden."

"Aha! Trying to turn me up sweet now. I know your tricks," he said, narrowing his eyes at her.

"Yes, yes, of course you do," Arabella soothed, taking the old man's arm. "Now where are Freddie and Bertram? Don't tell me you've lost them in the crowd?"

"No, no, that foolish woman has them in hand, I believe, though she will keep dawdling," he grumbled.

"That's because you terrify her, you big brute," Arabella said with a sigh. "I swear, if you run off another governess, I will throttle you with my bare hands."

"Is he still trying to intimidate everyone he meets? I thought he might have outgrown such nonsense, but he always was an overgrown, spoiled boy."

This tart pronouncement made the duke stiffen with real irritation this time and everyone turned towards the autocratic voice. Mr Barnaby Godwin—looking very much like he hoped a large hole would materialise for him to leap into—flushed scarlet and muttered *"Aunt!"* in a horrified tone, as this august lady was responsible for the scathing remark.

"Oh," the duke said, his grey eyes glittering. "It's *you.*"

"In the flesh, Axton," said Lady Balderston. "And you're not dead. Remarkable. I felt certain someone would have shot you by now."

The assembled company were utterly silent, watching the exchange with fascination.

"You know each other?" Arabella asked the duke. He had not taken his eyes from Lady Balderston. The lady returned his cool glare, looking regal and elegant in a gown of bright, fuchsia pink and matching turban with white feathers fastened with a large diamond brooch.

"Of old," the duke muttered darkly.

A prickling silence ensued.

"Still a scintillating conversationalist, I see," Lady Balderston remarked with a quirk of one elegant eyebrow.

"Why bother? No one can get a word in edgewise once you start. Tongue enough for two sets of teeth," Axton retorted, adding, "Did your husband go deaf, by chance?"

"No," the lady replied serenely. "He had the good sense to listen, which is why I married him."

The duke harrumphed, glowering. "I was sorry to hear he'd... shuffled off. A shame. He was a decent fellow, though a dreadful aristocrat." He stabbed at the ground with his stick, still scowling.

A fond expression crossed Lady Balderston's face, and she smiled wistfully. "He was, wasn't he? And thank you, Axton, quite a compliment coming from you."

The duke grunted. "Good, well, enough of that. Go away, you annoy me."

"Excellent, in that case, I'll stay," the lady replied with a dazzling smile, moving to take Rosamund's arm. "How are you, my dear, having fun? Introduce me to the children, would you, please?"

Lucian Barrington, Marquess of Montagu, closed the door behind him with a sigh of relief. The garden party was a magnificent success, his wife was thrilled, and that made him happy. He still could not wait for it to be over. There were things that needed his attention, not least his two sons, who were definitely up to something. Pip was in trouble if he had to guess, and Thomas was trying his best to help. They no doubt thought they were being discreet, but he was too adept at keeping secrets not to know when his children were trying desperately to keep things from him.

It would be easy enough for a man with his resources to discover what, exactly, his eldest son was hiding. The temptation to do so was tantalising, but Pip was no longer a boy but a man, and Lucian knew he must make his own mistakes and find his own way out of them. He hoped his sons knew they could rely upon him to help them, no matter what the circumstances, but he also knew they revered him enough not to want to appear foolish in his eyes. They also feared his displeasure, which was strange, for he had never thought himself an overbearing parent. He had never shouted, and certainly never raised a hand to them. Matilda told him his quiet, stern voice and obvious disappointment when he reprimanded them was punishment enough, and he supposed that must be it. Boys born to so much wealth and privilege needed a steady hand, though, if they were not to become spoiled and take their advantages for granted. And then there was Cat. He groaned inwardly even as a smile touched his lips. His daughter was the light of his life, and the reason for every white strand that appeared among his pale silver-blond hair. Matilda teased him mercilessly when he peered at the scattering of white at his temples with annoyance, asking him if he thought he could glare them into disappearing.

Lucian sighed, knowing he must return to the melee outside, but not relishing the thought. Perhaps he could persuade Matilda to slip away for an hour, he mused, the idea pleasing him. She would scold him, naturally, but she enjoyed it when he was wicked, despite her protestations. Making his way unerringly through the vast maze that was Dern Palace, he traversed the long gallery and stopped in his tracks as he saw a tall, dark figure staring up at his portrait. Damnation. How the bloody hell had *he* got in?

"You ought not be here," he remarked.

The man turned, unhurried and unsurprised, and Lucian found himself face to face with the Marquess of Kilbane.

"I was just wondering how you managed it?" Kilbane asked, his wicked mouth quirking into a grin. "Most men lose their looks as they age, but you seem to get more beautiful with each passing year. Do you think Lawrence did you justice? Have you had another portrait done more recently?"

"Last year," Lucian replied, wishing Matilda had heeded his advice and not invited the devil. "It's in the great hall by the entrance."

Kilbane nodded. "I would like to see it. Perhaps your beautiful wife would give me a tour if I asked her nicely. She knows how much I adore family portraits, you see."

Lucian kept his expression cool and utterly impassive, something that was second nature and had given him the reputation for being ice cold. Matilda had told him about her run-in with Kilbane, but he had suspected she had been kind as she always was and had protected the young man from his wrath by not giving him the entire story. She was too damned maternal, that was the trouble. No doubt she believed even this hell-born babe could be saved if someone loved him enough. Lucian knew better. The man was an amoral libertine and beyond salvation.

"Yes, she told me," he drawled, unmoved.

"I invited her to fuck, but she declined. A pity, that," he added with a dejected sigh, his violet eyes gleaming. "Not that I was being entirely selfish. I said you could come too."

A wicked smile touched his lips and Lucian fought to keep his hands still when he wanted to wring the bastard's elegant neck.

"How generous of you."

"Oh, I am generous," Kilbane replied with apparent gravity. "In bed sport, at least. Otherwise, I'm selfish to the marrow."

Lucian sighed, giving every appearance of being bored to death. "You astonish me. Now, if you will excuse me, I have one or two other guests to attend to. The great hall is that way, if you wish to view the portrait."

About to turn away in relief, Lucian froze as a soft voice piped up.

"I could take you to the portrait, Lord Kilbane, if you would like me to?"

"Catherine," Lucian said, his voice hard, betraying his concern. "Come here."

He held out his hand to her, his heart thudding unpleasantly. Had she heard that dreadful exchange?

His daughter ignored him, staring at Kilbane with a look of such obvious fascination his blood ran cold.

"Why, child, you are kind to offer," Kilbane replied, his eyes flicking from her to Lucian. "But I think your darling Papa might run me through if I accepted. There are rather a lot of deadly implements at his disposal, too," he added, gesturing to a display of glittering swords on the wall beside Lucian.

Cat, the wretch, grinned at him. "Papa is deadly with a sword. Everyone says so. Are you, my lord?"

"Oh, I'm far too indolent to exert myself—for the most part," he added, sending Lucian an amused smirk. His gaze travelled back to Cat, and he smiled. "My, but you'll cause a stir in a few years, my lady. You have your father's looks."

"Yes," Cat said with a laugh. "I know."

Kilbane snorted at her matter-of-fact acceptance that she would be a great beauty. "Oh, yes, quite a stir. Perhaps I'll marry you myself."

Catherine's eyes grew wide, and she grinned at him. "All right, then."

"Cat!" Lucian snatched his daughter's hand, and her eyes flew to his, startled by the fact he'd raised his voice, which he never did. "Go to your room. Now."

"B-But Papa—"

"Now!"

"Yes, Papa." She hurried away, pausing at the end of the corridor to glance back at them before running around the corner.

Lucian stalked towards Kilbane, the desire to skewer him with the nearest sword making his muscles leap. Kilbane watched him come, apparently unconcerned. Lucian stood toe-to-toe with him, the only thing restraining him from strangling the whoreson with his cravat the fact the devil would probably enjoy it.

"Did you hear what happened to the man who tried to hurt my wife, Kilbane?"

The marquess nodded, not taking his eyes from him. "Ah, yes," he murmured. "What was his name, Mr Brown? No, Mr Burton. You sliced him up into small pieces, as I understand it. At least, the scandal sheets would have it so," Kilbane replied, his attention entirely on Lucian.

"For once, the scandal sheets are quite correct, and if you so much as breathe in the same direction as my daughter, upon my honour, you will *wish* for such a fate," he hissed, only hoping the devil would give him an excuse to do it now so he wouldn't have to wait and worry.

Kilbane's sensuous mouth quirked. "Damn me, but you are magnificent," he said softly, before giving a sigh. "And much as it would be fun to drive you to lay hands on me, I'm not in the mood to cross swords with you, literally or figuratively. So I shall put your mind at ease. I've no interest in marrying, and I don't seduce innocents. Too much effort for too little reward, in my opinion. Your sweet little daughter is safe from my wicked clutches, I swear it."

Lucian studied his expression. He was an excellent judge of character, and he could smell a lie from a mile away. Hard as it was to swallow, he believed Kilbane was sincere. Relieved, he took a step back.

"You won't ever marry?" he asked, curious despite himself.

Having had the notion of his responsibility to the title driven into him with the force of a battering ram, such a dereliction of duty was beyond his comprehension.

Kilbane shook his head and then smirked. "And not because of my… wide ranging tastes, if that's what you're wondering. I adore women, of all varieties, I just believe in keeping my options open."

"Then why not marry?" Lucian asked, compelled to understand how he could let such an old title die out. "Are there other lines—"

"Not a one. I shall be the last marquess and with me the title dies," he said, with obvious satisfaction.

For once, Lucian's emotions must have shown, because the man laughed. "My God, you're notorious for being impervious to everything. You don't blink when I make it clear I want you and your lovely wife in my bed, but let drop I'm allowing my title to die out and you're aghast… and obviously so."

"But why?" Lucian demanded.

Kilbane spread his arms wide, one dark eyebrow raising. "You really want another like me in the world? I'm inclined to feel flattered. Except it might be worse than that, they might turn out like my father, or my brother. No, no, I'm depraved, I grant you, but I shan't be responsible for that. Hard you may find it to comprehend, I'm the white sheep of the family compared to those evil sods. Can you believe I disappointed my father daily for not being wicked enough? And I tried so *very* hard," he added, his tone derisive.

Lucian frowned, hearing truth in the words. For the first time, he thought about what the man had endured as a child. Lucian knew what it was to live with evil, to live every day in fear. Had Kilbane endured something of the sort?

"Oh, Christ, *don't!*" Kilbane snapped, his expression fierce now, the violet eyes flashing. "Don't pity me. I have no use for such saccharine sentiments. If you want to fuck, I'm all for it, but don't give me your bleeding heart."

Lucian controlled his feature, the icy mask firmly back in place, furious with himself for allowing it to slip, and aghast that

Kilbane of all men had managed to provoke it. Matilda was right, the boy deserved their pity, but she was wrong that there was anything left in him to save. The rot was too deep, too ingrained. Tragic as it may be, there would be no saving him, for he did not wish to be saved.

"Get out," Lucian said, his voice cold.

Kilbane smiled an unpleasant but satisfied smile. He swept a theatrical bow, mocking to the last.

"It's been a pleasure, Montagu, not the delicious pleasure I had hoped for it's true, but a pleasure, nonetheless. I wonder where I might find your wife?"

He walked away, the sound of his low laughter echoing down the long gallery as he went.

Chapter 10

Dear Aggie,

I am looking forward to seeing you at the garden party. It's been an age since we've all been together. We are all staying at Dern. Will you be there for the entire weekend? I have some excellent books for you, and I have done a drawing of an owl which I am rather pleased with. I thought you might like it as you were so pleased with the rabbit last time.

Felix and Emmeline Knight will be there too, though perhaps Felix will be too grand for us, now he's turned eighteen? Do you think he'll still want to build a fort in the woods? He was always the best at it, and we shall have to work hard without his skills. You will help too, won't you?

Jacob Carmichael (Viscount Ridley) is coming too, but I swear if he keeps making sheep's eyes at Torie, I shall draw his cork.

Oh, but for heaven's sake, don't let Cat lead you into mischief. You know what she is for causing trouble.

*—Excerpt of a letter from The Lord
Frederick Adolphus (younger son of Robert
and Prunella Adolphus, Their Graces, The
Duke and Duchess of Bedwin) to Miss
Agatha Smith.*

10th July 1842, The Marchioness of Montagu's Garden Party, Dern Palace, Sevenoaks, Kent.

Rosamund got up, needing to stretch her legs. Lady Balderston was a wonderful companion, but she had found some old cronies she'd not seen in decades and the three women were talking over each other in their haste to catch up on all that had happened in the intervening years. Not having a clue about the people they were speaking of, Rosamund moved to the opening of the marquee and looked out, enjoying the simple pleasure of watching people doing what people did when dressed up in their best and out to enjoy themselves.

The crowd parted as a couple moved along with their family in tow, and a familiar tall, athletic figure became visible through the gap. Lord Hargreaves, his wife upon his arm, was speaking to a group of people she did not recognise. Suddenly, he turned his head towards her, as if her gaze had a physical property he could feel. There was a swift flare of warmth and recognition in his eyes before his expression become carefully neutral and he turned back to the conversation. Rosamund's heart felt as if it were being squeezed in her chest as she saw the tight set of his shoulders. She too went to turn away, resigning herself to the inevitable, but something about his rigid stance must have struck Lady Hargreaves, for she looked past her husband, directly at Rosamund. The look she sent was one of pure malice, so shocking that Rosamund gasped.

Shaken, she turned away and went back to Lady Balderston.

"Are you well, Rosamund, dear?" the lady asked, pausing her conversation to regard her with concern. "You're white as a sheet."

"Oh, yes. Quite well," Rosamund assured her, though she did not feel the least bit well. "A little too warm, I think."

Lady Balderston passed her a beautiful painted fan with a sympathetic smile. "Take that, and drink another glass of lemonade," she advised.

Rosamund nodded, letting the ladies' chatter wash over her as she allowed the tension to leave her. She was being silly, getting herself all het up over something as silly as a glare from Lady Hargreaves. It was just the heat making her dramatic, that and the fact she had not slept well the past few nights, though she could not say why. Only that she was troubled and found it hard to settle herself to sleep with ease.

Over the next hour Rosamund drank two large glasses of lemonade as the ladies talked and laughed incessantly, with the inevitable outcome.

"I must find the necessary," she whispered to Lady Balderston, who nodded her understanding and returned to her conversation.

As Rosamund was staying at Dern Palace for the week with her family, she returned to the vast house, relieved to have a little peace. Though she hated to admit it when it was such a splendid affair, she was out of sorts and not in the mood to socialise. So, once she had seen to her personal needs, she remained indoors to make use of the magnificent library. Matilda always had a wonderful selection of novels, being an avid reader, so Rosamund was bound to find something to divert her.

On her way to the library, she ran into her brother, Jules, with some of his friends. Rosamund was surprised to discover Mr Humphrey Price among the group, for Jules had little time for the man. But then Jules, being the heir to a dukedom, often had to endure the company of sycophants and toadies with as much good grace as he could muster. Usually this wasn't a great deal, but he would not cause a stir at an event such as this, so Rosamund imagined he was gritting his teeth and bearing it as best he could.

"Ozzie? Where are you off to?" he asked, his brows drawing together. He lowered his voice to speak to her privately. "You ought not be wandering about alone."

Rosamund sighed, irritated. As if she didn't know that. "I thought the house was off limits to guests," she retorted, giving him and his friends a significant look.

Jules shrugged. "I had permission to show them the library. It's quite a marvel."

"Yes, well, that's where I'm going. I have a headache so I shall choose a book and go to my room where my maid will barricade me in and guard the door."

Jules glared at her, affronted. "Well, don't bite my head off for being a concerned brother!"

Rosamund groaned, immediately contrite. "I beg your pardon, Jules. I didn't mean it. I'm feeling rather out of sorts."

"Shall I stay?" he asked, concern in his eyes.

For once, Rosamund felt a swell of fondness for her big brother, whom she could often have cheerfully murdered. "No. I don't want to spoil your fun. I'll grab the first title that comes to hand and go upstairs, I promise."

"As you wish, but mind that you do," he said sternly.

Rosamund bit back the comment hovering on her tongue as her irritation rose again at his domineering tone. *He's training to be a duke,* she reminded herself, flashed him a sweet smile and hurried away before they started bickering again.

Sebastian sighed and wondered how much longer Adelia would want to stay. They'd taken rooms at a local inn for the weekend, and he wanted to return there and bury himself in a good bottle of claret. He'd not dared drink anything stronger than lemonade during the day, too on edge that Adelia might cause a scene if he didn't keep an eye on her.

She had complained bitterly, annoyed by his 'breathing down her neck.' But she had wanted him to stay, he reminded her placidly. So, he was staying. She couldn't have it both ways.

For the moment he was alone, however, a blessing he was relishing for as long as Adelia made use of the ladies' retiring room. He drew the line at following her into the necessary and only prayed she could not cause too much trouble in the distance between there and where he stood waiting for her. He kept his eyes on the path she must take to return to the party, determined she would not evade him.

Raucous laughter reached his ears and Sebastian frowned, scowling down at the drunken fools guffawing beneath the terrace where he waited.

"Hell, Kilbane of all men," one of them crowed. "And her a little innocent."

"Not for long," a man Sebastian identified as Humphrey Price sneered. "That devil will have her skirts over her head and her legs spread before she knows what's hit her. He's probably got her bent over a table as we speak. It's not like he's shy about taking his pleasure where he fancies."

Sebastian felt a chill of terror for whichever poor girl had got herself into the marquess' clutches. Cursing, but unable to ignore the girl's plight, he hurried down the stairs and grabbed Mr Price by the throat, slamming him against the wall.

"You knew the girl was alone with Kilbane and you did *nothing?"* he demanded with disgust, giving him a hard shake. "What kind of man are you?"

"The kind who knows better than to get between Kilbane and his quarry, that's what," Price smirked. "Silly little tart shouldn't have gone off on her own, should she? Asking for it, I should say," he added, making Sebastian want to break his damned nose for him, but if the girl was to be helped, there was no time.

"Where?" he gritted out.

"The library," Price's friend supplied helpfully. "That's what you said, wasn't it, Humphrey?"

"Yes, the library," Price replied, glaring at Sebastian with loathing.

Sebastian wondered at the vitriol in that icy glare but did not stop to consider it further, too afraid the young woman would meet her ruin if he did not hurry. Giving Price one last satisfying shake, he left the blackguard slumped against the wall and hurried into the grand house. Thankfully, he met a stream of servants, loaded trays in hand, on their way out to replenish the refreshments.

"Which way to the library?" he demanded of a young man who was trailing a little behind the others.

The fellow gawked at him before pointing to his right. "See that door on the left? Take that and then the third door to the right. Follow the corridor to the end and turn right, and then right again. Then take the next left and then the door right in front of you, the library door is at the far end of that room."

Sebastian groaned, remembering now what a bloody maze Dern was from having visited once before. Committing the instructions to memory, he hurried on.

Matilda kept her smile firmly in place whilst Miss Dudley gushed about how *simply divine* everything was. The food was divine, the gardens were divine, Matilda herself was divine, oh, and her daughter? Simply divine.

She was such a sweet lady, a spinster of middling years, that Matilda bore with her patiently though she was dying to find her husband. She hadn't seen Lucian in over an hour, and she knew he hated these affairs. If possible, she had hoped to let him persuade her to slip away and do something dreadfully scandalous with him somewhere secluded, but she would need to find him first. With one ear still on the conversation, she kept her eyes on the crowd, before noticing that wretched creature, Miss Hatchet. For reasons Matilda could never fathom, she was often in company with Miss Dudley, but unlike that kind-hearted lady, Miss Hatchet was a dreadful tattlemonger. Miss Hatchet was now speaking with Lady Hargreaves. Their bent heads dipped close together, both speaking urgently, no doubt having found some dreadful piece of gossip to devour. To Matilda, as beautiful as Lady Hargreaves may be, and as bright and lovely as her sky-blue gown was, the two of them resembled nothing more than carrion crows, picking over some poor, unfortunate creature.

Miss Dudley paused in her effusive praise as a little shriek of apparent dismay emanated from Miss Hatchet, though it sounded more like delight to Matilda.

"Oh, no, the poor child, and her a duke's daughter! She'll be ruined, of course."

Matilda's heart leapt with fright. "Who? Who will be ruined?"

"Oh, I told you not to tell anyone," Lady Hargreaves said, with such patently false ingenuousness, Matilda's hand itched with the desire to slap her.

"Who?" Matilda demanded, her voice frosty with dislike now.

Miss Hatchet paled and put up her chin. "It appears Lady Rosamund has been ill advised enough to speak privately with Lord Kilbane."

"Preposterous!" Matilda said at once. "She would never, never do such a thing."

"I saw her enter the library not five minutes ago, and a tall, dark-haired man slipped in after her a moment later. It looked like the marquess to me," Lady Hargreaves replied, her eyes full of malice.

Oh, the horrid woman was up to something. This was her revenge on poor Rosamund for daring to be friends with her husband, and Matilda did not doubt Miss Hatchet, the biggest gossip in England, was not the only person she had told.

"Stay here," Matilda commanded, hurrying back to the house, but the wretched women would not stay put, following her at a run, eager for the drama to play out.

Praying that she could find a servant, or better yet, Lucian or one of her sons to keep them at bay before she reached the library, Matilda rushed on.

Rosamund perused the titles, trying to choose as quickly as she could. The trouble was there were so many good ones, but Cat had mentioned something about The Devil and the Maiden, the new book by the scandalous and anonymous author of The Ghosts of Castle Madruzzo. Now *that* would give her an entertaining afternoon. After a fruitless ten minutes of searching, Rosamund gave up, remembering her promise to her brother not to dally. Unable to choose between The Fall of the House of Usher by Edgar Allan Poe, and The Captain's Daughter by Pushkin, she gathered up both. The House of Usher was only a short story, after all, so she ought to manage the two of them. Pleased with her selection, Rosamund had turned to leave when one of the two doors into the room burst open and slammed shut again.

Scanning the vast library, his expression fierce, was Lord Hargreaves.

Rosamund was so shocked she dropped the books with a squeak of surprise.

"My lord!" she exclaimed, staring at him.

Hargreaves started and spun to face her. *"Rosamund!* My God, where is he? Where is the blackguard?"

"B-Blackguard?" she queried, perplexed.

He paled, his expression changing from fury to terror in an instant.

"Oh, no," he murmured, before spinning around and grasping the door handle just as a definite, *snick,* indicated the turning of a key. Hargreaves tugged at the door. "Open this door, Adelia!" he bellowed, pounding on the thick oak.

Adelia? Rosamund's heart thudded with alarm.

"The other door," she cried, picking up her skirts and running to the door at the far end of the library.

"No, wait!" Hargreaves shouted, opening a window, but it was too late.

Before either of them could decide on the best exit, Mr Humphrey Price strolled into the room and made a great show of looking shocked.

"Good God, Lady Rosamund, and *Hargreaves!"* he exclaimed, eyes wide.

His friend guffawed loudly. "You was wrong, you said it was Kilbane, but... eh, wait a moment."

Whatever puzzled his friend, Price did not want to hear it and elbowed him sharply, glaring him into silence.

"You son of a bitch," Hargreaves said, advancing on Mr Price, only to stop in his tracks as a group of a dozen giggling young women entered, gasping and shrieking with apparent upset when all Rosamund could see was the delight in their eyes.

"A tryst!" one of them exclaimed. "With a married man! Oh, Lady Rosamund, for shame!"

"Get out!" This cool, furious voice came from Lady Montagu and Rosamund felt herself tremble uncontrollably at the compassion in her eyes. Oh, this was beyond bad. "All of you, out now."

"Oh, but we would not wish to miss this," Lady Hargreaves said, sweeping into the room behind her as if she was the wronged heroine in a bad play. "My sainted husband is not so very noble as we all thought, is he? Seducing innocents, Sebastian? How *could* you? Especially when you knew the poor child was already in love with you."

Rosamund felt giddy and ill and very much like she might do something as appalling as swoon, but the satisfied smirk on Lady Hargreaves' face made her stiffen her spine.

"You spiteful bitch," Lord Hargreaves said as the young ladies gasped in shock, the tone of his voice so terrible that Rosamund shivered. "I'll kill you for this."

He lunged forward, only the sudden appearance of Lord Montagu and Gabriel Knight holding him back, and still he fought to get to his wife, his face blanched with rage.

"I stayed, Adelia. I did everything you wanted! I stayed, *damn* you! I'll see you in hell for this, you see if I don't, you evil witch!"

Even his wife seemed taken aback by the power of his fury, staring at him with her chin defiantly raised, though she was chalk-white.

"My dear?"

Suddenly Matilda was in front of Rosamund, holding her hands, her face full of understanding.

"Don't let them see," she said, her voice very low, her hold on Rosamund's hands so tight it was almost painful.

Rosamund understood; she was not the daughter of a duke for nothing. She knew how to face the world and show nothing of what she felt. Though her knees felt odd, trembling as if they may not support her for long, she turned and faced the assembled company.

"Well, Lady Hargreaves. It seems you have accomplished your desire to ruin me and drag your poor husband into another scandal. Bravo. Of course, we all know this is an utter fabrication, but the truth has never been of much importance to you, has it? I pity you if you want the truth, but for now, I am tired of the circus you have created. If you will excuse me, I would like some privacy, and you will no doubt be eager to spread your poisonous gossip, so please do not let me stop you."

With Matilda at her side, Rosamund walked calmly out of the room, walking blindly as Matilda guided her to a small parlour. Once the door closed behind them, she managed only a few more steps before her knees buckled, and she sank to the floor, holding tight to Matilda as her chest heaved with sobs so overwhelming she could not breathe, but gasped and clutched at her bodice, which was constricting her lungs beyond bearing.

"Oh, my dear. Oh, love, I'm so sorry, so desperately sorry. That wicked woman. She won't get out of this unscathed, Rosamund, I swear it. By the time I'm done, there won't be a family in England who will receive her, you have my word."

But that was scant comfort now, when Rosamund knew by tomorrow morning the scandal sheets would be full of the story of her affair with a married man. Of all the things they could have accused her of, and of course everyone would believe it, because they had been friends. They had thought they could escape censure if they played by the rules of propriety, but in the end, they had been foolish, and Rosamund would pay the price.

The door opened, and Matilda looked up to see her husband and Mr Knight enter with Lord Hargreaves between them.

Rosamund gave a choked sob at the sight of him.

"My lady," he said, so obviously devastated that she tried her best to calm herself.

This was not his fault.

"Oh, Lucian, whatever is to be done?" Matilda asked, turning to her husband.

Montagu shook his head, his expression grave. "The story was spreading like wildfire before you even entered the room, only everyone was talking about Rosamund and Kilbane. They laid the groundwork well for this malicious piece of work. I can only promise you the people involved will pay, Rosamund."

Rosamund looked up into the austerely beautiful face of a man she had regarded as an uncle and saw the sincerity there. He would destroy anyone who hurt his family, and she fell into that category. It would not help her, though. It could not repair the damage.

"I want m-my mother," Rosamund said, aware she sounded like a child and not caring.

"Your mother and father took a boat out with Harry. Thomas has gone to fetch them," Montagu said.

Rosamund nodded and allowed Matilda to help her stand, sitting heavily in the chair closest to her. Lord Hargreaves approached her, kneeling at her feet, his countenance so bleak she could hardly bear to meet his eyes.

"Tell me what to do," he said, staring at her and then at Montagu and Mr Knight. "For the love of God, someone tell me what to do because I cannot live with this."

His voice cracked, such fierce emotion behind the words that Rosamund's heart went out to him.

"There's nothing you can do, my friend," she said gently, needing to comfort him even though she would bear the burden of this day's work.

Her entire future, which had seemed full of possibilities just hours ago, now lay in ruins because of a woman's desire to spoil the one bright spot in her husband's life.

"Friend?" he said, a bitter note to the word. "Some friend I have been to you."

"You have," Rosamund said firmly. "We were foolish not to see the danger we were in, but we did nothing wrong, and you *are* my friend. You always will be."

She held out her hand to him and Hargreaves took it, his larger hand engulfing hers, his grip warm and sure.

"I would do anything, anything at all, to save you from this," he whispered.

"I know," Rosamund said, blinking back tears. "But there is nothing you can do, except tell the truth to anyone who will listen. I… I think you should go now," she added, as her composure fractured, and she knew she could not remain calm any longer.

"So do I," Mr Knight said, his expression grim. "Bedwin will be here any moment, and this may not have been your fault, but he'll want to kill you anyway, Hargreaves. I would if it were my daughter. You'd best make yourself scarce until he's had time to calm down."

Montagu nodded his agreement. "He's right, I'm afraid. Come along. This way."

Hargreaves sent one last look at Rosamund, his frustration at there being nothing he could do to save her palpable, but he left the room, walking as though in a daze, numb with shock.

Chapter 11

Dearest,

I am broken-hearted for you. I know your family will take the very best care of you, but you need only say the word, and I will come.

We are all of us countering the vile story, telling the true version of events to anyone who will listen. Papa is making the rounds of the clubs, leaning on all those men who he holds in his debt, and Mama is frantically writing letters to all her most powerful friends. We both know your papa will tear down the city brick by brick and build it anew before he allows this to ruin you. Have courage, my dear. You have powerful allies and friends who love you. It may take some time, but we will prevail.

You may also take heart from the fact that Lady Hargreaves can never show her face in polite society again. Montagu saw to that. She may have ruined you, but she ruined herself in the process.

—Excerpt of a letter from Miss Evie Knight (daughter of Lady Helena and Mr Gabriel Knight) to Lady Rosamund Adolphus

*(daughter of Robert and Prunella
Adolphus, Their Graces, The Duke and
Duchess of Bedwin).*

Night of the 10^{th of} July 1842, Lansdown Place, Sloane Square, Chelsea, London.

Sebastian did not remember the journey back to London, only getting home, too blind with fury and regret to concentrate on what was happening. A vague memory of Gabriel Knight bundling him into his own carriage stirred in his mind, but he did not much care.

Adelia had ruined Rosamund's life.

Although she'd won, although he'd given in and stayed so she could continue to torment him, she'd had to break the only good thing in his life. He had turned his back on his friendship with Rosamund to keep her safe, had committed himself to never speaking to her again, and it had made no difference.

Impotent fury simmered inside him, the desire to break things overwhelming. So though it was stupid and base, sinking to her own spiteful level, he went straight to Adelia's room and broke everything he could get his hands on. China figurines and jewellery boxes were smashed against the wall. His wife's perfume—the one that he'd once thought so lovely, but which now made him ill—filled the room in an overpowering cloud that suffocated him as the delicate bottle exploded against the parquet floor, scattering glass shards. Yet he did not stop, pulling her clothes out of chests and wardrobes, ripping seams and tearing the fine fabric apart. He picked up the chair in front of her dressing table and smashed it down, breaking the looking glass into a thousand pieces. Seven years' bad luck be damned, he'd had a lifetime of bad luck due him the moment he'd said 'I do'. There was nothing for him in this life to look forward to. No joy, no love, no children, no family. Just Adelia tormenting him over and over. Well, she would have nothing too, then. He would leave in the morning and instruct the servants to close his houses and not allow her entry, and he would cut off her access to his money. He'd give her just enough to survive, but no longer would he pay for these fine dresses. There would be no more jewels and carriages. She'd have to find a lover, a real one this time, to pay for those fripperies if she wanted them that badly.

He was done playing the fool.

Adelia's lady's maid came in and gave a little shriek of horror as she saw the destruction he'd wrought.

"Don't you dare think about clearing it up," he barked as he stalked past her, heading down to the cellars, where he picked out two bottles of brandy. It was the only way to get through the next few days without doing something truly terrible. Perhaps, by the time he'd sobered up, Montagu, Bedwin, and Knight would have figured a way to save Rosamund, for they had made it very clear his help was not welcome. He would only make everything more difficult if he had a hand in whatever they did to repair the damage Adelia had wrought. The best thing he could do was to stay away and keep his head down. Ha! If only he'd done that from the first. If only he'd stayed away from Rosamund, instead of being drawn towards her kindness, her smile, and her laughter, the sound of which always made his heart feel lighter. It had been pure selfishness. He'd been lonely and wretched, and she had blazed across his world like a beacon of everything he longed for.

Sebastian drank, for no other purpose than to numb himself, though it did not work. All he could think about was Rosamund, how she had looked crumpled on the floor of the parlour, overcome with shock and misery. He had done that, and unless her father and Montagu and their powerful wives could perform a miracle, it could not be undone.

Someone would need to marry her, and quickly. If only he could have been the one to save her, instead of the instrument of her destruction. For a moment he allowed himself the unutterable torture of imagining Rosamund as his wife, of waking to that beautiful face, of all the ridiculous conversations they would enjoy, of the silly bickering and laughter, and sharing his life with her, his bed.

He slammed the door shut on the tantalising images, for that way lay madness, and he hovered on the brink of that state as it was. Hazily, he focused on the bottle in his hand, satisfied to discover he was emptying it with determined efficiency. Sebastian lifted it to his mouth and drank deep, closing his eyes and concentrating on nothing but swallowing as the liquor burned a path to his belly.

His bedroom door flew open and there stood Adelia, her eyes flashing fury.

"What have you done?" she demanded.

For once, his elegant wife looked rather dishevelled, her eyes red-rimmed as if she had been crying.

"My room is a shambles, you brute!"

Sebastian couldn't help but laugh. "Oh, poor, poor Adelia. Her pretty dresses are all spoiled and her room is a mess. How we ought to pity her. Do you think Lady Rosamund is weeping over such trifles?"

Her expression was cold, unrepentant, her tears for herself alone. "She's a duke's daughter, she'll recover. Montagu has ruined me for good with little more than a few words, the bastard. We will have to leave, go back to France."

Sebastian stared at her in wonder. Did she really believe she had that much power over him?

"The only reason I stayed was to protect Lady Rosamund. Well, you've lost that bargaining chip now, Adelia. I want nothing more to do with you. You'll get not a penny more from me, you'll not live in my houses, there will be no more expensive jewels and carriages, and you'll certainly not share my life. I might even divorce you for this day's work."

What little colour had remained in her cheeks drained away as the reality of what she'd done, of what he would do, hit home.

"You wouldn't dare shame me like that," she whispered, incredulous.

"Oh, the old Sebastian wouldn't have," he said, wanting to hurt her as much as she had hurt Rosamund. "But that man is dead. You killed him. Honour be dammed. There can be no honour when dealing with a creature like you. You did not bat an eyelid when you shamed Rosamund before all those people, and neither will I when I shame you before the world. It will be a crimcon they will talk about for decades."

"If you do, I'll counter sue. I'll name Rosamund as your lover!" she flung back at him, raising her voice now she saw he was deadly serious.

Sebastian got to his feet, swaying a little but remarkably steady as fury burned in his guts. "Go ahead," he growled, advancing on her. Whatever she saw in his face must have frightened her, for she backed up, out of his room and along the hallway as he followed her. "You do that, Adelia. I shall enjoy calling all the witnesses willing to swear that you set up this little scene today out of malice and spite. Montagu and Bedwin will enjoy presenting you as a heartless bitch who enjoyed her own affairs but could not allow her husband an innocent friendship. Do you really think that pretty face will save you against the might of those two families?"

"Oh, how I hate you! You never loved me!" she wept, but this time, Sebastian was utterly unmoved.

"Your crocodile tears are a waste of time. I'm done, Adelia. Done with this sham of a marriage, done with you. Get out of my house."

The words were quieter now, his anger retreating as fatigue, disgust, and misery rose in a great black wave. All he wanted was to go back to his room and keep drinking.

She flew at him, lashing out, clawing at his face. Sebastian grabbed her wrists, holding her off him with ease, which only made her increasingly furious. She kicked him in the shin, hard enough to make him curse and give her a shake.

"Stop it!" he roared. "Stop this insanity! Just leave me alone, you spiteful bitch. I want you out of my life, so leave, or you'll damn well regret it!"

Sebastian let her go so abruptly she stumbled a little, and he turned away before she could steady herself and fly at him again. Instead, he strode away, slamming the bedroom door behind him with nothing in mind but drowning himself in brandy.

Morning of the 11th of July 1842, Lansdown Place, Sloane Square, Chelsea, London.

It was the scream that woke him. Sebastian's brain moved slowly, wading painfully from the sodden depths of a drunken slumber to register the screaming did not stop but kept repeating itself. Then other voices joined it, shrieks and shouts and exclamations.

"Devil take you," Sebastian groaned, clutching at his head. What the hell was Adelia up to now that had the staff in such a taking? Blinking, he cracked open his eyes enough to see it was not yet properly light, his view of the sky a strange slash of scarlet and pink, visible through the partly open curtains as the sun rose upon a new day.

Red sky in the morning, shepherd's warning.

The old phrase rang unpleasantly in his ears like the toll of a bell, and his brandy-soaked brain reminded him about that scream. That awful sound had been because of something dreadful. Something truly horrible. Something had happened in this house. His heart thudded, an unpleasant chill of foreboding skittering down his spine as he forced himself upright, weaving across the room to the bedroom door and flinging it open. Somehow, he got out into the corridor, staggered to the landing, and leant heavily on the balustrade as another scream rent the air.

Sebastian looked down and saw one of the laundry maids pointing at him.

"Murderer!" she shrieked, and then fainted.

He registered the other faces, all of them staring at him with varying degrees of fear and suspicion. Then he saw the crumpled sky-blue skirts. With a sickening sense of inevitability, he leaned over the rail a little farther.

Adelia.

She lay in a heap at the bottom of the stairs, her head twisted at an unnatural angle, her eyes wide and sightless.

"Oh, no." He was uncertain if he had spoken aloud or only in his head, could not comprehend what he was seeing.

"What happened?" he whispered, staring at her with incomprehension. How could she be dead? Wicked, spiteful Adelia was too full of life to be so still and.... "What happened?" he demanded again, louder now.

"Why don't you tell us?" called a shrill voice from among his staff.

Sebastian clutched at the railing. No. No, he couldn't have… he… he couldn't… *Could* he?

Desperately, he tried to piece together the events of last night, but his brain refused to cooperate, the combination of alcohol and panic working upon him until he couldn't think. Adelia, dead? No. *No!* It was impossible, but there she lay, undeniable proof. Oh, Lord. His stomach roiled, horror and too much brandy souring into a vile mixture in his guts. He hadn't wanted her dead. He hadn't. Sebastian wouldn't have wished this on her… and yet an uncomfortable memory surfaced of having done just that. He recoiled as he remembered. *I didn't mean it. I didn't mean it!*

His pulse sped faster as he clutched at the railing, unable to look away from Adelia's crumpled form. She looked so small now. So frail.

He felt the judging eyes of his staff staring up at him. They had heard the rumours that he was having an affair with Lady Rosamund, had they heard too, that he had threatened to kill Adelia only yesterday? Had he meant it? When he'd said it, he had been blind with rage but... No. No; it was only words, a desire to frighten her. That was all. His chest was tight with fear as he tried to convince himself of that. He hadn't done this. He would remember, surely?

To his eternal relief, Peterson stepped forward.

"You there, fetch a sheet and cover Lady Hargreaves up. You, strong coffee and lots of it. Bring it to Lord Hargreaves, hurry now. The rest of you, stop staring and go about your work, at once. No one is to set foot up here again unless I order it. Go!"

It was testament to the force of Peterson's influence on his staff that they did as he bid them, many of them casting fearful glances up the stairs at Sebastian as they went.

Peterson, having apparently got over his own shock, mounted the stairs.

"My lord, I have had no choice but to send for the police, though it is clear Lady Hargreaves fell down the stairs. A tragic accident, but an accident all the same. I am sure this matter can be dealt with quickly."

Sebastian stared blankly at his butler.

"She fell down the stairs, my lord," the butler said, his voice firm.

It occurred to Sebastian to wonder if Peterson truly believed that or if he just wanted to limit the scandal. Did he think Sebastian had pushed her? Of course, it did not matter what people believed. The police would find what Peterson had said. He was a peer of the realm. His wife had fallen down the stairs. A tragic accident. That's what the official line would be. What people said in private, however…. How fortuitous that the woman standing between him and the lady he was having an affair with was now dead.

Everyone would believe he'd done it. Perhaps Rosamund would believe it too.

Had he?

The question circled his head until his stomach rebelled, and he fled back to his room to vomit.

Chapter 12

My dears,

I am sending this to every one of you. A meeting is most urgently required. We must do all in our power to counter this vile scandal before it gets completely out of hand. Please come to Dern, at once.

—Excerpt of a letter from The Most Honourable Matilda Barrington, Marchioness of Montagu, to the Peculiar Ladies.

12th July 1842, Dern Palace, Sevenoaks, Kent, London.

Rosamund looked up from her book at a soft knock on the bedroom door. Not that she'd been reading, only staring at the pages as the words danced before her eyes. She could not seem to settle to anything. The family had elected to remain at Dern. Here, her father and Montagu could present a united front as their mothers rallied their own troops. It was also a private fortress, and Lord Montagu was forbidding enough that no one with any sense would come within ten miles of it without invitation.

"Come in," Rosamund said, trying to inject some force into her voice when she felt utterly listless and drained of hope.

Everyone was tiptoeing about her, being so kind and reassuring, constantly checking she was all right and not about to take a hysterical fit until she was seriously tempted to scream and rant so they could stop worrying she might. At this point, a hysterical fit looked terribly appealing. The trouble was she was far too pragmatic and strong-minded to indulge in such a display. A pity, really, for she suspected she might feel better for it. Looking up, she saw her brother, Jules, had entered the room.

"Morning, brat," he said softly.

She summoned a smile for him, praying he would not feel the need to apologise again. He blamed himself for her demise, berating himself over and again for leaving her alone. But how could he have known?

He walked towards her, his expression kind and careful, and she wanted to shake him. Jules only ever teased and was dreadfully rude to her, as any older brother ought to be to a sister. Anyone would think there had been a death in the family.

Her heart turned over as she realised he was pale, and steeling himself to tell her something dreadful.

Rosamund took a deep breath and reminded herself that being ruined would not kill her. Her family and friends loved her. They would stand by her; they would weather the storm.

"Whatever it is making you look so Friday faced, you'd best get it over with," she said, aiming for a light-hearted tone but only sounding breathless and terrified.

"I know, Ozzie, only... only I don't know how. You ought not have to bear this burden."

"I won't break, Jules," she said, her heart thudding harder as he pulled up a chair in front of her own and sat down.

Leaning forward, he took her hand in his, such an affectionate gesture from her big brother that her eyes prickled.

"Of course you won't break," he said scornfully. "The women in this family are made of steel. Oh, father and I make out like we're the backbone of the dukedom, but it's only a front. We know it's Mama that keeps Papa from losing his mind, we know it's Eliza and Lottie and you, and soon the other young female brats who always keep the family name upheld whilst I gallivant, pretending I'm doing the important job of learning to be a fat, lazy nobleman."

Despite everything, Rosamund's lips quirked. "My, it must be bad if you're being nice to me."

Jules nodded, holding her hand tighter. "It is, sis."

"Tell me."

"Lady Hargreaves is dead."

Rosamund stared at Jules as the words sank in. "B-But that... she can't... *How?*" she finally demanded, uncertain Jules hadn't misunderstood whatever information he'd been given.

"The police enquiry states she fell down the stairs and broke her neck," Jules said, his expression impassive. "The staff found her yesterday morning."

Rosamund swallowed, an awful buzzing in her head accompanying the dizzying speed at which her heart was beating.

"Hargreaves was with her?"

"In the house, yes. Drunk out of his skull. He had retired to his room and Adelia... fell down the stairs."

"But that's not what people think."

It was obvious what people would think, in the circumstances.

Jules shook his head. "No. They think Hargreaves pushed her."

Rosamund snatched her hand from his grip and stood, forcing him to shift sideways as she stumbled away from him, heading to the window. She unlatched it and swung it wide, leaning out and gasping for air.

"No!" she said, shaking her head, sucking in lungfuls of air that seemed never to allow her to breathe. "No! He didn't. He didn't! He *didn't!*"

Jules ran to her, taking her by the shoulders. "Breathe, Rosamund. Breathe in, breathe out. You'll faint if you don't calm yourself."

"I never faint!" she retorted furiously, glaring at him over her shoulder and then shrugging out of his hold. "And I am not hysterical. I'm damned furious!"

"Ozzie, you have got to admit, it's suspicious. Everyone heard him tell her he would kill her, and hours later she's dead," Jules said, his voice calm, patient, as if speaking to an overwrought child.

Rosamund called on years of training to hide her thoughts and feelings, slamming her public mask into place and speaking with such cold calm that Jules stared at her.

"Lord Hargreaves is the kindest, gentlest man I have ever known. He would never lay a hand on a woman. This I believe. He is not capable of murder."

"No one said anything about murder," Jules said, his expression softening. "But he tore her room apart, smashing everything he could get his hands on, furniture, china, jewels and clothes, he destroyed everything she owned. He was out of his head drunk by the time his wife got home. She came back and confronted him, and they had one hell of a row. The night staff heard them at it."

"And did they see him push her down the stairs?" Rosamund demanded. "Did they witness it with their own eyes?"

"No," Jules admitted. "They heard the door slam to his room, and it went quiet, so they thought the show was over. It must have happened once they'd gone downstairs, for no one found her until the staff were about their morning chores."

"So, she likely fell down the stairs like the police said. If she was overwrought, she could have missed her footing, or tripped on her skirts," Rosamund said furiously. "It's easily done, I assure you."

"She could have." Jules nodded, though there was enough doubt in his eyes to make her want to hit him.

"But no one wishes to believe that," Rosamund said, her voice dull. "Everyone thinks he killed his wife so he could be with his mistress."

Jules' jaw flexed, and she saw the effort it took for him to control his temper. "Anyone who implies anything of the sort in my hearing will regret it," he muttered.

"They won't say it in your hearing, but they'll say it," Rosamund said, her knees wobbling. She found her way back to her chair, suddenly exhausted. "Thank you, Jules, for telling me, and for your kindness. You are an excellent big brother."

Jules made a sound of disgust, but Rosamund shot him a look that silenced him.

"If you wouldn't mind, I would like to be by myself for a little while."

"Of course." Jules moved closer to her, laying his hand on her shoulder for a moment in a gesture of reassurance. "If you need me, just shout. If there is anything I can do, anything at all—"

"I know, Jules," she said, covering his hand with her own for a moment. But that was the devil of this situation.

Jules could go out and proclaim her innocence from the highest tower, but people had minds of their own, and wasn't the lurid version of events always so much more appealing.

Jules left her alone and Rosamund thought furiously. She remembered and re-examined every conversation, every interaction with Lord Hargreaves, and the way he dealt with everyone else in his life. Refusing to see anyone else who asked after her, she turned over everything she knew of him, every piece of gossip, every scandal sheet heading. The afternoon was growing late by the time she felt she had put him before her own personal jury. Her opinion remained unchanged.

Lord Hargreaves was a gentleman in the truest sense of the word. Despite years of provocation, he had continued to treat his wife with respect, certainly in public. Yes, of course it was possible that he had abused her in private, but Rosamund had looked into his eyes and... and she did not believe him capable of such behaviour. Her mother had told her quite bluntly about the life one could expect if one married the wrong man. Rosamund's grandfather on her mother's side had been a brute and a bully and had abused her grandmother. Rosamund knew such men could be charming in public and something else in private. Yet, she could not believe that the case here.

If Lord Hargreaves had been abusing his wife, it would not be him giving up Rosamund's friendship but Adelia giving up her many beaus. If he had held all the power, it would not have been him feeling helpless to stop his wife's scandalous behaviour. He was far bigger and more powerful and the threat he would hold over her life would be more than enough to keep her in line if he were so inclined. Of course, if he were that kind of man, he could have simply locked her up and declared her mad. Men did such things.

No. Lord Hargreaves was everything she had believed him to be. Of that, she was certain.

Rosamund got up and paced back and forth, her mind racing. Of course, the obvious thing for a woman in her position was to marry and to do it quickly.

Her heart gave a hard thud as she considered the idea. It was madness. It would simply confirm everyone's suspicions. But they were going to think it, no matter what.

"Oh, Lord. Oh, Lord. Oh, Lord," Rosamund repeated over and over, pacing up and down and wringing her hands together, uncertain if she were praying for help or blaspheming.

Was it possible to do both at once? Wishing she had thought to ask Jules for his hip flask, Rosamund longed for a little nip of something to calm her agitated spirits. With no other option, she braced her hands against the wall, trying to steady her breathing, for her corset was suddenly far too tight. With one hand, she reached back to massage her neck, turning her head from the left to the right to ease the tension, and her gaze flicked to a large, battered hat box sitting atop her wardrobe.

Cat had given it to her when she had arrived at Dern, doing her best to cajole Rosamund into taking her dare. So far Rosamund had avoided all demands from her friends and from Cat, but now... now she felt as if a little push might be just what she needed. After all, her Mama had taken a dare before doing something dreadfully scandalous. So had Lady Montagu. If Rosamund's dare propelled her into doing something they might not approve of, well... they could hardly complain, could they?

Before she could think about it and change her mind, Rosamund dragged the chair Jules had sat upon earlier over to the wardrobe and climbed onto it. Carefully, she lifted down the hatbox, jumped off the chair and carried the box to the bed.

The hat was old and rather tatty and smelled faintly of mothballs, and the pleasanter scent of dusty old paper that permeated the very best libraries. Rosamund stared down at the dares. There were dozens and dozens of them now, and the old one always got put back in too.

"Fine," she said aloud, squaring her shoulders. "Come on, hat. You got my mother to marry the right man, and everyone else who took one of your demands to heart. Help me," she begged, wondering if the hysterical fit was really so farfetched after all.

Was she already in the midst of one? She was talking to a top hat, for heaven's sake!

Deciding things were unlikely to get any worse, she plunged her hand into the hat. The papers rustled as she sifted through them. Closing her eyes, Rosamund took one of the tiny, folded pieces and drew it out.

"Oh, well," she said breathlessly, and revealed the dare.

Matilda clinked her teaspoon against the fine china cup, the ringing sound bringing everyone to order. The ladies settled at once, every one of them turning their attention towards her. Despite the situation, or perhaps because of it, she felt of rush of love and affection for the women here. They had begun as wallflowers, as misfits, all of them unwelcome, unmarriageable … and now here they were, among the most powerful women in the *ton*. If one of them was in trouble, the others came running. For someone to mess with the happiness of their children—that was a big mistake.

"Well, how is our campaign coming along?" Matilda demanded.

Rosamund's mama, Prue, sat stoically beside her, outwardly calm while inside she was stewing with the desire to rage at the world. Matilda understood the impulse and reached out a hand, taking hold of Prue's fingers and squeezing.

"Anyone speaking of Hargreaves in a less than flattering light or implying that Rosamund behaved with the slightest impropriety is being shown the door of Hunter's, no matter who they are or what influence they wield. We cannot stop them thinking it, but Nate has made it clear any member of the club will have their membership revoked if he hears of any such talk," Alice said, referring to her husband, Nathanial Hunter, who was also Matilda's brother. "I have been making the rounds and ensuring all those members' wives who so enjoy Hunter's ladies' nights are aware the situation applies to them, too. And of course, Bainbridge is up in arms and has promised to smash the heads of anyone who dares to say such vile things. His father is likewise invested in causing havoc, so that ought to have an impact," Alice said with a wry smile.

Matilda nodded, remembering when Alice had been too shy to speak up for herself, her lack of confidence in herself and her abilities profound. There was no trace of that now.

"That's excellent work, Alice," Matilda said, smiling.

"Arabella and I have already given the cut direct to the mamas of those awful girls who so delighted in Rosamund's misery. They will not receive invitations or be acknowledged by any of us again until we have received abject apologies. Arabella has already received one and I expect the others to follow by the end of the week," Alice added with obvious satisfaction.

Aashini, Lady Cavendish, Kitty, the Countess of Trevick, and Harriet, the Countess St Clair, all had similar stories to tell, with letters being written and furiously copied out by the dozen, clarifying that anyone paying credence to these vile and fictitious rumours would be dropped from all and any social events. Harriet in particular was famous for her parties and political dinners, where the great and the good gathered. Such a threat would not be taken lightly. Ruth, the Countess of Morven, revealed a neatly written and quite staggering plan of action that detailed the dozens of influential women she would visit over the next week, having delayed her return to the Highlands to help her friends save Rosamund's reputation.

Mrs Bonnie Cadogan and Mrs Minerva de Beauvoir held less social status than their friends, but their influence was still far-reaching among the artistic and scientific communities, and especially through their children who had married well.

"Solo is out with Viscount Kline as we speak, doing what they can," Jemima offered, speaking of her husband, Baron Rothborn. "Kline's wine import business is doing terribly well now and many of the grandest clubs and hotels rely on his supply. I believe Solo is looking forward to helping Lord Kline with a touch of blackmail," she added, with such an innocent expression even Prue smiled. "I will be out with all the other ladies shortly, of course, making morning calls and ensuring the true story is told."

"And I'm calling on the Duke of Sefton," Lady Helena Knight announced as everyone gaped at her.

The duke was an old bully and an ill-tempered brute, though he wielded a great deal of power among the *ton*. Matilda and Aashini, who had both had run-ins with his daughter, now Lady Steyning, a spiteful gossip, both spoke at once.

"Helena!"

"Oh, my dear, is that wise?"

Helena waved their concerns away. "Evie is coming with me. Don't ask me how she's done it, but the old devil has a soft spot for her. Only, if one of you breathes a word to Gabriel, I shall not be responsible for the consequences. He'll die of fright if he knows we're anywhere near Sefton. He's been awful to Gabriel in the past, the great snob."

"Yet Evie has charmed him? And she's brave enough to face him and ask for his support?" Jemima said in wonder.

"I will be forever in her debt, though it does not surprise me in the least. Evie charms everyone," Prue said, smiling, her eyes shining with gratitude.

"That she does," Helena replied dryly. "If that child ever realises the power she wields, she'll have the world at her feet. She won't listen to me, though," she added with a sigh of frustration.

"I cannot thank you ladies enough," Prue said, her voice quavering a little.

"Don't be foolish, Prue," Bonnie replied with an impatient tut. "When I think of the kindnesses you've done all of us, the support you and Bedwin have lent us when it was required…. We will do all in our power to support dear Rosamund. She'll be back where she belongs as society's darling in no time at all."

"Hear, hear," Minerva said, as the other ladies all agreed enthusiastically.

"Society, look out, the Peculiar Ladies are on the march," Jemima said with a grin, and everyone laughed.

Matilda laughed too, squeezing Prue's hand, but beneath the bravado, they both knew that stories like this were not so easily crushed. It was too deliciously salacious, and whilst people might say all the right things in public, what they said in private was another matter, as Matilda knew all too well.

Chapter 13

My Lord,

I do not believe for a moment the vile things people are saying about you.

I must speak with you at once and in private. I will be at The Vine in Sevenoaks on Tuesday morning at ten o'clock. I beg you will come.

—Excerpt of a letter from Lady Rosamund Adolphus (daughter of Robert and Prunella Adolphus, Their Graces, The Duke and Duchess of Bedwin) to Sebastian Fox, Viscount Hargreaves.

15ᵗʰJuly 1842, En route to The Vine Cricket Ground, Sevenoaks, Kent, London.

Sebastian stared at the note for the fiftieth time, smoothing it out over his thigh. He stared at the words, his heart giving a little skip of relief at the first line. Rosamund did not think him capable of such a heinous act. He wasn't, he reminded himself, but that little niggle of doubt lingered in his mind. If only he could remember, if only he could be entirely certain. Yet the harder he fought to remember that night, the quicker the images slipped away from him. He had never, would *never*, lay a hand on a woman, he knew that, but could he have done it accidentally?

Rosamund thought not, but she was the embodiment of everything that was good and kind, her mind would baulk at the idea of her friend doing such a thing for she saw the good in everyone. But she was not a fool, he reminded himself. Yet asking him to come to her seemed foolish in the extreme. If anyone were to discover them together, it would only add fuel to a fire which was burning quite adequately despite her family and friend's efforts.

I beg you will come.

But how could he refuse such words when he heard the desperation behind them? Rosamund would never have written such a thing lightly. She truly was begging him to meet her.

Despite his worry for her, despite everything that had happened, his heart felt lighter at the prospect of seeing her, of speaking to her when he had believed he should never do so again. Perhaps it truly would be for the last time, but he would snatch at the chance, no matter the risk.

He had dressed in his most conservative clothes, aiming to look like a plain *Mr* rather than Lord Hargreaves. Walking from his home to Eaton Square, he hired a hackney to the outskirts of London before changing again at Camberwell to lessen the chances anyone would recognise him. He had the carriage drop him half a mile from The Vine and instructed the driver to wait for him at The Chequers Pub, which was a short walk away.

Sebastian tried not to hurry, for he was at least half an hour early and did not expect to see Rosamund before the appointed hour. Indeed, he was prepared to wait for her, knowing it might be difficult to get away from Dern unnoticed. So, as he crossed the neatly cut green, his heart did an odd little somersault behind his ribs as he noted a lady lingering in the shadow of a great oak tree. The slender frame came to attention as she saw him and

Hargreaves picked up his pace, certain now that this was Lady Rosamund.

As he drew closer, he saw she had worn a hooded green cloak, though the morning was mild.

"My lady," he said as he reached her, unnerved to hear his voice sound so uncertain.

"I never thought it of you. I knew it was impossible," she said fiercely.

Sebastian swallowed, so touched by her unwavering belief in him, his chest swelled with emotion. Yet guilt followed hard on its heels, and he felt the overwhelming need to confess to her. "Then you know better than I. You see... I was drunk, quite out of my head and we had the most god-awful row and... and what if I—"

"No! I don't believe it." Her words were so vehement that Sebastian took courage from them. "Even drunk, you would never have hurt her. *Would* you?"

Sebastian racked his brain, though he'd already tried and tried to remember. So far, he had only grasped at fragments, snatching at broken shards of that last terrible row. Now, though, with Rosamund staring at him with such certainty, such trust, the clouded memory of that night returned to him little by little. He remembered the fury raging in him when he had smashed the things in Adelia's room, then the exhausted desperation of losing himself in brandy. After that, Adelia's return and that dreadful argument, the things they'd said. For the first time, he spoke aloud what he remembered of that night.

"She attacked me," he said, seeing his wife's beautiful face distorted with rage as she flew at him. "Tried to scratch my damn eyes out, but... but I held her off. I told her to leave me alone." His heart stopped as he remembered, staring at Rosamund. "I... I walked away."

He let out a shuddering breath, leaning on the trunk of the gigantic oak they stood beneath as relief washed through him.

"Of course you did," she said, as if she had never doubted it for a moment.

"I walked away," he said again, closing his eyes. "Oh, God. She was still there when I closed the bedroom door. She was alive."

He leant against the oak, needing the support to hold him up as the nightmare of not knowing, of not trusting himself, resolved itself because of Rosamund. Because she trusted him to be a good man.

"Oh, Hargreaves," she said, blinking back tears as she closed the distance between them and took his hands, holding on tight. "Oh, what an ordeal you must have suffered. I am so desperately sorry. I know your marriage was not a happy one, but you loved her once, and... and I am sorry. Truly, I am."

Sebastian stared down at her in wonder. His wife had destroyed Rosamund's life—her chance for happiness—out of sheer spite, and yet her concern was all for him, for what he had suffered and for his loss.

"She ruined you," he said, choked now.

Rosamund shrugged, her lips quirking. "I do not feel ruined. I feel no different from how I did last week. It is only people's perception. Those I care for know the truth. I have decided this matters more than the good opinion of people too ready to believe the worst of me."

"You are very brave, and that is well and good, but you may feel differently when you face them all at the theatre, or the Queen's Levee, or a ball."

"Yes, my courage may fail me then," she admitted. "But my friends will bolster me, I know."

She squeezed his hands and Sebastian stared down to where her slender, gloved fingers held his. Her gloves were a pale fawn, the colour startling against his sombre mourning black. His thumb caressed her knuckles absently, needing the contact with her, until he realised what he was doing and tugged his hands free.

"Forgive me," he said stiffly, glaring at the ground and cursing himself. What would she think of him? His wife was barely cold, society accused him of murder under its breath, her reputation hung in tatters, and he was *flirting* with her?

"My lord." Her voice was softer now, a note to it that made his gaze fly to hers. She reached for his hand again, holding it between both of hers now. "I need to ask you a… a rather indelicate question. Or perhaps it is a delicate one? I am uncertain which, but we can discuss that later, I suppose. I'm certain my mother would know the answer, but I could hardly ask her before I left. Oh, dear. Now I am babbling. I always do when I'm nervous, I'm afraid."

"You do?" Sebastian asked, perplexed. "I hadn't noticed."

"That's because I am never usually nervous with you, but today… well, the question, you see. But it's because of that ridiculous hat, though to be truthful, the idea was already in my mind. Then that dare appeared, though, and it seemed like fate. Do you see?"

"I'm afraid I don't," he admitted. "I am entirely befuddled, which is likely my fault. I seem unable to think clearly of late."

"Me either. Hardly surprising, is it?" She gave a little laugh, higher than usual, her nerves showing.

Sebastian shook his head, unable to tear his gaze from her beautiful face, drinking in the sight of her and committing it to memory. It had been foolish to come here, to remind himself of everything that was lost to him, for he was no closer to her now than before he had so abruptly become a widower. And now, now that he saw her here, alone with him, her hand in his, a shaft of longing pierced his heart. *Not just a friend,* he admitted to himself. *I don't want her to be just a friend.*

"Say something outrageous to a handsome man," she blurted suddenly, her cheeks tinged with pink.

Sebastian blinked. "I beg your pardon?" he said, wondering if he'd missed some crucial part of the conversation. It seemed possible as the realisation he could fall head over ears in love with Lady Rosamund with the slightest encouragement entered his brain and refused to budge, distracting him from whatever she'd been saying.

"That was the dare," she said, which still made no sense to him whatsoever. "So, that's what I'm going to do. It's an old one. The dare, I mean. I think perhaps it was Ruth's—the Countess of Morven now—or was it Aunt Alice? Oh, no. Hers was a kiss in the moonlight, of course."

"A kiss?" Sebastian murmured, having completely lost the thread of the conversation now. His gaze fell to her lips as that painful sensation filled his chest, a longing so profound it hurt.

She nodded absently. "Yes, Alice's dare was a kiss. Mine is the outrageous one. To say something. Outrageous. To a handsome man. So, there's my question, you see."

She really was babbling now, he thought with affection. How lovely she was.

"Of which handsome man are you to ask this outrageous question?" he demanded, wishing he hadn't.

He could not bear to think of her with another man. Not now. But that was just his own stupidity and selfishness. Of course, she must find herself a husband now. She must marry, and quickly. She had wanted to marry, of course, but now it was urgent. It would smooth away most of the problems she had. Society would forgive much of a married lady that was beyond the pale in a maiden.

"Well, *you*, obviously. Really, Hargreaves, do keep up. This is difficult enough for me. The least you can do is pay attention."

Her dark brows drew together, her lush lips pressed together so firmly it was almost a pout. Sebastian gave himself a stern talking to and ignored the temptation her indignant expression beguiled him with.

"I beg your pardon. I am paying attention, my lady. You wish to ask me a question. An... outrageous question?" he added doubtfully, distracted by the idea she found him handsome but hoping that he'd gleaned that much.

Apparently so, for she nodded and sighed with relief.

"Yes, my lord. So I shall just get on and ask."

"Please do."

"Lord Hargreaves, would you do me the great honour of becoming my husband?"

Sebastian stared at her. Her cheeks were flaming now, the colour also flushing the length of her slender throat. Well, she would be nervous, if she'd just asked him to marry her, but she hadn't... he was suffering a nervous collapse. It was only to be expected in the circumstances. It was also the only explanation.

"My lord? Did you hear what I said?" she asked fretfully.

Sebastian shook his head. "No. That is, I heard words but... but they seemed so unlikely I rather doubt I heard them correctly."

"Oh, you did! You know you did, you great oaf! Oh, do stop funning with me at such a moment. I am perfectly serious," she scolded him.

Sebastian sucked in a breath. "Marry? You want to marry *me?"*

"Yes, of course," she said, stiff with embarrassment. "Who else should I wish to marry, may I ask you? It is the perfect solution. We shall face the *ton* together and dare them to think ill of us. We shall t-tell everyone it was a marriage of convenience, but that it suits us both very well for we are friends a-and, as your wife put me in such a wretched position, it was only fair you get me out of it."

She stammered through her explanation, but held her chin up, holding his gaze with sheer determination. Good Lord, if she blushed any hotter, she'd set herself on fire.

He was too stunned to present a proper argument, but even his poor, beleaguered brain could grasp the basic point. "They'll think it all true. The affair, and that I murdered Adelia."

Rosamund shrugged. "They think it anyway."

Sebastian's heart had stopped beating some time ago, well, precisely at the moment she had proposed to him. She had proposed. *To him.* With difficulty, he swallowed down the hysterical impulse to laugh. Except then he remembered all the reasons marrying him was a terrible idea and he did not wish to laugh ever again.

"You would do far better to marry someone else, my lady, though I should be honoured to do so, if it were possible."

"Oh, drat you, Hargreaves. It *is* possible. It's scandalous, I grant you, but as we're in the eye of the storm anyway, what does it matter? And... And I wish to marry you," she said stoutly.

Sebastian had been wrong. She turned an even deeper shade of red, but there were still no signs of her bursting into flames. Perhaps he would, then. He felt hot. And indecently, incandescently happy. It had been so many years since he had felt anything of the sort, it took him a moment to realise what it was.

"You *wish* to marry me?" he repeated, hardly daring to believe it.

She nodded, a nervous, jerky up-and-down movement he found ridiculously endearing. "I am very f-fond of you, my lord, and you are my friend. If there is anyone I believe I can face this... this ordeal with, and survive it with my wits intact, it is you."

"Rosamund," he said, her name spoken on a soft breath as the idea caught him up and wound itself about him, binding him up so tightly he could barely speak. He could marry her. Have a life with her. Have a *family* with her. "It's madness," he said, needing to give her the chance to see sense, even if his heart was crying out for him to get on and say yes.

"Perhaps," she admitted, staring at him. "But I will be content to be thought mad, if you will too."

He swallowed, allowing a smile to curve his mouth, astonished that such a thing was even possible when he had sunk to such miserable depths just days ago. "You're sure? Have you really thought this through?"

"I have."

She gave another nod, her expression so fierce and determined he ached with the desire to take her in his arms. Instead, he answered, feeling as though he was living in some outlandish dream where terrible and wonderful things happened every day.

"Yes, my lady. It would be the greatest honour of my life to marry you."

Rosamund's hand tightened on his, and her smile made his heart hurt.

"Oh," she said, giving a breath of relief. "Oh, thank heavens."

Sebastian grinned at her. They were both out of their tiny minds. The scandal would reach fever pitch, and now he did not give a damn.

"Now we just need to persuade my parents it's a good idea," she said brightly.

His grin faded abruptly. *Hell.* Bedwin was going to rip his bloody head off.

Chapter 14

Louis,

I took it upon myself to pay a visit to the wife of your old master. The lengths I will go to for you surprise even me sometimes.

The vile creature lives out of pure spite, I am certain. I think the devil does not relish her nagging tongue in hell so keeps her alive, if barely. She looked far too pleased with herself but even my presence could not induce her to give me anything of interest. Perhaps because there was nothing to give, though I admit my gut tells me otherwise. Sadly, even my villainy draws the line at menacing sick old ladies. Though if I ever changed my mind on that, she'd be the woman to do it. How did you survive her? And to think she terrified you less than the old man. You had balls of steel, mon amie, even as a child. I think I shall have nightmares.

I have nothing to report that we did not know. She relished giving information to your Mr Knight's informers, naturally, boasting of all the things she had told them. Sadly, none of it was untrue, though I am certain she presented

*the information in the worst possible light. I
promised her I would dance on her husband's
grave on your behalf. I would have said her
son's too, except then I remembered that there
had never been a body retrieved from the
ashes, and not because we hid it.*

*As far as I can tell, the dead are still dead, but
there was that smug look in her eye that
haunts me still.*

**—Excerpt of a letter from Wulfric 'Wolf' De
Vere to Louis César de Montluc, Comte de
Villen.**

15th July 1842, Dern Palace, Sevenoaks, Kent, London.

"Have you taken leave of your senses?" Bedwin bellowed at
Sebastian, which was hardly a surprise.

It might even be true.

"Darling, please stop shouting. You are giving me a headache
and the least we can do is hear them out," the duchess said, giving
her husband a meaningful glare.

"What the devil is he even doing here?" the duke demanded,
sending Sebastian a look of such wrath he was hard pressed not to
flinch. He was an imposing devil when his temper was lit.

"I wrote and begged him to come here, to the cricket pitch,"
Rosamund replied, quite calm now. "I slipped out early this
morning to meet him in secret. It was all my idea. In fact… I asked
him to marry me."

Sebastian looked at her, rather awed by her serenity, for they
faced not only her parents, but Lord and Lady Montagu and Mr
Gabriel Knight, who had arrived at the same time they had, in
search of his wife. He had missed Lady Helena, who had just

returned to town. Sebastian could inform Mr Knight of this as he had passed her carriage on his way down that morning.

Bedwin stared at his daughter. "You…" he began and then sat down, put his head in his hands and groaned.

"Darling, you told us there was nothing but friendship between Lord Hargreaves and yourself," her mother said, studying her daughter closely.

"Yes, Mama, and that was true. *Is* true. But I am fond of his lordship, and I believe we shall weather this storm better together than apart."

"That is undoubtedly the most ridiculous thing I have heard yet this week, and it's got some stiff competition," her father said irritably. "Do you not see that everyone will believe you were having an affair, and that Hargreaves here pushed his wife down the stairs to make way for you?"

"People think that anyway, Papa. At least, the ones who wish to believe the worst of us. If we brazen it out, however, perhaps they'll think twice. For surely, we'd not be so blatant if it were true?"

Her father gaped at her, but Lord Montagu was considering them with interest.

"She has a point, Bedwin. It would take one hell of a nerve to do something of the sort if Hargreaves were truly guilty."

"You're not serious?" her father said, obviously astonished.

Montagu shrugged. "I think they might handle this better together than alone. Besides, they make a rather handsome couple," he said, his piercing silver eyes resting on Sebastian in a way that made his neck feel hot.

He pitied the man's sons. Poor devils likely never got away with a thing. Bedwin took a deep breath and pinched the bridge of his nose. Sebastian was under no illusion that only his wife's presence had stopped the duke from breaking *his* nose on sight.

"Let me get this straight. He's supposed to be in mourning for his dead wife, the one the *ton* thinks he murdered on Rosamund's behalf, and you believe if she marries him it will smooth everything over?"

He directed the question at Montagu, who nodded. Lady Montagu, who had also been studying both Sebastian and Rosamund with interest, did likewise.

"It's so outrageous no one will believe the rest of the story can be true," she declared. "Especially not once the Peculiar Ladies have worked on it and spread it about."

"The Peculiar...?" Sebastian began but Rosamund shook her head.

"I'll explain later," she whispered.

"Is this to do with—"

"The hat, yes," she said, gravely.

Sebastian nodded, as if that made complete sense. If he was losing his mind, he was inclined to let it happen so long as he ended up married to Rosamund.

"Is this what you want, Rosamund?" her mother asked suddenly. "This was your idea. You invited Lord Hargreaves here, you proposed to him, but is it actually what you want?"

Sebastian's heart, which had endured some harsh treatment over the past days, trembled as Rosamund turned to face her mother. "Yes, Mama. It is what I want."

"Well, then," the duchess said, perfectly calm. "That's that, then. Robert, you had best get up to Doctors' Commons at once. We shall need a special licence."

The duke stared at his wife in stunned silence but uttered not a single objection.

Sebastian smothered a grin.

Rosamund stood by the door as her father accepted his hat and gloves from the footman. She waited until the staff retreated and walked out of the front door with him. Her younger brother, Fred, was going too to keep him company and was already waiting in the carriage.

"Rosamund," Papa said, turning to her. "I know everything that has happened has upset you deeply so perhaps you are not thinking clearly. I don't want you to rush into some foolish marriage when we can simply wait for this scandal to be replaced by another. In a couple of years, with the weight of my name and our friends' support, this will have died down. You are certainly young enough to wait that long. There is no need for this, truly."

"But I want to marry him, Papa," Rosamund said, colour tingeing her cheeks.

"Oh," her father said, obviously taken aback by the determination in her words.

Rosamund put a hand on his arm. "I didn't lie, Papa. He was only my friend. I never allowed myself to think of him in any other way and would never have done so, but things are different now and the truth is… I like him very much. I admire him, and when I am with him I feel—"

Her father took her hand and gave it an encouraging squeeze. "Yes?"

"I feel entirely myself. Not Lady Rosamund, daughter of the Duke of Bedwin. Not the public face, the façade, but *me*."

"Well, then," Papa murmured, his expression softening. "I had better get this licence, hadn't I?"

"Yes, please."

He smiled at her and leaned down to kiss her cheek, before turning and climbing into the waiting carriage.

Rosamund watched him go and then went back indoors to find her mother waiting for her.

"Have you set his mind at rest?" she asked with a smile.

"Yes, Mama."

"Good. Well, in that case, you had better do the same for your fiancé. I believe he is walking in the garden. He looked rather overwhelmed, the poor dear. He's had quite a tumultuous few days. I think you had better go and talk to him."

"Thank you, Mama," Rosamund said, and hurried outside.

She found him sitting on a bench in Matilda's private garden. Hidden by high brick walls, the white garden was hidden from the rest of the property and arranged in a formal knot with low hedges of cut box. The planting in between was far looser and more romantic, though, and everywhere there were white flowers studding the green like pearls upon velvet. Extravagant climbing roses tumbled over the brick walls, filling the garden with their lush perfume. Bees droned lazily and the sound of birdsong filtered into the space, but other than that there was no interruption from the outside world. It was a little corner of paradise where one could simply escape from everything.

Rosamund paused just inside the arched doorway, watching Lord Hargreaves in silence and feeling suddenly shy. He looked up and met her gaze, and a prickle of awareness shivered over her. She had never allowed herself to look at him this way before, as a potential suitor, but now she *saw* him, now she acknowledged the attraction she had buried down deep and an odd, fluttering sensation stirred low in her belly.

"Don't wake me up," he said, keeping his voice soft, as if he might disturb the peaceful atmosphere if he spoke too loudly.

"Are you sleeping, then?"

He smiled, a wistful quirk of his lips that did odd things to her insides. "Dreaming," he corrected.

Gathering her courage, Rosamund closed the door to the garden and walked towards him.

"Then what are you dreaming about?"

He sat back, staring up at her as she paused at the edge of the path, her skirts not quite touching his boots.

"It began as a bad dream, actually, and then it became a nightmare from which I thought I would never wake. But now…."

He stared up at her, as if he could not believe she was real. The silence stretched out as Rosamund waited, needing to know what came next.

"But now?" she whispered, her heart picking up speed as her patience frayed.

"I never dared to think of you," he said, his voice rougher now, a sense of desperation lingering behind the words. "I thought I had lost any chance for happiness because I'd been such a naïve fool, so idiotic as to marry a woman I did not know nor understood when we were both too silly and shallow to know better. I swear, Rosamund, if I could have just been your friend, I would have counted that as the greatest of blessings."

"I know," she said, blinking back tears at the emotion in his voice.

He put his head in his hands, fingers clutching at his hair. "This is wrong. I know it's wrong, but I want to do it anyway. God, I must be wicked to the core."

Rosamund watched him, aware of his turmoil, uncertain what to say to make it right, for there was no right. It was wrong of them to marry so fast, and yet, life was short, and Adelia had set this chain of events in motion.

"You are not the least bit wicked, but… but you can change your mind if you don't want to…"

He laughed then, looking up at her with such despair in his face. "Don't want to? My God, Rosamund. You are offering me everything I have ever dreamed of. Do you really think I am strong enough to walk away from that, knowing that you want it too? But at the same time Adelia *is dead*. She's dead and—" He groaned and shook his head.

Rosamund hesitated, choosing her words with care. "I know. I understand how difficult this is for you because you are honourable and true. I know what people will think of us too, but we know the truth, Hargreaves. I certainly do. You are a good man who deserved better. Let me give you better. I swear I will try my best."

She watched as he lifted his head, staring at her. He reached out then, and she did the same, a jolt of awareness running through her as his large hand closed around hers. "Surely it is wrong to feel this much joy after everything that has happened? I keep experiencing this overwhelming sense of relief and happiness and just as quickly, I am swamped with guilt that I could move on with my life with so little regret. Adelia was young and full of life and, even though she made me so bloody wretched, I did not want this for her."

"I know that," Rosamund said, stepping closer to him so that her skirts billowed about his legs. "You *are* a good man, my lord, and I do not think it is wrong for you to find happiness when what happened to your wife was not your fault."

"Would you sit with me?" he asked, never taking his eyes from her, as though afraid she might disappear if he looked away.

Rosamund nodded, and he made room for her, keeping a firm grip on her hand. His gaze was so intent that she lowered her eyes, for his nearness made her insides feel all hot and muddled.

"If your father is successful, we could be married this night," he said.

Rosamund let out a shaky breath and nodded. She felt him raise her hand and turned to see him press it to his lips. She was not wearing gloves and the feel of his mouth upon her skin made her breathing hitch and her heart race.

"Is this really what you want?" he asked, clasping her hand between his.

"Yes," she whispered.

He frowned, studying her with such intensity she felt as if he wanted to stare inside her head and read her thoughts. "You need to be very certain of that, Rosamund. I know what it is to marry in haste and to spend my life repenting for it."

"I know you," she said breathlessly as she reached out her free hand and cupped his cheek. "I am certain."

He closed his eyes and turned his face into the caress, holding her hand in place as he pressed a kiss to her palm. Rosamund felt giddy and oddly like laughing. Her blood surged in her veins and a strange restless sensation rolled over her. "The devil with it, then," he said, his voice firm.

Rosamund gasped as he opened his eyes and she saw he had made his choice.

"The devil with it," she agreed.

"I should like very much to kiss you."

"I-I should like that too," she managed, rather astonished she had got the words out.

He smiled then, his expression one of such joy it felt as if the fates had given her the greatest power in the world, the ability to make this lovely man happy. Still, kissing him was a rather daunting prospect, even though she wanted to, very much.

"Don't be anxious," he said, correctly interpreting her sudden attack of nerves.

"I'm sorry, it's only I... I've never done this before," she blurted out, embarrassed.

He stared at her. "Never? Not even a stolen kiss under the mistletoe?"

She shook her head. "After Eliza... well, Papa is rather overprotective, you see."

Not wanting to reveal exactly how scandalously her sister had behaved when pursuing her husband, she did not elaborate. Not that Rosamund found it scandalous; her sister's determination had only impressed her... which probably accounted for their father's anxiety.

Sebastian grinned, a rather wolfish grin that made her stomach lurch.

"Stop looking so pleased with yourself," she scolded him.

"Impossible, sorry," he replied, still grinning.

Rosamund blushed and looked away and he chuckled. "Let us start slowly, then. Come here."

He slid his arm about her, and with gentle pressure, urged her closer. Rosamund leaned into him, relaxing against his body until she was nestled against him, her head on his shoulder. She closed her eyes on a sigh, her nerves melting away as the rightness of it sank into her bones. He nuzzled her hair, inhaling.

"You smell divine," he murmured. "Like strawberries."

She bit her lip, glancing up at him. "Lady Aisling gave me a wonderful recipe for my hair to keep it shiny. It's made with crushed strawberries."

"Ah," he said, clearly amused. "I approve."

"I always wondered if you would smell spicy," she said and then felt silly for having admitted such a thing.

He quirked an eyebrow in surprise but looked pleased, so she reached up, daring to smooth her fingers over his brow.

"Why?" he asked, holding still beneath her touch as her fingers trailed over his cheek.

"Because your eyes are the colour of spice. Like gingerbread sprinkled with brown sugar," she said, getting lost among the flecks of gold she saw now she was so close to him.

"And do I?"

Rosamund dared to turn her face into him, the fabric of his coat soft beneath her cheek. Inhaling, she smiled, delighted. "You do," she exclaimed. "There's a woody scent, cedar I think, and... and nutmeg, but something else too, something sweeter, citrus and... *Oh,* lavender," she said in surprise.

"Ah, for that you may blame my housekeeper. She insists on sachets of dried lavender in every drawer and wardrobe."

"You smell good enough to eat," she said, laughing, though her laughter died abruptly as she noted the way his eyes darkened.

"My lord?" she said, nervous now.

"Sebastian," he corrected her, stroking her cheek with the backs of his fingers. "We're engaged, remember?"

"I remember," she whispered, finding it hard to breathe.

"Rosamund," he murmured, and slid his hand to the back of her neck as he leaned down and pressed his mouth to hers.

Rosamund closed her eyes, overwhelmed by the sensation. His lips were soft and warm, gentle upon hers, but the reaction his kiss provoked inside her was not soft and warm but electric. His kiss burned with a fiery heat that made her blood feel like brandy in her veins, ready to burst into flame. Rather stunned, Rosamund pulled back to stare at him.

His warm gaze searched hers, full of concern. "No good?" he asked, and she heard the anxiety in his voice now.

She blushed, uncertain how to tell him that his kiss was dreadfully provoking. Looking away, she focused her attention on an elegant group of white delphiniums that swayed in the breeze.

"Do you trust me?"

His voice shivered over her, but she still could not meet his eyes. She nodded. His fingers touched her chin, turning her face back towards him.

"I must speak plain, Rosamund, so I beg you will forgive me, but I will not marry a woman who does not want me. This time, I will have a real marriage in every sense. I want to share my life with you, to have children with you, and I will *not* bed a woman who regards my touch as a chore, as something to be endured."

Rosamund gasped, wanting to avoid his gaze but he would not let her evade him.

"Does my touch, my kiss, displease you?"

She shook her head, wishing she were braver, but this was happening so suddenly, and though she had instigated the whole thing herself, it was overwhelming. If only there were more time.

"Are you certain, Rosamund? Because there is far more than just kisses ahead of us, and if you cannot endure even that…."

Squirming with embarrassment, Rosamund could see only one way out of her predicament if she could not tell him what it was she was feeling. She grasped his lapels and kissed him.

He stilled at once, his breath catching, though he made no move to reach for her. Rosamund pulled back warily, finding him watching her with interest but he held still, not saying a word. Encouraged, Rosamund leaned in again and pressed her lips to the corner of his mouth. His warm breath fluttered against hers, but he only watched her. Feeling a little bolder, Rosamund closed her eyes and pressed her mouth full against his, jolting with shock as she felt his tongue touch her lower lip.

Pulling back to stare at him, she saw a glint of something devilish in his eyes that made her insides quiver. Determined not to be thought missish, she kissed him again, and this time, when his tongue touched her lips, she did not pull away. He traced the seam of her lips, seeking entry. She opened to him, quickly beguiled by the sensation of his tongue sliding against hers.

"Oh," she murmured, breaking the kiss to take a deep breath.

"Is that a good, '*oh*'?" he asked.

Rosamund forced herself to nod.

"Tell me, then. Tell me you like my kisses," he said, not taking his eyes from her.

"My lord," she protested, torn between laughter and feeling very foolish.

"Sebastian," he corrected, his voice firm. "And I am not joking, Rosamund. I will not spend the rest of my days wondering what you are thinking, wondering if you are doing your duty or if you desire me. You must talk to me, you must tell me what you think, what you feel."

"But it's so…." She fidgeted, wishing this wasn't so awkward.

"Difficult, yes, I know," he said, his voice gentle now. "But I am on your side, Rosamund. I only want to make you happy, and how am I to do that if you are not honest with me? Do you even know what happens in the marriage bed?"

Rosamund fought the urge to run. "Yes," she said, remembering the matter-of-fact way her mother had described the physical act, and that there was pleasure to be found in it with the right partner.

He lowered his voice, and once again it seemed to shiver over her skin like a caress. How strange, to find the tone of his voice as arousing as his words. "And can you imagine the two of us doing that, touching so intimately?"

Rosamund leapt to her feet, feeling as though she might combust as the images flickered behind her eyes of his powerful, naked form wrapped around hers. Having never allowed herself to think of him that way, the force of her attraction to him was shocking. She wanted to press herself against him and to pull him down on top of her, to feel the weight of him crushing her, overpowering her, and the realisation that she felt such visceral things for him was startling and frightening and wonderful, and she could not help but wonder what he would think if he knew of the lewd images in her head. Though Mama vehemently disagreed, society believed women ought not to have such thoughts, or even enjoy the marital bed. But Mama was an exceptional woman and powerful enough to be scandalous. Most men would think badly of an unwed woman having such wicked thoughts. Only whores took pleasure in it. Would Hargreaves think that, especially after the way his wife had taunted him?

"Oh, God. This was a bad idea," he said, the misery in his voice so audible it shook her.

"What? N-No, it isn't," she said, turning back to him.

He shook his head. "If you cannot even bear the idea of it, then—"

"That's not why!" she cried, wringing her hands, frustrated that he was so very wrong, and she was too shy to explain herself. "It's j-just all too fast. It's happening so quickly. You were my friend and… and now…."

She watched as he got to his feet and came to her, taking her hands in his. "Forgive me. I am an unfeeling brute for treating you with such impatience, only I am afraid too, Rosamund. I don't want to marry you and for either of us to regret it. Perhaps we should wait like your father suggested. In two or three months, when you've had time to get used to the idea—"

"No!" she shook her head. "People will expect us to wait until the scandal dies down a little before we marry. It will only make us look guilty. If we do it at once, they are more likely to believe our side of the story or else they must convict us of being utterly cold and ruthless. I do not think people could believe that of either of us."

"Do you *really* believe that?" he asked, obviously sceptical.

"I do," she said, before forcing herself to explain. "And I can, yes."

"Can what?"

She squeezed her eyes shut, hoping it might be easier to tell him if she could not see him. "I can imagine it. *Us*. I can."

There was a pause.

"And do you think you would like that?"

"Oh, damn you, Hargreaves, this is mortifying, but if you must have it out loud…. Yes! Yes, I think I should like that very much, and I like your kisses too, and I should like you to do it again, and to put your arms around me, but it's all rather too much after everything that has happened. You cannot go from friend to husband in the space of a few hours! Well, you can, of course. You will. Indeed, I asked you to do so, but it's terribly… terribly… discombobulating."

There was another silence and Rosamund covered her face with her hands in case the urge to peek overcame her. Facing him now was simply beyond her.

She heard him move nearer, felt his hands touch her waist and urge her closer. With a sigh, she leaned into him, removing her hands from her face in favour of burrowing against him. His arms closed about her, holding her, and suddenly she did not feel so overwhelmed, or so silly and frightened. The tension left her shoulders as a large hand stroked up and down her spine and she let out another shaky breath.

"Discombobulating," he said, a thread of amusement behind the word.

"Yes," she replied, her voice muffled against his chest.

She felt him nod. "Yes. I ought to have considered that. I'm a horrid brute."

"No, you're not. You just don't want to get rushed into making another mistake. I know that."

"Did you know I had not touched my wife in years?"

She looked up at him then, astonished.

"She couldn't abide me. Could not bear my hands upon her, my kisses. I swear I was kind, Rosamund, gentle. I tried. I asked her to explain to me what the problem was, to talk to me, I kept trying, but she would not explain, not help me to understand her. I think perhaps her mother gave her a disgust of the entire process and so any evidence of desire on my part disgusted her, too but that is only a guess. I do not wish to guess at your feelings, or for either of us to suffer that."

"That is not the problem," she said, staring up at him, willing him to believe it.

"It isn't?"

She shook her head. "No. When you kiss me...."

The words stuck in her throat, and she made a sound of frustration.

"Don't be shy, love. Not with me. You never were before."

"That was a bit different," she retorted, a little indignant.

He smiled. "So it was. If it helps, I can tell you that I want you very badly. I never allowed my thoughts to linger on you before, but now... Rosamund, I want to marry you. I want to take you to bed and show you how much pleasure we can find together. I want that so badly I could weep, but I will walk away from it if it is not what you want too."

Rosamund took a deep breath, encouraged by the sincerity of his words, the warmth in his voice. "Your kisses make me feel hot and m-muddled up inside. Like I can't think straight, and I want—"

"Yes?" he said, and his voice was rough, his eyes so dark with wanting that it gave her courage. She looked away from him, though, braver when she could not see his face. Instead, she smoothed a hand over his waistcoat, too aware of the muscular body beneath the fine fabric, of the power she felt beneath her palm.

"I want to touch you, to feel the weight of you upon me," she managed, the words said in a rush.

She dared a glance up at him.

He let out a harsh breath, and smiled then, his eyes shining. "You desire me."

She nodded, relieved to have made the point. "Does that mean you still want to marry me?"

"Little nitwit," he said with affection. "I never stopped wanting to, but you cannot blame me for being a little wary."

"But you know me better than you did Adelia, I think?" she asked him.

He nodded then. "I do. And I know you desire me because you have explained yourself. So now I can be as patient as you need, sweetheart. So, if you need time, you have it. Do you understand?"

His gaze was tender, full of understanding, and Rosamund let out a breath. She had been right about him from the start. He was gentle, he would never hurt her, and he would be her husband.

"You're saying I could delay the wedding night if I wanted to?"

He nodded. "If you want to get comfortable with the idea first, with *us*, I understand. Though, I insist we share a bed from the outset. Is that agreeable?"

Rosamund nodded. Though it was dreadfully unfashionable, her parents shared a bed every night. Mama hated it when Papa went away too, for she complained she could not sleep alone.

"Yes."

He smiled then and stroked her cheek. "Then we shall be married, and I will be the happiest of men."

Chapter 15

I do not know what is to become of me. I feel I am living some strange half-life. I am Persephone, tricked into eating pomegranate seeds that condemn me to spend half my life in the underworld. My father believes that is where the man I love belongs. I cannot deny there is truth in it, for I see the darkness in his eyes. I always have. Now I am lying to my family, pretending I have banished him from my thoughts when he consumes them from the moment I wake, and I cannot escape him, even in my dreams.

The moments when I am not with him, I am restless and miserable, consumed with the craving to be with him again. I never knew such desire, such a profound physical connection, was possible. When he is near, I am too reckless, so thoroughly under his spell I fear what I might do. I fear what he wants from me and wonder if I can keep denying him.

When did this happen? How did I fall so thoroughly under his sway? I crave him as some crave opium and that frightens me. I do not want this madness that infects my blood

*and makes my body ache with the need for
him. I long for his touch, for his kisses. How
can I bear it? How can I marry a man so full
of secrets, a damaged, beautiful man who I
can forgive for murder without a second
thought? What else would I forgive, what else
would I turn a blind eye to, just to keep him?
How can I turn my back on my family and do
the one thing they have forbidden me to do,
and how can I live the rest of my life when I
know Papa is right? He will take me into the
darkness with him. Yet I fear I love him too
much, want him too badly to keep saying no.*

**—Excerpt from the diary of Miss Evie
Knight (daughter of Lady Helena and Mr
Gabriel Knight).**

15th July 1842, Doctor's Commons, Knightrider Street, City of London.

To Fred's eye, the sombre red brick houses had the look of irritated old men, fusty and outdated as they glowered down at the shaded courtyard. His father headed for a large green baize door, studded all over with great brass nails. Being the Duke of Bedwin, he strode in with the obvious expectation that everyone would leap to do his bidding. He was not disappointed. A lot of red-gowned and white-wigged men surged to their feet with exclamation and hovered about his father like so many chickens, fussing over the last pieces of grain. Fred wondered how his father bore it, for he did not enjoy sycophants, though Fred suspected he was rather used to having things done his way. It was part of the job of being duke, though, and his father bore with them all patiently, greeting everyone politely and without the slightest hint of impatience.

"I'll leave you to it then, Pa," Fred said, eager to be away from the old men and the overpowering stench of decay and mouldering paper. He might understand his father's position, but he could not be sorry that Jules was the heir and not him.

His father turned away from the officer of the court, recognisable from the tight grip he had on a large silver-headed staff. The look on the duke's face was not encouraging.

"I'll be fine, don't fuss," Fred said, trying to keep the whine from his voice by reminding himself he was a grown man of fifteen years and not a silly child who needed a babysitter. Whining would not highlight that point.

"You'll take Granger," his father said, with a tone that brooked no argument.

"Oh, but, sir," Fred protested.

"You will take Granger," his father repeated, and Fred was not idiotic enough to make him do it a third time.

His father was a fair man, and Fred admired him beyond anyone, but it did not do to irritate him. Still, it rankled that he could not roam about on his own like his older brother did.

"Yes, sir," he said, resigned to his fate.

At least it was Granger this time, who was a decent sort, not like that old fusspot Morris, who would snitch on Fred for the least little thing. Irked all the same, Fred hurried out of the stuffy building, eager to be free of the stench of worm-eaten books and musty old robes.

It wasn't so bad in the end. He had an enjoyable visit to St Paul's Cathedral and lingered in the crypt and the churchyard, fascinated by the ancient tombs and gravestones of the long dead. After that, he got a hackney coach to Berkeley Square and went directly to Gunter's where he ordered three cream cakes. It was an extravagance he never would have indulged in if anyone was with him, but Granger had a sister working in the house across the square and had gone to visit with her, so Fred was free to enjoy his own company for once.

He had just sunk his fork into the second cake—a splendid creation of choux pastry, vast amounts of cream and chocolate icing—when the voice to his right struck him as sounding familiar.

Glancing sideways, Fred recognised Humphrey Price, the sneaking little rat. He was the miserable arse that had done his bit to ruin poor Ozzie. Fred could barely restrain the urge to pummel the disgusting prick, but he was not an idiot. For one, Price was bigger than he was. That alone would not have stopped him, but he was with a companion. Mr Travers was a great deal bigger than Fred, and if he made a scene, it would only make things worse for Ozzie, and—and this was the clincher—it would *displease* his father.

Seething with fury he could do nothing to divert, Fred pushed the cake away, having thoroughly lost his appetite.

"But if she were there that night, Humph, well, it don't look good, does it?"

"Shut up, and don't you dare breathe a word. If anyone gets hold of that information, they'll find out why she was there, and then they'll find out about the brat, and I ain't marrying her."

"Brat's yours, though," the big fellow said, his slow speech showing he wasn't the brightest of fellows.

"So?" Price growled ominously.

Fred writhed with the desire to knock the fellow's teeth down his throat. The miserable wretch. Not content with aiding the late Lady Hargreaves to ruin his sister, he'd also got some poor girl in the family way and would now abandon her to her fate. His stomach roiled with revulsion as he wished he could do something. But perhaps he could. If he could figure out who the girl was, then maybe he could help her? Uncomfortable with playing the part of eavesdropper, Fred reasoned it was in a worthy cause and smothered his finer feelings.

"Still reckon she ought to speak to the police. What if Hargreaves *did* push her down the stairs? If your girl was there to confront his missus, she might be a witness to murder."

Fred felt an icy rush down his back.

"Keep your voice down, you blithering imbecile!" Price hissed, glancing around him as Fred ducked his head and pretended to concentrate on the cake he'd abandoned.

The girl had been there that night. Fred had never believed the story that Hargreaves had murdered his wife. Rosamund's certainty aside, and in his cups or no, he was too good-hearted for that. Fred had met the fellow several times over the years, and he was a thoroughly decent fellow, the kind who never treated you like an annoying brat but had a proper conversation with you. If Fred could only talk to her, perhaps, if she had seen anything, he might convince her to speak up. And if he knew who she was, he could also make sure she and her babe were safe, perhaps force Price to marry the poor girl, though that was such a depressing fate for the unknown young woman that Fred felt quite ill.

He racked his brain, trying to figure out who would know all the latest gossip, before sitting back in his chair with a grin. Well, of course. The answer was obvious.

Aggie.

15ᵗʰJuly 1842, The Phoenix Charitable School for Young Ladies, London

"Your father is going to have my guts for garters," Granger muttered as Fred leapt down from the hackney coach.

"He won't even know," Fred scoffed, though a squirming sensation in his belly reminded him he'd better not dilly dally or they'd both be in the basket.

Granger shook his head, his expression tense. "His grace has a sixth sense, I'd like to remind you. He knows everything, I swear, though the Lord knows how. If I lose my position for letting you gallivant about visiting your girl, I'll—"

"She's not my girl!" Fred exclaimed, blushing to the tips of his ears. "She's a friend, that's all, and… and I need to speak to her about something urgent. I won't let you get into trouble, I swear it."

"Right you are, my lord," Granger said dryly. "I'll wait here. Only for fifteen minutes, mind. Hopefully you can't get up to too much mischief in a girls' school in that time," he added with a low chuckle.

Fred returned a look of contempt he'd seen his big brother give people he deemed *de trop* and stalked off. Clearly he needed more practice, for Granger's chuckle continued, following him all the way to the front gate.

Slipping through the entrance, Fred darted from the path into the garden that led around to the girls' recreation area. Aggie had told him the older girls were allowed twenty-five minutes of fresh air in their own private part of the garden after lunch before returning to their lessons. If he had calculated right, that was about now.

Crouching down behind a hawthorn bush and feeling dreadfully shifty, Fred peered around at the girls. Hell's bells, he'd be in so much trouble for this if he got caught.

Much to his relief, and not greatly to his surprise, he saw Aggie sitting on a bench by herself reading one of the books he'd sent her. He grinned as he noted the expression of rapt concentration on her face, and groped in the dirt beside him for a small pebble. Waiting to be certain no one else was looking, he chucked the stone, which hit her lightly on the shoulder.

Jumping a little, Aggie turned in surprise, her eyes widening as they fell upon Fred peering out from behind the bush. He gestured for her to hurry and ducked back out of sight to wait.

"What the devil are you playing at?" she demanded a moment later, once the two of them were out of sight.

"I need your help," Fred whispered urgently, and told her everything he'd learned.

15th July 1842, Dern Palace, Sevenoaks, Kent, London.

Voices from outside the parlour had Rosamund leaping to her feet and rushing to the door. Sebastian could not help the smile that curved his lips as she turned back a moment later, despondent to discover it was not her father returning from town with their marriage licence. She wanted to marry him. The thought settled beneath his skin, warming him. He wanted very badly to kiss her again, to soften the pout of disappointment pursing her lips until he teased her into kissing him back, sliding her tongue against his like she had done earlier. Desire heated his blood in an instant, his body reacting to the idea like gunpowder touched with a flame. He shifted on the settee, uncomfortably aware of her mother sitting at the writing desk in the corner, the scratch of her pen the only sound at present.

Rosamund sighed and came to sit back beside him. He took her hand in his, taking pleasure in curling his fingers about hers, and from the shy smile she returned. Such a simple, foolish pleasure, and yet how many years had it been since anyone had touched him with affection? It was on the tip of his tongue to suggest they go for another walk in the hope he could be alone with her, when her mother got to her feet and gathered up her writing things.

"I just remembered I have something I need to do," she said, giving them a bright smile. "I had quite forgotten I needed to do it, but now I've remembered. So I'd better... erm... get on and do it. Excuse me."

She hurried out of the room, and either the thing she needed to do was so urgent she was distracted, or she was going to be the best kind of mother-in-law because she forgot to leave the door ajar, closing it firmly behind her.

Sebastian turned to Rosamund to find her blushing and staring at the carpet.

"Was that...?"

"On purpose, yes, of course it was," she said, darting him a quick smile.

"Oh," he said, feeling suddenly ten years younger. "She's rather splendid, isn't she?"

"She is," Rosamund agreed.

"Your father is terrifying," he added with a wry smile. "And that's coming from someone who has considered him a friend for some years."

"He's a duke," she replied, as if this answered the question admirably, which it did.

Sebastian studied her face, willing her to turn towards him, hoping she might want him to kiss her. She shifted on the settee, inching closer and leaning into him. He slid an arm about her waist, to which she did not object. Slowly, she turned her head, staring up at him, before tilting her face to his, offering her mouth to him. He pressed his lips to hers, careful not to spook her as a bolt of pure hunger shot directly to his groin.

In an instant, Sebastian's heart had rocketed from a steady thud to career about behind his ribs. *Calm yourself, you damn fool;* he cursed inwardly, but it had been too long, so very long, since a woman had wanted him for himself. Oh, perhaps the ladies he occasionally visited at the Orchid House had desired him, but when there was money on the table it was never possible to be certain of that, and Sebastian had never favoured such bloodless couplings with no emotion involved. Not a problem now, he thought wryly. Years of unspent lust warred with the desire to protect Rosamund from the least harm. He would not ruin the chance he'd been given by taking things too fast, not if it killed him… which was a distinct possibility, considering he was already hard as a rock, and he'd barely kissed her. He kept his kisses careful, gentle, aware that he had overwhelmed her earlier. Unintentionally to be certain. She'd overwhelmed him, too, and threatened to do so again as her tongue darted out to touch his lips.

His breathing hitched, but he was not about to deny the lady if she wished to explore. He opened his mouth for her, allowing her to take the lead, encouraging her by pulling her closer into his arms. She came willingly, relaxing against him, and Sebastian experienced a thrill of elation. Good God, he was acting like a schoolboy, but how could he not? He was too used to feeling rejected, to having Adelia stiffen with disgust if he touched her, turn her head away to avoid a kiss, though he had given up on even that years ago. Thoughts of his wife dampened his ardour as his guilt resurfaced at once. Rosamund pulled back, immediately aware of the change in him.

"Did I do something wrong?"

His heart clenched at the worry in her eyes.

"Sweet girl, as if you could," he said, stroking her cheek. He shook his head, giving her a crooked smile.

Rosamund studied him, not finding it difficult to unravel his thoughts. "She was cruel to you, Sebastian. She shut you out and did everything in her power to torment you. I know one ought not speak ill of the dead, but she was not kind. I do not pretend to understand her, and perhaps if I did I might have more sympathy, for I do not believe she was happy, but she made you unhappy too, for years and years, and that grieves me. You don't owe her another day of unhappiness. You have given her enough of those already."

He stared at her, his throat tight with emotion, with gratitude for her words. "I am falling in love with you at a quite startling rate, do you realise that?"

There was a quick little intake of breath as her eyes widened, and then she smiled, bright and so dazzling he felt blinded by it. "Kiss me," she demanded, and reached for him.

Happy to oblige, Sebastian pulled her close again, kissing her deeply as she sighed and wriggled closer.

"Oh, bloody hell!"

Rosamund squeaked with alarm and pushed at his chest before turning to glare at the door where her brother stood. "Jules!" she exclaimed furiously. "Go away!"

"Damned if I will. Really, Hargreaves, I know you're marrying her, but can't you wait?"

"Argh!" Rosamund exclaimed, getting to her feet and stalking to the door. She gave her brother a push, both hands flat on his chest.

Blackstone just stood there, glowering.

"Mama will have something to say about this if she finds out, Ozzie," he said, folding his arms and glaring at her.

"Oh, stop trying to look ducal, Jules. It does not impress me, and Mama already knows. She closed the door to give us some privacy."

Jules blinked. "She did?"

"She did," Rosamund gritted out.

"Oh. Very well, carry on, then. Apologies for the interruption, Hargreaves."

With that, he walked out again.

Rosamund muttered something that sounded rude and closed the door again.

"Sorry," she said, shaking his head. "He's an idiot."

Sebastian grinned and held out his hand to her. "Come here."

She did, and did not protest as he patted his knee, perching on his legs as though she might flee at any moment.

"That doesn't look very comfortable," he observed.

"Not really, no."

He tugged her back against him, settling them both upon the cushions. "Better?"

She rested her head on his shoulder and nodded. "Lovely."

Rather bewildered by his good fortune, Sebastian enjoyed the delight of cuddling his wife-to-be, toying with a lock of her hair and revelling in the lush weight of her soft body relaxed against his.

"Hargreaves?"

"Sebastian," he corrected.

She sighed, shaking her head. "It's difficult to get used to that, and I like Hargreaves."

He chuckled. "Very well, but I insist on Sebastian when we are intimate. Hargreaves reminds me of my father."

"Oh!" she said, blushing. "Very well, then."

"What did you wish to ask me?"

"Well…." She hesitated, glancing up at him.

"Go on," he urged her. We can talk about anything, I promise.

"Even subjects that are rather… uncomfortable?"

"Especially those," he assured her.

Absently, she traced a hand over the embroidery on his waistcoat. It was a light satin and her touch tickled through to his skin, making him wonder if she knew she was circling his nipple and making his nerves leap.

"Well, I just wondered if Adelia had enemies?"

His excitement died instantly at the mention of his wife, and he frowned, concentrating on the question. "There were certainly plenty of people who disliked her, but enemies? No, I do not think so. Why?"

She shrugged, giving him an apologetic glance. "What if she *was* pushed? Just not by you."

He frowned at the idea. "Isn't it more likely she tripped, like you said?"

Rosamund nodded but her expression remained troubled. "Yes, probably, but now I have the idea in my head it's sort of stuck there. What if she was rude to one of the staff and they lost their temper, or... or what if one of the men she was flirting with tired of being led about by the nose? It might not have even been on purpose, but.... Oh, am I being ridiculous? Too many Gothic novels, I expect."

"You could never be ridiculous," he assured her, but he was disturbed by her words and rather wished she'd not said anything because now he was considering it too. "She was always vile to the staff. Why would they react now, though, after so long?"

"Perhaps it was the last straw?"

Sebastian frowned, remembering that Adelia's lady's maid had acted rather oddly when he had dismissed her with a letter of recommendation and a generous last payment. He'd assumed it was because she thought him a murderer and blamed him for losing her position, but could it have been something other than that? Surely not.

Rosamund was quiet for a moment, but it was clear she did not wish to let the matter drop. "What about her flirts? Who was a part of the group always trailing after her? Would any of them do such a thing? That awful Humphrey Price was always with her, and we know he and his friend Travers helped her to set us up in the library."

Sebastian battled a swell of fury at the reminder of Price and his crony. One day, he would have the satisfaction of breaking their noses if there was any justice in the world. Sadly, justice was in short supply most days, but one lived in hope.

"But the staff would have said if someone had come to the house," Sebastian pointed out, all too happy to accuse the men of a heinous crime but not so dishonourable as to condemn them with no evidence.

"Unless they didn't know, or they were covering for them," Rosamund suggested.

"My word, what a Machiavellian mind you have, child," he said, staring at her in wonder.

She pulled a face at him. "Just because it works quicker than yours, *old man*."

Sebastian smothered a grin, delighted that she was comfortable enough to provoke him again. "Old man, is it? Well, you asked this wicked satyr to marry you, might I remind you, so you must have a fondness for decrepit old goats."

She pinched his chin, a mischievous look in her eyes. "Perhaps I just felt sorry for you, seeing as how you're so ancient. Thirty, at least," she added, all innocence.

"Next year," he grumbled, glaring at her but he could not keep looking cross even in fun when she was so adorable. "I want to kiss you," he said, not wanting to think about Adelia anymore, even though they must.

"I want to kiss you too, but this is important, isn't it?"

He nodded and leaned towards her, pressing his mouth to hers. "Just one kiss," he promised.

"J-Just one," she agreed breathlessly, sliding her hands into his hair and pulling him closer.

It was only one kiss, he reasoned sometime later, for their mouths had not yet parted but the kiss was growing hotter, deeper, and he was on fire. Rosamund shifted on his lap, her skirts billowing up and getting in the way. Sebastian pressed them back down with a growl of annoyance as she wriggled again, moving to straddle his lap. Oh. Oh, that was....

He gasped as she shifted closer, her sex cradling his erection so perfectly he forgot how to breathe. Rosamund sucked in a breath, her eyes widening as she discovered how beautifully they fit together.

"Oh!" She clutched at his shoulder, a look of such innocent surprise in her eyes that Sebastian grinned.

"That feels good, doesn't it?" he whispered.

She nodded and gave an experimental push with her hips, increasing the pressure. Her breath hitched and Sebastian groaned, resting his head on her shoulder.

"It does. Very good," she whispered, and did it again.

Dropping the hands that held her waist to her hips, Sebastian held her tight against him and tilted his hips, rubbing his cock repeatedly against her sex as colour rose high on her cheeks, and she closed her eyes.

"I want to make love to you," he whispered, knowing he could not do this for long, he was too close already. "I need to be inside you, beautiful girl."

She pressed her mouth to his, kissing him fiercely and making soft little erotic sounds that made him wilder still.

Outside the door, the sound of voices echoed. The duke was home. Rosamund heard it too and gave a squeak of alarm, leaping from his lap and almost falling on her backside. Sebastian grabbed her by the waist and put her firmly back on the sofa as he shifted away and sat back with his legs crossed and his hands in his lap to cover the fact he had a raging cockstand.

A moment later the duke strode in with Rosamund's little brother, Fred, a girl Sebastian did not recognise, and the duchess.

"Do you have it, Papa?" Rosamund said eagerly.

The duke nodded, waving a folded piece of paper at them. "Better than that, though, I have information. Though Fred must take the credit for it. He's been quite the detective this afternoon."

"Oh, but Miss Agatha helped too, sir," he said gallantly, earning himself a quick smile from the young lady.

"Indeed, she did," Bedwin replied, laying a hand on the girl's shoulder.

"Well, don't keep us in suspense, Pa," Rosamund insisted. "Tell us everything."

Chapter 16

Wolf,

He's not dead. He's not dead. Mon Dieu. Either that or I am losing my damn mind. Perhaps the devil animated his foul corpse to torment me. He's been in my rooms. More than once now. I can feel him watching me. I have come home again tonight to the smell of those filthy cigars lingering in the air.

My brother, my friend, and my valet huddle together and whisper about me, for they think I am becoming paranoid. They think my mind is unravelling. I cannot pretend that isn't true. I have just torn the place apart, certain he had left something, some tangible proof he had been here. You know how he loved his little games. I found nothing, but I know it's here. I know it's here. I cannot sleep and jump at shadows. If only he would show himself so I might kill him again and make certain he stays dead. He will succeed in killing me this time if I do not strike first. I would beg for you to pray for me, but we both know God stopped listening a long time ago.

—Excerpt of a letter from Louis César de Montluc, Comte de Villen to Wulfric 'Wolf' De Vere.

15th July 1842, Dern Palace, Sevenoaks, Kent.

"So then I went to see Aggie," Fred said, his excitement obvious. "Because her guardian lets her read the scandal sheets when she visits, and she always knows all the gossip. I was right, too: she said Mr Price has shown interest in several young ladies this year, and so we made a list."

The evening was drawing in, twilight settling over the skies outside the windows.

"Fred, did it never occur to you that you ought not sully the ears of a young lady with such a sordid tale?" his father asked, his tone gently reproving.

Fred turned scarlet.

"Oh, that's all right, your grace," Aggie said, waving this concern away. "I saw far more terrible things before Monsieur Le Comte rescued me from the streets."

Everyone fell silent as this appalling truth settled between them. Aggie had learned her lessons well, so well it was impossible to believe she wasn't a well brought up, sheltered young lady like Rosamund or any of her sisters.

"Come and sit by me, Aggie dear," Matilda said, patting the empty seat on the settee beside her.

Obligingly Aggie did as she asked, sending Matilda a curious glance as the lady hugged her.

"You said you made a list, my dear?" Matilda said, smiling at her.

Aggie nodded. "Yes, Fred has it."

Before Fred could speak, Matilda raised her hand. "We must all solemnly promise to keep this to ourselves," Lady Matilda said, her expression one of concern. "If one of these girls is really with child, she will be terribly frightened and if words gets out...."

"No one here will say a word, love," Montagu said, his voice firm.

Matilda nodded and let out a sigh. "No, of course, I know that. Oh, but, Lucian, the poor girl."

Her husband, who sat on her other side, took her hand. Matilda clung to it, her expression taut with concern.

"Who is on the list, Fred?" Rosamund asked, though she knew at least one name that would need to be there if it was not already.

Fred read out the names and Aggie spoke again once he'd finished. "I know Mr Price showed quite an interest in Miss Knight too, but she sent him packing, so we can certainly discount her."

"I should think so!" Prue exclaimed, shocked.

Aggie hurried on. "Oh, of course. I did not mean to suggest... only that he had shown her interest. But Miss Evie is far too clever for such a nasty fellow and obviously an excellent judge of character, for she didn't like him at all and said that he was a loathsome toad."

"Miss Morcombe," Rosamund said, her expression anxious.

"The young lady you took under your wing?" Sebastian said, remembering having seen them together.

Rosamund nodded. "She had hopes of Mr Price, I think. I tried to dissuade her, for she has no dowry and Mr Price only ever attends to heiresses, but she would not hear a word said against him. I cannot help but fear it may be her."

Aggie nodded. "I put her and Miss Childe at the top of the list. Both have found favour with Mr Price of late. Neither is especially plump in the pocket, though Miss Childe is a distance relation of the Duke of Sefton."

"Miss Childe strikes me as being an eminently sensible girl who does not suffer fools, but Miss Morcombe is prettier, and her nature sweeter," Bedwin said with a concerned frown. "Exactly the kind of girl a rogue might take advantage of."

Rosamund frowned, and would have agreed at once that she was a sweet-natured girl, if not for the catty way Miss Morcombe had spoken about Lord Hargreaves and his wife. But then if her lover had left her pregnant and had promptly fallen under the sway of Lady Hargreaves....

"I think it might be Miss Morcombe," she said in a rush.

Everyone stared at her.

"Why?" Sebastian asked.

Rosamund hesitated, not wanting to repeat what the young woman had said about Sebastian not letting his wife make such a fool of him. "She spoke rather sharply about Lady Hargreaves. Said she had an excess of animal spirits. Her dislike was rather marked."

Sebastian frowned, and she reached for his hand. How horrid this must all be for him. He smiled faintly at her touch and curled his fingers around hers. "The poor girl."

"We cannot be certain she is the young lady Fred heard Mr Price refer to," her father said, accepting a glass of wine from Montagu, who had decided everyone needed a drink. "And so we must tread very carefully indeed. Though I admit, I am at a loss to how we ought to proceed."

"I will speak to her," Rosamund said, her voice firm. "She trusts me, a little at least, and she was very grateful for the support I lent her over the season. Perhaps I can get her to confide in me? Though for that, we will need to return to town."

"Montagu and I were going back tomorrow anyway," her father said. "We are both needed in the House. It will not be so very astonishing if everyone returns with us."

"Very well." Rosamund nodded her agreement but could not help adding, "But Lord Hargreaves and I will still be married before we go. Tonight. *Now.* You said we might, Papa."

Her father stared at them, his gaze lingering on their joined hands before he looked at her mother.

"Prue?"

To Rosamund's relief, Mama nodded her agreement. "I think it is a good match, Robert. And you know how much I enjoy shocking the *ton.* We'll set the cat among the pigeons with this, that's for certain."

Her father sighed, looking resigned to the inevitable fallout. "Very well, then. Montagu, you said we could use the chapel? Is that still possible?"

Montagu nodded, unperturbed. "Of course. Let's see, it's six thirty now. Give me until eight o'clock and everything will be in place. Matilda, my love, I believe I require your assistance."

Matilda leapt up to follow him, her face alight with pleasure. "How exciting. Oh, I do love weddings."

There were no two ways about it: marrying again just five days after his wife had died—or been killed—was utterly beyond the pale. It was scandalous and wicked, and Sebastian was drowning in an excess of emotion. Guilt churned in his guts, but the overwhelming rightness of this moment battled it down. Rosamund's hand was in his, and she was staring up at him as she recited her vows, her gaze so solemn that he knew without question she meant to honour the words.

For Sebastian speaking the sacred words again ought perhaps to have terrified him. Once again, he was rushing into marriage with a woman he had not known for very long, yet everything was different. He was old enough to know his own mind, old enough to be a far better judge of character, and his heart was in no doubt at all that he would never live to regret this decision. Rosamund was a part of him, was so familiar to him that he finally understood what people meant when they spoke of their other half. It was as if she was woven into the fabric of his soul. He had realised she'd been missing from his life the moment he'd first seen her. He'd been a clumsy oaf and thrown champagne over her, but it had been the shock of recognition that had hit him, and that moment still lingered in his mind, like being struck by lightning. Sebastian had not allowed himself to dwell on it and had pushed the knowledge way down in the dark recesses of his mind. Knowing he could fall in love with her in the blink of an eye was one thing, but allowing his feelings to follow where they wanted to was quite another. But now he had been set free. Poor, unhappy Adelia had paid a terrible price for his freedom, but as much as he wished that were not so, he could not find it in himself to regret the opportunity it had given him: an opportunity he would not let slip from his grasp. He knew he must live with the guilt he felt for a long time, but he would not let Rosamund go and lose his one chance for happiness. Not for any price.

Somehow, Lady Matilda had worked a miracle. The chapel had been decked with flowers, making it feel beautiful and intimate, instead of the hasty, scandal-driven affair most would view it as. Rosamund also carried a bouquet of white and yellow roses: white for purity and innocence, and yellow for friendship. The thoughtful gesture touched Sebastian deeply, for above all she was still his friend and, though he longed for more, he did not wish to lose the connection that had brought them together.

The minister, who must have been well-acquainted with the gossip circling society and had been giving Sebastian dark looks through the entire service, lingered for an uncomfortably long moment to ensure no one had any objections to the marriage. To Sebastian's relief, and to the minister's obvious disappointment, no one spoke up. Despite his misgivings, the fellow finally pronounced them man and wife, and Rosamund smiled. It lit up her face, lit the little chapel brighter than the lamps that were chasing away the darkening skies as night fell, and lit up his heart like a beacon guiding him home.

Sebastian bent and kissed her, a chaste brush of lips so as not to scandalise the minister any more than they already had, but he heard Rosamund's swift intake of breath, and longed to be alone with her. The small congregation comprising Lord and Lady Montagu, their daughter Cat, Miss Agatha, and the Bedwin clan, gave a little cheer of glee. Everyone bustled forward to congratulate them before bearing them back to the grand house where a lavish dinner had been prepared to help celebrate their nuptials.

Before they went in for dinner, Montagu drew Sebastian aside.

"I've had the Dower House prepared for you, and had yours and Lady Rosamund's belongings taken there. I beg you will forgive my presumptuousness, but I rather suspected you'd prefer not to spend your wedding night under the same roof as her father."

Sebastian let out a breath and hoped Montagu could see how grateful he was. "My lord, you have been everything that is kind and honourable, but for all you have done today, for Lady Rosamund and myself, I shall never be able to repay you."

Montagu shrugged, his silver eyes glinting. "Oh, well. You never know about that," he replied, reminding Sebastian that Montagu was not known as the most powerful man of the *ton* for nothing. "But either way, I was glad to help. My lady and I are very fond of Rosamund, we wish for her to be happy. So long as you continue to make her happy, I shall consider that repayment enough."

Sebastian could not fail to hear the implicit threat in the words, one which it had not surprised him to hear from the duke too, shortly before they'd spoken their vows.

"I have every intention of doing so, I assure you," he replied, noting with relief the amusement in Montagu's expression.

"I know, and so does the duke, which is the only reason Bedwin let it happen. Good luck to you, Hargreaves. I know what it is to cause a scandal by marriage. I hope you have a robust constitution. You will surely need it."

With these encouraging words, Montagu let him go into dinner.

Sebastian endured the next two hours in a tumult of anticipation. He tried to do justice to the excellent meal provided but the knowledge that Rosamund was his wife now consumed him so completely he could have been eating stale bread for all the attention he paid the food.

Finally, dinner was over, and he guided a blushing Rosamund out to the waiting carriage, which would take them the short distance to the Dower House. Once they had bade everyone farewell and the carriage door closed on them, the night became still and silent, the only sounds the horses' hooves and the turn of the carriage wheels.

"No regrets," he asked softly, trying to make out her face in the shadowy interior of the carriage.

"Not so far," she replied, and he heard the smile in her voice.

"Well, that's a relief." He reached out and took her hand. "We're still friends, Rosamund. I hope, as your husband, I can be far more than that to you, but I want you to know you can trust me. I would never hurt you, never betray you by word or deed. I swear it."

Rosamund shifted closer on the seat, leaning into him. "I know that, and I do trust you. How could I not? I have seen you act with honour and dignity despite the worst kind of provocation, but I can promise you I mean to honour my vows, too. You need never doubt me."

Silence fell between them again, and Sebastian racked his brain for a way to put her at ease. They had never been uncomfortable with each other before, but... well, this was a rather unique situation.

Sebastian was uncertain if the Dower House appeared too soon or not quickly enough. It was hard enough to speak what was in his heart in the dark confines of the carriage. Once in the brightly lit Dower House, he felt a certain restraint fall over them as the strangeness of what was happening came rushing in upon them. The housekeeper was a friendly but brisk woman of middling years who showed them to their room, told them baths were being prepared and would be ready momentarily, and left them alone in the luxurious confines of their bedroom. Rosamund glanced at the bed and quickly away again, her fingers knotted tightly together.

"Do you remember what I said?" he asked, watching her as she inspected the paintings on the bedroom wall.

"I do." She nodded, not looking at him and concentrating instead on tugging her gloves off, one finger at a time. "You said I could wait if... if I wished to."

"I meant it when I said I would not rush you, not when everything has happened so quickly and in such a way. I want to make you happy, Rosamund, not to cause you a moment's disquiet. We may have married quickly, but there is no need for everything else to follow suit."

She nodded, still not looking at him.

Sebastian waited, studying her as she moved about the room, touching the heavy brocade curtains and inspecting the selection of novels displayed on top of an elegant chest of drawers.

"And... And if I don't want to wait?"

Sebastian's breath caught, hardly daring to believe he had heard correctly.

She darted a sideways look at him, her cheeks pink. "Have I shocked you?"

He shook his head. "No," he murmured unsteadily. "I just… I still can't believe it, that you're really my wife. This is too extraordinary to be real. How can I be this lucky after everything that's happened? Rosamund, I am living in constant terror of waking up and discovering it was all a dream."

"Not a nightmare?" she asked him, her voice quiet as she trailed her hand over the ornately carved bedpost.

"There have certainly been nightmarish moments. You know that as well as I, but this is beyond my wildest dreams, for I would never have allowed myself to imagine such a gift as you."

She smiled at that and turned to face him. "I'm real, and… and I cannot deny I am nervous, afraid even."

"Of me?" he asked in alarm.

"*No*! Oh, no," she said at once, shaking her head vehemently. "No, I'm not afraid of you. I just… I don't want to disappoint you. You told me how difficult such things were with—"

She clamped her mouth shut, obviously as reluctant for that name to be spoken in this room tonight as he was. Sebastian's heart ached that she should worry about it for his benefit. "There's no need to worry about that."

She sent him an anxious glance. "Isn't there? I just so want things to be good between us."

"Then they will be," he said simply. "Because that is what I want too."

He closed the gap between them and pressed a kiss to her mouth. He did not linger, did not dare kiss her more than once, for his desire for her was becoming difficult to manage. "Take your bath, love. I'll see you when you're ready and we'll talk more."

Rosamund nodded and moved to the connecting door to the bathing room, though he was pleased when she stopped and looked back at him, seeming as reluctant to leave him as he was to let her go.

Rosamund returned to the bedroom an hour later, dressed in a simple white cotton nightgown which she had fretted was not at all the thing for her wedding night. Her mother, however, had only given a soft laugh and told her to stop being foolish.

"If Lord Hargreaves' jaw does not hit the floor upon seeing you, he is not the man I think he is," she had said with a laugh.

Rosamund had exclaimed with shock at her mother's words, though they'd had the desired effect, for she'd felt reassured... until now. Alone in the bedroom, she waited for him. With nothing else to occupy her, she sat down at the dressing table and began brushing out her long hair until she heard the door open on the far side of the room.

In the looking glass she saw him then, standing barefoot in the doorway. He wore a dark blue banyan and, as was clear from the triangle of skin exposed beneath his throat, nothing else. Rosamund swallowed as a knot tangled in her belly and a combustible mix of excitement and nerves fizzed in her veins.

He closed the door behind him and came closer, moving slowly as if he feared she might bolt at any moment. Foolish man. She might be anxious and embarrassed, but she was going nowhere.

"My word," he whispered, reaching out to touch her hair with a reverent hand. "You are lovelier than I dreamed possible."

Rosamund set down the brush and turned on the stool to look at him. "Thank you."

He put his hand out, and she took it, allowing him to pull her to her feet. "Would you be comfortable sitting on the bed with me? If not, we could—"

"That would be fine," she said quickly, not wanting him to talk himself out of it.

He grinned then, a quick, boyish expression that made him look far younger and made her heart glad. It was so good to see him smile.

A moment later and they sat side by side, propped up by pillows, their legs stretched out in front of them. Rosamund stared at his legs, or at least what was visible beneath his robe. They were long and powerful and covered with dark hair. The urge to stretch her foot out and slide it along his calf to see how it felt was intense, but she resisted.

"It's been quite a day," Sebastian said, his tone wry.

Rosamund laughed. "That it has."

The tension between them eased a little and they talked, hesitantly at first. Rosamund asked him where they would live, listening with rapt attention as he described the properties he owned. They spoke about their childhoods, about their hopes for the future, about the possibility they might have children of their own.

"A girl," Sebastian said in answer to her question. "An heir would be a fine thing, but I never want you to feel you must provide one. I have a cousin who will be delighted to inherit, and I want only for you and any children to be happy and healthy. That will be more than I ever thought I would have. It is more than enough."

Rosamund smiled, and Sebastian reached for her hand and brought it to his lips, kissing her knuckles one by one, and then her palm before setting it upon his chest.

"Can you feel my heart thudding?" he asked.

Rosamund nodded, feeling the steady beat beneath her hand.

"It's rather fast," she noted, looking at him.

"Because you're close to me. When you are near, I cannot think of anything else. Since you allowed me to kiss you, I can think of nothing but doing it again."

"I'd like that," she offered.

He held her gaze, his eyes darkening in a way that made her heart race far faster than his.

"Come to me, then," he said, opening his arms to her.

Wriggling closer, she fitted herself against him, her breath catching as he moved, keeping her in his arms but easing her onto her back.

"Nothing you don't want," he murmured, leaning down to brush his mouth over hers. "Just a word from you and I'll stop, and I won't be cross, I promise."

Rosamund's breathing became increasingly erratic as he kissed her again and again, soft little presses of his mouth against hers. He encouraged her to join in, to ask for what she wanted, to demand more. Emboldened, she sought his mouth, darting her tongue along the seam of his lips as he had taught her to do. He gave her what she asked for at once, opening to her and teasing her further, encouraging her to grow bolder with the tantalising slide of his tongue against hers.

Her limbs grew heavier, languid, though there was a strange tension coiling inside her. Her breasts tingled, her nipples aching as a distracting pulsing sensation began between her thighs. Restlessly, she moved within his embrace, trying to press closer, to ease the maddening sensations.

"Hargreaves," she said, struck by the breathless quality of her own voice.

"Sebastian," he corrected with a chuckle. "Yes, love. Is it too much? Should I stop and let you catch your breath?"

"No!" she replied at once.

"What, then?" he asked, infinitely patient. "Tell me."

Oh! Why must she always explain herself? Why couldn't he just get on and... but that was foolish. *Why* was obvious, and he had already told her he needed her honesty. He was relying on her to tell him how she felt, no matter how mortifying it was.

She swallowed, trying to put the rather exasperating sensations into words. "I... I feel... impatient," she managed, surprised when he looked delighted by her admission.

"You want more?" he asked, stroking a finger down her throat. Even that slight contact made her shiver, a flood of damp heat pooling between her legs. Sebastian watched her and moved his hand to her waist, then slowly higher to cup her breast.

Rosamund arched into his touch as pleasure rippled through her.

"Good?" he asked, to which she had no reply beyond a nod.

This must have been enough, though, for he continued, gently squeezing her breast and then her nipple, not pinching hard enough to hurt but certainly enough to send a shaft of pleasure arrowing directly to the place between her thighs. Rosamund gasped, pressing her legs tight together, desperate for relief from the increasingly demanding throb that only grew louder as he continued.

She watched, a little hazy now, as Sebastian reached for the ribbons holding the front of her nightdress closed and tugged each one undone. With infinite care, he drew the simple cotton to one side to expose first one breast, then the other.

"So lovely," he said, his voice growing low and husky, which only worsened the insistent pulsing that craved more, that craved something—*him*.

Fascinated by the change in him, she watched, bemused, as he lowered his mouth to her breast and suckled, the sensation so shocking her reaction almost catapulted her off the bed.

"Oh!" she exclaimed, gasping for breath.

He teased, licked, and kissed her breast quite thoroughly before turning his attention to her other nipple and starting all over again. By the time he raised his head to judge her reaction, she had lost all possibility of coherent thought.

"Have I shocked you?" he asked, studying her expression with concern.

Rosamund only shook her head. "N-Not yet," she managed. "Please keep trying, though."

He gave a startled laugh, his expression one of pure delight. "My God, I love you," he said, and then stilled, realising what he'd said. "You don't mind? I know it's too soon, but it's true and I can't pretend otherwise. I don't expect you to say it in return, but it's bursting inside me and—"

Rosamund reached for him, dragging him down on top of her, bringing his mouth to hers. She kissed him, purposefully and with no ambiguity, and she pressed her body against his, seeking the friction, the weight of him she needed so badly.

"Take it off," she urged, though she was uncertain if she meant her nightgown or his robe.

All she knew was that she wanted them both gone, *now*. Anything that kept her skin from his was wrong and needed to go at once.

With more urgency than grace, Sebastian tugged at the tie to his robe and shrugged out of it, tossing the banyan to one side. He froze as Rosamund gasped, staring at him with wide eyes.

"Too much?" he asked, watching her warily.

Rosamund's gaze roved over him, part of her wanting to agree that he was most certainly too much, far more than she had ever imagined. He had broad shoulders and a powerful chest quilted with muscle and coarse dark hair that she had the strangest urge to rub herself against, to feel it brush over the softness of her breasts. That hair continued in a trail, leading her directly to that most masculine part of him, which, despite her mother's warning that it was unlikely to resemble the Greek statues she'd seen, was still rather shocking. Hargreaves looked nothing like a Greek statue *there.*

"You'd never cover *that* with a fig leaf," she said before she could think better of it, and then clapped a hand to her mouth.

Her husband stared at her in shock for a moment and then roared with laughter.

Rosamund bit her lip, uncertain whether laughter in the bedroom was a good thing or not, until he flopped down beside her, still chortling, with an arm slung over his eyes. "Oh, love. You are utterly perfect," he said, the affection in his voice overriding any remaining qualms.

Reassured, Rosamund dared to reach out her hand and touch his chest, feeling the hair rasp beneath her fingers and his muscles flicker and leap as her hand drifted lower. Her gaze flicked to his as he moved his arm to watch her.

"Don't stop," he said, his chest rising and falling faster. "Touch me. *Please*, touch me."

Rosamund heard the plea behind the words and remembered what he had told her, how his wife had reviled his touch, and realised that meant she would not have willingly touched him either. He had been without love, without affection, for such a long time, with no one to tell him—to *show* him—how wonderful he was. Overcome with tenderness for him, Rosamund leant down and pressed a kiss over his heart, intrigued by the soft warmth of his skin beneath the hair. As she leaned over him, her naked breasts brushed his chest, and the sensation was every bit as delicious as she had suspected. Delighted by her discovery, she smoothed her hands over him, stroking over his chest and belly, over his lean hips. She investigated his strong thighs, honed to pure muscle from years of horse riding, and then, inevitably, the thick thatch of dark hair and his arousal that twitched with anticipation as her hand grew closer.

He let out a low moan as she dared to stroke a finger down the length of him, startled by the intense heat and the silken texture. How strange it was to be here like this, with this man. He had been only her friend such a few short days ago, and yet it was not strange at all to know they could be more than that now, for beneath everything else he was still her friend. Being with him was the perfect mix of excitement and anticipation and discovery of the unknown, and the certain knowledge that she would find nothing to hurt or disappoint her.

Rosamund curled her fingers carefully around him and stroked, aware of the throbbing pulse that seemed to echo that insistent ache in her own body. She watched with fascination as she continued to caress him, slow and careful, up and down. Sebastian's hips bucked and an urgent sound escaped him.

"I'll come," he bit out, shaking his head. "Best stop, love… I can't… Please."

Rosamund released him with regret, but she suspected he would allow her plenty of opportunity for further exploration at another time, if she wanted. And she certainly wanted.

"Can we take this off you?" he asked, gesturing to her nightgown.

Rosamund nodded eagerly, only too happy to be rid of it. She sat up and raised her arms as Sebastian tugged it over her head and flung it to the floor. His expression made her blush as he sat staring at her, the blatant desire in his eyes enough to make her body prickle all over with anticipation. His chest rose and fell faster now, and he let out a ragged breath.

"Is it foolish that I feel like I have endured everything that came before this so I might be worthy of this moment?" he asked, and she heard the tremble in his voice, the sincerity. "I know now how precious this is, Rosamund, this chance to try again."

"I know," she whispered, feeling the same overwhelming surge of emotion, of the beginning of something wonderful. "And it's not the least bit foolish, it's lovely. You're lovely, Sebastian."

He laughed, reaching for her. "I think I'm supposed to say that to you, and you are, you know. Quite extraordinarily lovely."

He kissed her then, and Rosamund sighed as he lay her back down, enchanted by the heat of him, giddy with delight at the feel of his body against hers. He was an unexplored landscape of silken skin and coarse hair, of soft lips and hard muscle, and she revelled in her discovery of him, her hands roving over him and charting every sinew and curve. All the while he kissed her, with occasional diversions to trail his lips down her neck to her breasts and to kiss and lick and torment her tender nipples until she was squirming beneath him. Her sex was slick with desire now, his arousal sliding back and forth in the most beguiling way, sending little sparks of heat glittering through her blood until she was teetering on the edge of something explosive.

Rosamund opened her legs wider, tilting her hips harder against him, seeking more, needing relief. He stared down at her, colour cresting his cheeks and his breathing erratic.

"Shall I make love to you?" he asked, his voice oddly scratchy and uneven.

She nodded, staring up at him, knowing now that was what the clamouring, empty sensation meant, that was what she wanted.

"I need the words, Rosamund. Tell me," he said again, firmer now. "Because if you need to wait—"

"No! I mean yes. *Please.* I want you to. I don't want to wait," she added, hoping that her garbled answer had been enough.

He let out a sigh of relief and reached between them, touching the place that was already so dreadfully sensitive with a delicate finger. Rosamund closed her eyes, her head thrown back as pleasure washed over her. Carefully, he circled the delicate nub of flesh until she was dizzy, gasping and clutching at the covers, and then he slid a finger inside her. Rosamund gasped, startled, and then he shifted lower down her body and ducked his head, gently sucking the taut little bud into his mouth as he slid another finger inside her.

Rosamund shattered, stars exploding behind her eyelids as the room whited out. Joy surged through her, stealing her breath, shutting out everything but the feel of his mouth upon her most private flesh, the intimate slide of his fingers, and the dazzling pleasure that stole her wits and left her languid and boneless as he teased the last, lingering ripples from her body.

When finally she found energy enough to raise her eyelids and remembered she was in bed with Sebastian, not floating in some distant galaxy, his expression arrested her. He was staring down at her with a mixture of smug male pride and such joy that his eyes sparkled a little too brightly.

"Oh, Sebastian," she said, reaching for him, pulling him down to her. "That was… you are… wonderful. Thank you."

He made a choked sound and sought her mouth, kissing her hard, so passionately that she knew he was overwhelmed. She wrapped herself around him, encouraging him to take his place, to join them as they both needed to be joined.

"I'll be careful," he whispered, breaking the kiss as he pressed the head of his arousal against her, but Rosamund shook her head.

"Don't. Don't be careful. I want you. I want you inside me now."

Using her thighs, her hands, the angle of her hips, she urged him inside her. It was easy, her body so slick and ready that he slid inside with little resistance. Rosamund gasped all the same, very aware of how completely he had filled her. Sebastian groaned, tremors running over him like chills as he held himself still.

"Did I hurt you?" he demanded, but Rosamund only laughed and shook her head.

"No. No, you could never hurt me. Love me, Sebastian. Show me how it's supposed to be."

He did as she asked, worshipping her with his body, with his mouth and his hands, until Rosamund was so enraptured by him, so tangled up in him that she could not imagine how she would ever bear to be without him again.

"I love you," she sobbed, the pleasure overwhelming, pulsing through her as he thrust harder and deeper and cried out, his powerful frame shuddering in her embrace while he came inside her in a searing rush.

She stroked his passion-damp skin as the orgasm shattered him, leaving him trembling and spent until at last he grew still, his breath rushing hot and ragged against her neck. He collapsed on top of her with a quiet moan.

Gradually he came back to himself, his gaze focusing on her, his eyes all dark spice and sated lust, and such tenderness that her breath caught.

"My love," he whispered, his smile one of such joy her she felt her heart might burst.

"*My* love," she replied, and kissed him again.

Chapter 17

Dearest Evie,

Good Lord, everyone is talking about Rosamund and Hargreaves. The scandal is upon everyone's lips, every headline. How will they bear it? It is a relief to hear there are those who are defending Hargreaves, saying that he was always kind and decent, and that he would never do such an appalling thing, but there are still those who delight in all the salacious details.

As parliament is still in session anyway, we have all come back to town. We are armed and ready to attend the same events as they do and stand at their backs. Mrs Belvedere's ball this evening is going to be an absolute crush as everyone attends to get a glimpse of them. Still, they will have Montagu and Bedwin at their backs, among others. They will not be alone, but I fear Rosamund will find it overwhelming. I do not envy her. It is enough to make me wish I were not out yet when I have fought so hard to be given the privilege. How terrifying it is though, for if someone as perfect and well behaved as Rosamund can get

*into such a dreadful scandal, what hope is
there for me?*

**—Excerpt of a letter from Lady Cara Baxter
(daughter of Luke and Kitty Baxter, the
Earl and Countess of Trevick) to Miss Evie
Knight (daughter of Lady Helena and Mr
Gabriel Knight)**

17th July 1842, Mrs Belvedere's Ball, Bloomsbury Square, Holborn, London.

"I feel sick," Rosamund admitted as the carriage crawled towards the grand house and venue for tonight's ball. The entire *ton* looked to have turned out, if the number of carriages cramming the roads were any indication.

"We don't have to do this," Sebastian said, taking her hand. "I can get the carriage to turn around and take us straight back to the hotel. We could have a nice little supper and go to bed early," he added, his tone hopeful.

Despite the sick sensation roiling in her stomach, Rosamund smiled at her husband. Her *husband*! She still had not got over the delight of saying that—even to herself—and would readily have turned the carriage around if the circumstances were different.

"We can't. It is the perfect opportunity to speak to Miss Morcombe for one, and for another, we must do this, Sebastian. It is not enough that we married, we must look them in the eye and show them we have nothing to be ashamed of. You did nothing wrong. It is no secret your marriage was an unhappy one, but you did her no harm. You did your very best for Adelia, and so now you must hold your head up high, and we shall discover who our friends really are."

Sebastian stared at her, admiration shining in his eyes. "I could not be prouder of you. Very well then, wife. We shall stride in there as if they are lucky indeed to have our divine selves in their presence and anyone who doesn't like it can go to perdition."

"Exactly," Rosamund said, still feeling as though she might cast up her accounts but determined to go through with it.

"Though, I have to say, love… I think we know very well who our friends are."

Rosamund smiled and took a deep breath as the carriage finally rolled to a stop. "Yes. I think we do."

By design, they had set off in convoy from Brown's, the hotel Sebastian had booked them into, for the idea of returning to the house in which his wife had died and where he'd been so unhappy was more than either of them could face. So, everyone had rendezvoused outside the hotel before setting off for Bloomsbury, and the carriages ahead of their own carried Lord and Lady Montagu, Rosamund's parents and her eldest brother, Jules, the Earl and Countess of Trevick and their daughter Lady Cara, the Earl and Countess St Clair, and Lady Helena and Mr Gabriel Knight, with Evie and her younger brother, Felix. Already inside, Lord and Lady Bainbridge and Lord and Lady Roxborough waited with Rosamund's older sisters, Lottie and Eliza, and their husbands, Viscount Oakley and Mr Demarteau. There had also been many letters promising support from friends, including Muir Anderson, Leo Hunt, Larkin Weston, the Earl and Countess of Vane, the Comte de Villen, Mr Barnaby Godwin, and Mr Cyril Hadley-Smythe.

The knowledge that they were not alone, that there were many people among the vast gathering who would not only lend their support but raise their voices against the awful gossip, gave Rosamund the courage to nod at Sebastian as he gave her one last enquiring look before getting out of the carriage. It was his presence, though—his hand reaching out for hers—that gave her enough fearless pride to raise her chin and step outside to face everyone else. He was her husband now. Hers. And no one would make her feel anything less than the most fortunate woman in the world. Never again would he stand alone in the face of gossip and scandal. She would stand with him and protect him as he protected her, no matter what it cost her to do it.

As soon as they turned to face the grand building, they found themselves flanked on all sides by their friends and family. Her father and mother had both dressed to the nines, making certain that there was no mistaking the fact they were the highest ranking peers attending that night. Lady Montagu also looked stunning, with the marquess at his arrogant best beside her, his ice-cold demeanour daring anyone to breathe a word in their direction.

Still, their friends could not protect them entirely. When they entered the ballroom, it grew eerily quiet. The moment didn't last, and the murmur of scandalised whispering followed them about the grand ballroom like the buzzing of angry wasps, effectively chasing away the silence.

"Well, this is fun," Lord Bainbridge said, his strident voice easily heard over the whispering and gossip. He gave Hargreaves a hearty slap on the back. "You remember how you said you'd cut your throat before causing Lady Rosamund the least bit of trouble—"

Sebastian paled.

"Bainbridge!" his wife exclaimed, glaring at him. "Stop misbehaving."

"*Me?*" he said in outrage, pressing a hand to his chest, his eyebrows flying up. "It's not me they're all talking about, love. Unusual, I admit, but true."

"Yes, but we're not going to hold our breath, are we, old man?" Viscount Roxborough cut in, smirking at him. "It's only a matter of time."

"Well, I like that! As if you're a blasted angel, and I'll have you know I'm a damned saint these days. Bella, tell them," Bainbridge demanded of his wife, who patted his cheek in an effort to soothe him.

"I know, darling. You've been a very good boy. Mostly."

Bainbridge harrumphed and accepted a glass of champagne, still scowling at his best friend.

Smothering her laughter, Rosamund glanced up at Sebastian to find his expression taut and unhappy, his expression distant and unfocused.

"Hargreaves? My lord." She tugged his sleeve.

His attention snapped to her at once and he returned a crooked smile. "I did say that, you know. That I'd cut my own throat before I caused you any harm. Well, look how that turned out."

"Yes, isn't it splendid?" Rosamund replied serenely, holding his gaze.

Slowly, his tense expression eased, replaced by something warm and mischievous. "You know, you're absolutely right. Well, apart from the fact everyone thinks I'm a murderer, and we're the scandal of the century, but yes…. It *is* splendid."

Relieved by his smile Rosamund looked around them and stiffened.

"Oh, look, there's Miss Morcombe," she whispered, standing on tiptoe to see above the crowd. She strained to get a better look at her, trying to detect any noticeable change to her waistline but there were too many people between them to tell. "I must speak to her. I think if I can get her alone, she might confide in me."

Sebastian frowned. "To get her alone, you'd need to be alone, too. I think you ought to stay close, love."

Rosamund laid her hand on his arm and smiled. "You're sweet to wish to protect me, but this is the reason we came."

"I thought we came to show people we have nothing to be ashamed of," he countered, watching her.

"Of course, that too. But they would know that all the quicker if there was a witness who could prove you were free of any wrongdoing. It's worth a try, Sebastian, and these people don't scare me. Let them talk if they wish to, they will not shame me. I shall not allow it."

He still looked unhappy at the idea of letting her out of his sight, and outside the protective circle of their friends and family, but pride shone in his eyes, too. "Very well. I know better than anyone how strong and brave you are. Go on, then, but know I will not be far away."

"That is the reason I am strong and brave," Rosamund assured him, before steeling her nerve and setting off in pursuit of Miss Morcombe.

It really was an absolute crush with upwards of four hundred people in the ballroom alone, never mind those who were making use of the card rooms or walking in the gardens. Rosamund did her best to ignore the stares and none too subtle comments. Head up, she reminded herself she outranked many of the people here and that she didn't give a fig what they thought of her. By the time Rosamund had caught sight of Miss Morcombe again and pushed through the crowd in pursuit, she was hot and irritated beyond endurance. With every step, she heard more whispers, gasps, and giggles from behind fluttering fans. Some people delighted in speaking loud enough to ensure she heard their vile insinuations, others just tittered and smirked, but there were those who stopped her and offered congratulations, or a kind word and an encouraging smile. She took heart from those encounters.

"Rosamund! Oh, I've had such a battle to get over here," Evie said, hurrying up to her, flushed and breathless. "Are you well? Congratulations, Lady Hargreaves, I'm so *proud* of you, and all those tattle mongers can go and *boil their heads,*" she added, speaking loud enough that everyone around them could certainly hear her.

Rosamund laughed and took her arm. "Thank you, Evie, but come along, quickly. I'm in pursuit of Miss Morcombe. I must speak to her privately."

"Oh, an intrigue? What's happening?"

Not wanting to risk being overheard, Rosamund shook her head. "I can't explain right now, but I must speak to her."

Evie nodded, and Rosamund knew she was too good a friend to press her for anything more.

Instead, she nodded. "Very well. I understand."

"Oh, we'll never catch her in this crush," Rosamund exclaimed as she glimpsed Miss Morcombe exit the ballroom through the press of bodies ahead of them.

"Well, she must be going to either the retirement rooms or for refreshment. Felix is a great friend of Mrs Belvedere's son, you know, and I've been to the house several times. I know a shortcut. This way." Evie grasped her hand and towed her in the opposite direction, the two of them forcing their way through the throng. The crowd thinned and Evie paused as she saw the Comte de Villen watching her intently from the far side of the room. The searing look in his bright blue eyes made Rosamund gasp and glance at Evie, who blushed scarlet.

"Evie?"

"Not now," she whispered, her voice taut. "I can't explain now either. Let's find your Miss Morcombe."

"Very well," Rosamund said, following her, but promising herself a private talk with her friend as soon as possible. "Where are we going?"

"This way." Evie opened a door into a private parlour and hurried through it to another door on the far side that opened onto a long picture gallery. They hurried past the paintings without so much as a glance at them, and out of another door.

To Rosamund's relief, they eased back into the crowd near the refreshments room.

"There she is," Evie said, gesturing to where Miss Morcombe was slipping through the door to the ladies' retiring rooms.

"Thank you, Evie," Rosamund said with a sigh of relief. "I'll catch her on her way out and take her somewhere private to talk."

"You're welcome. Though I insist you explain everything the next time I see you," she added with a smile.

Rosamund nodded. "I will if you will," she said wryly.

The two of them stood quietly, catching their breath after their run through the house.

"Goodness, it's hot," Evie complained, fanning herself vigorously. "I wonder if I can stand the crush in the refreshments room. I'm dreadfully thirsty."

"Mademoiselle," said a soft voice as a silver tray appeared before her. *"Un cadeau de monsieur le comte."*

Rosamund started as she saw the servant. He was neatly and precisely dressed, as all of Madam Belvedere's servants were, but his face was badly scarred, so severely that Rosamund had to fight not to stare at the poor man.

"From the Comte de Villen?" Evie said in surprise as she saw the glass of chilled champagne he offered her.

The servant raised a finger to his lips, one side of which was twisted into a permanent smile. He offered her the glass.

Evie frowned, hesitating. Rosamund suspected she did not wish to insult the man by questioning him further in case he thought the look of him had unsettled her, so she took the glass.

"Merci," she said as the servant bowed and slipped away.

"Louis ought not to take such risks," Evie muttered crossly. "If my father finds out...."

She closed her eyes, her expression pained. Sighing heavily, she lifted the glass to her lips and took a sip of the champagne.

"What's wrong?" Rosamund asked her with concern.

Evie shook her head. "Nothing. At least nothing I can tell you tonight. I will explain everything next time I see you… Oh, *look!* There's your quarry."

Rosamund started, turning to see Miss Morcombe as she hurried back into the crowd. "We will speak soon, Evie," Rosamund promised her, before setting off in pursuit.

Rosamund almost lost the young woman again in the crowd, but reached out and grasped her wrist before she returned to the ballroom.

Miss Morcombe started with surprise and whirled around, her already wan face blanching stark white when she saw Rosamund.

"My lady," she whispered, staring at her in shock. "You came!"

"As you see," Rosamund replied. "And I need a private word with you, my dear."

"Oh. Oh, no, I-I really must get back, m-my aunt is chaperoning me tonight, and you know what an old fusspot she is," Miss Morcombe protested, tugging at her wrist.

"This won't take above a moment, I promise you," Rosamund said, holding on tight. "Come along if you would, please."

Sensing a will far greater than her own, Miss Morcombe gave a taut little nod and followed Rosamund until she had retraced her steps to the parlour she'd run through with Evie.

Guiding Miss Morcombe to the nearest settee, Rosamund sat down and tugged her down beside her. The young woman sat, stiff and unhappy, her jaw set.

"What did you want to talk about?" she asked, her voice flat.

Rosamund reached out and took her hand, holding it between both her own. "Miss Morcombe. We don't know each other terribly well, but I'd like to think we are friends, aren't we?"

Miss Morcombe gave a derisive little sniff. "You mean I'm your charitable project? Your good deed?"

"My what?" Rosamund said, taken aback. "Is... Is that what you think? Is that how I've made you feel?" she asked, horrified by the idea.

Miss Morcombe's face was set in hard lines as she turned to meet Rosamund's gaze, but then all at once the rigid mask fell away, replaced by a look of sheer misery. Her eyes filled, and she shook her head. "No. No, I don't think it. Oh, my lady, you were only ever kind to me. *He* said that's what you thought of me. He said you weren't really my friend, only pretending to make yourself look good, but then he said a lot of things that weren't true, and I was a fool to listen to him."

"Oh, my dear." Rosamund's heart clenched at the agony she heard in the woman's voice and fumbled for her handkerchief as she saw the first tears roll down her cheeks. "I'm so sorry. Oh, if only I'd known, but... but this man you speak of. Is it... Is it Mr Price?"

Miss Morcombe nodded, sobbing now. "And you warned me, didn't you? You told me over and over not to take him seriously, but I thought I knew better. He was so kind at first, you see. So attentive, and he promised... he p-promised...."

She put her head in her hands and wept, and Rosamund could do nothing but hold her as the poor girl broke her heart.

"Miss Morcombe," Rosamund began, and then tried again, for she could not ask such a question of the girl in such a formal manner. "Hannah, I hope you believe that I am your friend, for I swear it is true. And because I am your friend, I can promise you that if you were ever to find yourself in... in a *difficult* situation, I would help you. You can trust me, I swear you can. I will do all I can for you, if ever you should need me."

Miss Morcombe stared up at Rosamund, a look of such utter resignation in her eyes, Rosamund wanted to weep herself.

"You know, don't you?" she said, her shoulders slumping. "Not that it matters now. I shan't be able to hide it much longer. Then everyone will know I'm ruined. Soiled goods. A—A harlot."

"Oh, no!" Rosamund said, taking her hands and holding on tight. "No, Hannah. I shan't let that happen. We will find a way, I swear it. We will make it all right, I promise. Papa will help us. He's a duke, remember, and if anyone can help you—"

Before she could say another word, the young woman leapt to her feet, her face creased in such misery and anger, Rosamund could only stare.

"You can't!" she shouted. "You can't help me, no one can! Not after... not after... Oh, leave me alone, please!"

She ran, fleeing for the door with such speed, Rosamund could not hope to stop her. She tried all the same, hurrying out, but Miss Morcombe had already plunged into the crowded ballroom and disappeared.

"Oh, my word," Rosamund said, agitated. Well, there was nothing else for it. She must find her father and Hargreaves. She needed help.

Finding her Papa and Sebastian was rather easier than Miss Morcombe. The two men stood with Lord Montagu and Gabriel Knight, and most people seeing the Duke of Bedwin, Lord Montagu and Mr Knight standing together, knew better than to approach them at such an event unless they were family or close friends. As everyone knew well that they were here for a reason and were ready to wring the necks of those gossips who insisted on throwing mud at Hargreaves and Rosamund, it was unsurprising to discover a large area of clear space between them and the rest of the room.

"Papa!" Rosamund said, hurrying up to him. "I spoke to her. It's just as we feared, but the poor girl is in such a state. She's terrified, and she ran away before I could persuade her we would help her."

Her father muttered a curse. "Well, we must find her."

"Did she confirm the father's identity?" Sebastian asked quietly.

Rosamund nodded, wringing her hands together. "Oh, Sebastian, she's so frightened and unhappy. I could weep for her. Humphrey Price ought to be horse whipped for what he's done."

"Price?" growled Mr Knight, his expression darkening. "Why, that slimy, disgusting excuse for a man."

"Gabriel?" Montagu frowned at his friend.

"The bastard only spoke to me yesterday," Gabriel said, his fury evident.

"What about?" Rosamund asked.

"He wanted to ask permission to court Evie. Well, I know full well Evie doesn't like him, so I told him to sling his hook, but he did that, knowing full well…." His eyes glittered dangerously as his temper rose. "I'll bloody kill him!"

"Wait, Gabriel," her father said, reaching out to take the man's arm and finding it closing on air.

"Oh, the devil take him, now we're for it," Montagu muttered. "Come along, before he murders the wretch."

"Very well, but I must ask, *why* are we stopping him?" Papa demanded, hurrying after Montagu as Sebastian and Rosamund followed. "Do we care?"

"For Mr Price? Not a whit," Montagu returned. "But I'll not have Gabriel gain a reputation for murder and brawling when I've worked so damned hard to make him respectable."

"Fair enough," Papa replied, nodding, as they rushed out of the ballroom in pursuit of Gabriel Knight.

Chapter 18

Jacques,

Prepare the fortress for an extended visit. I have a bad feeling Louis is going to need to disappear for a while and you know I prefer to prepare for the worst. We'll need extra security in place at the club, too. I'm taking no chances. If his suspicions are correct, I fear for him. I'm not sure he can endure this again.

—Excerpt of a letter from Wulfric 'Wolf' De Vere to Jacques Toussaint, Manager of Rogue et Noir, Paris.

17ᵗʰ July 1842, Mrs Belvedere's Ball, Bloomsbury Square, Holborn, London.

To the relief of all concerned, Gabriel was not so far out of his mind with fury as to cause a scene before the entire ton. Instead, he whispered in Mr Price's ear that he wanted a private word, giving the fellow the kind of smile any other fool would have recognised as bad for one's health.

Mr Price, was not so bright as he might have liked to believe, and swallowed the murmured enticement about a lucrative investment hook, line, and sinker. The moment Gabriel got him outside and in private, however, he took hold of his cravat and shook him like a rag doll.

"You son of a bitch!" he growled, as Mr Price's eyes bulged with shock. "You vile excuse for a man. You dare to come sniffing about my daughter? My *daughter*, when all the while you've got some poor girl in the family way? You miserable worm!"

"Oh, c-come, sir," Mr Price stammered, clawing at Gabriel's wrists to no avail. "Hannah is no better than she ought to be. I admit the child is a shame, but it's one of those things. She ought not to have—*ooof*!"

Mr Price sucked in a breath as Gabriel grabbed hold of his balls and twisted. Montagu and Rosamund's father winced but did not intervene.

"You, Mr Price," Gabriel growled, his voice low and menacing. "*You* ought not to have. *You* are supposed to be a gentleman, not a low life rat who goes about preying on innocent girls. That young lady is going to have to pay a high price for her mistake, because the poor creature is going to have to consider the prospect of marrying you! But you are going to offer for her, Mr Price."

"No!" Price squeaked, his voice several octaves higher than usual. "I c-can't! M-Mother will kill me if I don't marry money."

"Then I foresee a great deal of pain in your future, Mr Price, but I can promise you it will be worse if you do not!" Gabriel twisted a bit harder, and the man shrieked in alarm.

"Fine, fine, I'll talk to her… I will," Price said, his eyes watering, gasping and clutching at Gabriel's arm. "Please!"

With obvious reluctance, Gabriel let him go, but before he could say another word, Price kicked him in the shin and ran.

Mr Knight uttered a profanity Rosamund had never heard before—which, considering she had brothers, she found rather impressive—and set off in pursuit.

Montagu sighed. "That was quite obviously too easy. He ought to have kept hold of his balls until he passed out. Always best to err on the side of caution in my experience."

Rosamund glanced at her father, who nodded his agreement with this statement. She turned to stare at her husband.

Sebastian shrugged. "Yes. They're terrifying," he agreed. "So, I'm promising you right now I'll be the model husband. I had no intention of ever putting a foot wrong, but I swear I never will. Please don't set them on me."

Despite everything, Rosamund smiled. "Idiot," she muttered fondly, before hurrying after them.

They made their way back into the ballroom, searching for Mr Price, who had gone to ground like the snake he was.

"Have you seen Humphrey Price?" Mr Knight demanded of Lord Bainbridge, interrupting his conversation with Gabriel's son, Felix Knight, and Rosamund's brother, Jules.

"No. Don't wish to, either," Bainbridge said, blunt as ever. "Man's a prat. Why d'you want him?"

"Unfinished business," Gabriel muttered darkly.

Bainbridge perked up at once. "Oh, a mill, is it? Need a hand?"

Gabriel shrugged. "If you can find him, certainly."

Bainbridge, being one of the tallest men in the room, scanned the ballroom. "Follow me," he commanded, waving them on as he strode through the gathering, scattering lesser beings as he went.

They were halfway across the ballroom when Mr Price caught sight of them and gave a little shriek. He turned to run, only to find Miss Morcombe standing in his way. She slapped him, hard.

Gasps and exclamations followed as the gossip mill blazed to life at once, the promise of another scandal carrying through the room like a spark chasing gunpowder.

"Get out of my way, you little slut. Haven't you done enough?"

Price pushed her aside savagely. Miss Morcombe stumbled, and Sebastian lunged forward, grabbing hold of her before she could fall.

"You swine," he growled at Price, and Rosamund's breath caught as she saw the fury in his eyes.

"What? You going to murder me now?" Mr Price shouted back, sneering at Sebastian. "Or is it only helpless women you terrorise?"

The room was deadly quiet. The only sound Rosamund could hear was the thudding of her own heart. *No, oh no,* repeated a panicked voice in her head as she struggled to think of something to do or say to stop this awful moment.

"I never laid a hand on my wife," Sebastian said, advancing on Mr Price with such a look in his eyes all the hairs on the back of Rosamund's neck stood on end.

"Murderer!" Mr Price shouted, pointing at him. "He's a murderer!"

Voices murmured among the crowd, some vehemently against Mr Price, but others… others agreeing, shouts of *shame*, and *villain* echoing through the room.

Rosamund felt sick. She turned to Miss Morcombe, knowing she was their only hope.

"Hannah," she said, pleading in her eyes. "Hannah, I think you know Lord Hargreaves is innocent. If… If there is anything you can say to help him…."

Rosamund's voice broke. Hannah stared at her, fear in her eyes, her skin so white the veins shone blue at her throat. Tears rolled down her cheeks, her breath coming in short little gasps, and Rosamund knew it was hopeless. She turned back to go to

Sebastian, to stand beside him so he was not alone amid this awful scene, but Hannah's voice cut through the melee.

"He's no murderer!"

Everyone turned to stare at her, this fragile young girl, trembling with terror as the eyes of the *ton* turned towards her.

"He's no murderer," she said again, putting up her chin. "Nor an adulterer. He never had an affair with Lady Rosamund. Lady Hargreaves—Adelia Hargreaves—ruined her on purpose."

"Shut your mouth, you little bitch!" Mr Price shouted, advancing on her. "Don't you dare speak her name, you weren't fit to kiss her feet, you cheap who—"

He did not finish the sentence as Sebastian hit him, knocking him onto his backside so that he sprawled on the floor, clutching at his bloody nose.

"I'd stay there, if I were you," Montagu drawled, looking down at Mr Price with distaste. "The lady is speaking and does not wish to be interrupted. Please carry on, Miss Morcombe."

Miss Morcombe nodded, two spots of colour burning high on her cheeks. "Lady Hargreaves set the whole thing up. She got Mr Price to gossip about some poor girl who was alone with the Marquess of Kilbane in the library. Mr Price whispered this nonsense in front of Lord Hargreaves. She knew he was too decent to let any woman face ruin in such a way, and so he walked into a trap. Mr Price had told her Lady Rosamund was there alone, and it was the work of moments to get Lord Hargreaves there too. Then she told everyone there was a scandal about to reveal itself, and ran to watch the scene unfold."

"That's a filthy—"

Mr Price let out a squawk of indignation as Bainbridge hauled him up by his mangled cravat.

"Shut it, or I'll make it permanent," he said, before dropping him again. Mr Price subsided in a heap on the floor and Bainbridge wiped his hands with a show of revulsion. "Apologies, Miss Morcombe. He's rather an arse, isn't he?"

"Yes," she said, a faint smile at her lips. "I wish I'd seen that sooner, my lord. Sadly, I did not. I believed his promises of love and marriage and now… and now…."

Her voice quavered and more tears streamed down her face.

"Oh, my dear," Rosamund said, her heart breaking. She ran to Miss Morcombe and put an arm about her. "You're very brave," she said, feeling the way the poor woman was trembling, but Rosamund's words seemed to give her courage.

"I'm carrying his child."

The whispers and exclamations reached a fever pitch, and two young ladies fainted, much to Rosamund's disgust.

"I believe he did care for me, at first, until Lady Hargreaves got her claws into him," Miss Morcombe said, fighting for control. "But she dazzled him until he convinced himself he was in love with her. She never cared for him, any fool could see that, but Humphrey believed he had a chance with her, the numbskull. I thought… I thought if I could only speak to her in private, if I could explain my situation, perhaps she… she might take pity on me. She might…."

"Oh, no," Sebastian whispered, as Hannah began to shake uncontrollably.

Rosamund held onto her, trying to lend her strength, and suddenly Mama and Matilda were there too.

"It's all right, my dear," Mama said, gently, taking her hands. "We're here. We'll take care of you. Just tell us what happened."

Hannah looked up, staring at Rosamund's mama, who was smiling kindly at her, and at Lady Matilda's soft blue eyes, so full of compassion.

"I knew Lady Hargreaves' lady's maid," Hannah said, speaking quickly now, as if she could not wait to unburden herself. "She's walking out with our butler. No one is supposed to know, but I caught them together and I went to her that night. I told her I'd tell everyone about their affair if she didn't let me in to speak to Lady Hargreaves."

"So you went to speak to Lady Hargreaves the night she died?" Mama asked her.

Hannah nodded. "I told her about the baby, about Humphrey. I begged her to stop playing with him, for she didn't really want him. She was just toying with him."

"That's not true!" Humphrey Price exclaimed, his face twisted with hatred. "She loved me! Adelia loved me best. She told me so. We were going to run away together, she promised me. We would have been happy if *he*... if he hadn't killed her!"

He pointed at Sebastian, his eyes glittering with malice.

"You fool!" Hannah said, her words hard and contemptuous as she stared at the man she had once loved. "She didn't give a snap of her fingers for you, and Lord Hargreaves didn't kill her. I did."

The silence was so absolute, Rosamund felt it ringing in her ears.

"Hannah?" she whispered, hardly able to believe she'd heard correctly.

Hannah's face crumpled. "I didn't mean to," she said, sobbing hard now. "I swear I didn't, but the things she said to me. She called me names, told me I w-was a s-slut and a whore, and that I'd better get used to it b-because that's all that was left to me. I was so angry and upset with her and I... I pushed her. Not hard, I swear, b-but she stumbled, tripped on her skirts and then... and then she was falling. I reached for her. I tried to stop her falling, I swear I did, but... it was too late."

"Oh, Hannah. Oh, my dear," Rosamund said, stunned and too shocked to know what else to say.

Hannah breathed in ragged little gasps, staring at Rosamund and clutching at her arms so hard there would be bruises tomorrow. "I bribed her maid to keep quiet, but she's been blackmailing me since, and I've used all my pin money and given her all my jewellery and now… I've nothing left. I've nothing left. I've nothing left," Hannah moaned, sounding dazed. She swayed and Rosamund held tighter, keeping her upright.

"You bitch! You killed her! You killed Adelia, and I *loved* her!" Mr Price raged, scrambling to his feet and lunging at Hannah.

Sebastian intervened, pushing him away before he could get close. Mr Price ricocheted backwards, stumbling into two men who shoved him roughly aside. Wild with fury, he lashed out, catching one of them on the chin. Suddenly, the two of them were exchanging blows and the atmosphere in the room, already combustible, became charged with the threat of greater violence. They crashed into another man, who spilled his drink on his neighbour's wife. The woman screamed and her husband cursed the idiot for his clumsiness. Before Rosamund could blink, the two of them were at each other's throats.

"Oh, dear," Mama said with a sigh. "It only needed that. Come along, we need to get Miss Morcombe out of here."

Rosamund looked around to see the fight was escalating as men tried to intervene and stop the melee, only to get dragged into it. Rosamund saw someone jostle Arabella, almost sending her flying. Bainbridge's face darkened with rage.

"Yes, I think perhaps we ought to leave at once," she said, trying to get Hannah moving, but the girl was on the verge of fainting.

As Sebastian hurried towards them, Rosamund caught sight of a dark shadow from the corner of her eye. She turned and found

Mr Price reaching for Hannah, his face twisted with anger. Rosamund could see no option but to let go of her. She made a fist, just as her brother had taught her many years ago and swung it hard. The contact with Mr Price's already bloody nose made her catch her breath as pain radiated up her arm, but his head snapped back and he staggered, which was so thoroughly satisfying that Rosamund didn't care about the pain one bit.

"You bastard!"

She jumped in surprise as Sebastian tackled Mr Price, taking him to the ground with a thud. Sebastian looked like he might have come to the end of his patience and was strongly in favour of doing Mr Price an injury.

"All right, young man, that will do," her papa said, hauling Sebastian off him. "I think he's had enough."

Indeed, Mr Price lay in a heap on the floor, moaning and clutching at his nose. Rosamund turned in horror to look for Hannah, to find she had passed out and Lord Montagu had lifted her into his arms.

"Oh, Lucian, the poor child," Matilda cried, her eyes filled with tears.

"There, there, my love. We'll see her safe, don't worry," Montagu said softly. "But let us get out of here before there's a riot."

Matilda gazed adoringly at her husband, but nodded, following him out.

"Come along, Bella," Bainbridge boomed as he guided his wife out of the ballroom, guarding her from the jostling crowd by baring his teeth at anyone who got close. "Damned place is not safe for civilised people. I tried to knock some sense into them," he added, shaking his head.

"Yes, darling," Bella said ruefully, hurrying beside him. "I saw."

"Well, it's not my fault they didn't listen," he protested, putting a protective arm around her. "I told them I'd knock their heads together if they didn't stop. I *did* warn them."

"Yes, dear," his wife said with a sigh. "I know you did."

"Rosamund?"

Rosamund turned to see Sebastian in front of her. His usually immaculate clothes were dusty and rumpled, and his hair was a mess, and Rosamund thought he had never looked more handsome.

"Oh, Sebastian!" she cried, and flung herself at him.

Sebastian held her tight for a moment before swinging her up into his arms.

"Oh!" Rosamund exclaimed. "There's no need to carry me, I can walk."

He shook his head, staring down at her. "I want to know you're safe, and besides, it's nice to play the hero for once, even if it's a minor role."

"Not to me, it isn't," she said, putting her arms around his neck. "Oh, Sebastian, it's over. Everyone heard her say it. They know we were not having an affair, and no one can accuse you now, your reputation will be restored."

"Well, I married you with rather scandalous haste," he said, grinning at her. "So, I think I'm probably still a *bit* villainous."

Rosamund laughed and shook her head.

"No," she said, patting his cheek. "I'm very sorry, my darling, but you were never cut out for the role of villain. You have always been and shall always be my hero."

"Ah, well," he said with a shrug. "I suppose if I must, I must."

He laughed, and Rosamund pressed a kiss to his mouth, not caring who saw.

"Lady Rosamund!"

They both looked around and saw the Comte de Villen hurrying towards them, his beautiful face taut with concern. "Have you seen Miss Knight?"

"Evie?" Rosamund said, shaking her head. "No, not for a while."

"When?" the comte demanded, and Rosamund felt a tremor of anxiety as she heard the urgency in his voice. "When did you see her last?"

"Not since you sent her that glass of champagne," Rosamund said.

"Champagne?" he repeated in confusion, and then paled. "Excuse me."

He turned and disappeared, pushing into the crowd.

"Do you think she's all right?" Rosamund asked with concern.

"I expect so, just caught up in the chaos. Besides, Mr Knight is no doubt rounding his family up as we speak, and Villen won't stop until he finds her, that much is obvious."

Rosamund frowned at him. "What do you mean?"

Sebastian laughed, shaking his head. "I mean, he'll ensure she's safe because the poor devil is mad for her. Knight will have his balls in a vice next, though, if he finds him near his daughter."

Rosamund stared at him in shock. "You know?" she whispered.

Hargreaves rolled his eyes. "I'm not blind, love. I've seen the way he looks at her." He smiled and tightened his grip on her, holding her close. "And I know what a man in love looks like now."

Rosamund sighed.

Epilogue

Elton,

Leave everything and get out. You know where to go.

—Excerpt of a letter from Louis César de Montluc, Comte de Villen to his valet, Mr Elton Carter.

The early hours of the morning 18ᵗʰ July 1842, Brown's Hotel, 33 Albemarle Street, London.

Sebastian closed the door to their hotel room and leaned against it for a moment.

"Well," he said. "That was another eventful evening."

Rosamund gave a huff of laughter. "You could say that. My word, poor Mrs Belvedere. It sounded like there was a riot going on as we left."

Sebastian shrugged. "Oh, I don't know. She'll be able to dine out on everything that happened tonight for years. If I know anything about society hostesses, they want their parties to be memorable. I suspect she'll consider a bit of wear and tear worth it."

"Memorable," Rosamund repeated, shaking her head. "Well, it was certainly that. Oh, but poor Miss Morcombe. She'll certainly never be able to show her face in society again, but do you think she'll go to prison?"

"No, love. It won't come to that. Montagu and your father agreed she had suffered enough. They'll intervene to stop it from going to court. It was obviously an accident and, as sorry as I am for what happened to Adelia, her cruelty was what killed her in the end. Montagu promised he would settle Miss Morcombe somewhere she could live safely and happily with her baby. He's a man of his word, you know that."

Rosamund nodded. "Papa promised his help too, so I know she'll be safe, but I'm so sad for her. And I know she will carry the guilt about what happened to Adelia for the rest of her days."

Sebastian moved closer, pulling her into his arms. "That is certainly punishment enough without having her child born in prison. She has been ill used, and she made some bad choices, but she is not alone in that. I'm glad she has a chance to start over and do better this time. There aren't many of us who get a second chance, but for my part, I know I am blessed indeed."

"You have nothing to make amends for," Rosamund said firmly. She smoothed her hands over his chest, still surprised that she could do that now, that it was her right. "I am so glad I married you."

Sebastian put his hand beneath her chin, tilting her face up to his. "Are you certain? Now our reputations have been restored, don't you wish you had waited? Perhaps—"

Rosamund stood on tiptoe and pressed her mouth to his, kissing him hard, grasping the back of his neck to keep him in place as she pressed her body against his. She did not wish for him to have the slightest doubt that she regretted her decision, that she might not want him. Her fingers sought the buttons on his waistcoat, undoing them as quickly as she could before tugging his shirt free of his trousers. Her hands slid underneath, coasting over his bare skin as his breath hitched. He deepened the kiss, tugging at her hips until she could feel the shape of his aroused flesh, hard against her. Desire surged through her, making her bold enough to take what she wanted.

Sliding her hand between them, she caressed his rigid length, delighted by the moan that escaped him. She searched for the buttons to release him from the confines of his trousers as he broke the kiss to stare at her with surprise. Rosamund flashed him a smile before pushing his trousers down his hips, her own breath coming faster as his cock sprang free, demanding her attention.

"You don't ha—" he began, and then clamped his mouth shut as Rosamund knelt before him and nuzzled into the thatch of hair at his groin. She inhaled the purely masculine scent of him, clean linen, soap and male musk.

"You always smell good enough to eat," she murmured, only realising how he might interpret her words as he let out a strangled sound and closed his eyes, his hands clenched into fists at his sides.

Biting back a giggle, she returned her attention to his arousal and pressed her mouth to the hot, silken skin. He jolted under her lips, which she took to be a good sign and so carried on, pressing kisses down the hard length of him. Emboldened by the way his breathing sped up, she licked her way back up again. Sebastian shivered.

"Take it in your mouth," he pleaded, staring down at her, his eyes dark with desire.

She obeyed willingly, wanting to please him, to learn how to bring him as much pleasure as he had given her since they'd married. Carefully, she slid her mouth down over him as far as she could and back up again.

"Like that?" she asked.

"Don't stop, don't stop, don't stop," he commanded through gritted teeth.

Apparently, that worked, she thought happily, repeating the move over and over until he'd tangled his hands in her hair, holding on to her, guiding her as he gasped, his hips rocking as she worked him with her mouth.

"Stop! Stop now," he begged, and pulled her to her feet.

Before she could ask why, his mouth was on hers, hard and demanding. He lifted her, carried her through to the bedroom and deposited her none too gently on the bed. With no preamble, he tossed up her skirts, his fingers sliding between her thighs.

Rosamund squirmed under his skilful caresses, already hot and ready for him, wanting him.

"Please, Sebastian. I need you. *Now,*" she demanded, pulling him closer.

He tugged her hips to the edge of the bed and thrust into her, joining them in one smooth movement that had Rosamund throwing her head back, eyes closed as the pleasure of it made her cry out.

Sebastian braced himself on his arms over her and she wrapped her legs about his hips, holding on whilst he thrust harder, faster, until she trembled beneath him, clutching at his coat she shattered with a harsh cry.

"Rosamund," he rasped, succumbing to the same fate with a shout that tore through him as he spent, over and over, flooding her with all he had, his love and his joy and the very essence of him.

They came back to themselves, still dressed but clothes awry, staring at each other in shock as they tried to steady their breathing.

"Rosamund," Sebastian said unsteadily, frowning as he stared down at her. "I'm so sorry, I... I ought not to have...."

"What on earth are you sorry for?" she demanded, before he could say anymore.

Emma V Leech

"I didn't even undress you!" he exclaimed. "I mean to be tender with you, romantic, not… not…."

"Not exciting and demanding and perfectly wonderful?" she asked, tilting her head to regard him curiously.

His eyebrows went up. "You didn't mind?"

She snorted, a little incredulous. "Did it sound like I minded?"

"No," he admitted, his lips quirking into a pleased smile. "Actually, it didn't."

"Well, then." She tugged at his coat and he moved, collapsing beside her on the bed as she snuggled against him.

"You wanted me," he said in wonder, reaching out and tracing the shape of her mouth. "I have never been wanted like that before, like—"

"Like I needed to rip your clothes off?" Rosamund cut in ruefully. She blushed, avoiding his gaze, suddenly a little anxious. "I suppose it wasn't very ladylike."

She gasped as Sebastian pushed her back onto the bed, moving over her again, settling back between her thighs. "You were splendid, and you were honest, and you wanted me. I am the luckiest man alive and, if you ever want to rip my clothes off again, just so you know, I'm all for it."

Rosamund grinned, sliding her arms around his neck. "That is good to know," she murmured and then gasped as he slid his burgeoning arousal against her sex, making the sensitive skin throb in response.

"Again?" she asked in surprise.

"I want you," he said, his voice low as he ducked his head and nipped at her ear. "And I may not be a villain after all, but I do know a thing or two about sinful behaviour."

"Show me," she demanded, pulling him down into a passionate kiss.

And so he did.

Next in the Daring Daughter series...

To Dare the Darkness
Daring Daughters, Book 13

Turn the page and keep reading for a scintillating teaser of Louis and Evie's book.

18th July 1842, La Forteresse du Loup Noir. 5th Arrondissement, Paris.

Wulfric De Vere, known as Wolf to his few—very few—friends, or *le loup noir* to those who feared him, poured two drinks. He handed one to Jacques Toussaint, the manager of Paris' most exclusive, and most notorious club, Rouge et Noir.

"Vous êtes certain? You're sure he'll come?" Jacques asked, frowning down into his glass.

Wolf shrugged. *"Non,* but I would. If you must battle an enemy, better to do it on familiar territory, and where you have men enough to fight an army.

"I don't think he needs an army, if what you've said is true. It's just one man, *n'est-ce pas?"* Jacques said with a shrug, waving Wolf's concern away as him being overprotective as usual. "Louis can look after himself, we know that. He's done it often enough."

Wolf sighed, and sat down, the chair giving an ominous creak as it accustomed itself to his massive frame. He stretched out his legs, glowering into the fire which was blazing even though it was the middle of July. Paris might enjoy the warm night outside the vast stone walls, a bit too warm if you were in proximity to the fetid drains and the less salubrious parts of the city. Here in the depths of the fortress, however, there was no sun, no warmth, and a fire blazed all year round. This was the place Louis had created as a haven in case of trouble, the first property he had ever bought for himself. It had been a wreck then, but he'd seen the potential, a defensive position with secret tunnels in and out, but only one obvious entrance, and that impenetrable. It had been Wolf's haven, too. The first place he had ever felt safe. It was his now, a gift from Louis, and the storerooms were full to bursting with booze and silks and spices and caviar and all the most expensive things the rich of Paris were clamouring for. If you wanted something decadent, something exclusive, something forbidden, you came to

Wolf—providing you were prepared to pay the price for it. Though if you wanted someone disappeared, or dead, you'd come to him for that too.

Wolf ruled this city, or at least, the bits polite society and polite people pretended were not there in daylight hours.

"But it's not that simple," he said in reply to Jacques words. "Not just one man. He's a ghost, one of the demons that haunts Louis' dreams. He'll come, and the devil will follow him," Wolf said, certain of that much.

Louis would want Wolf at his back if that evil bastard was truly not dead. Though how? How was it possible? The place had been an inferno and Etienne had been in it. Christ, Wolf had only just got Louis out in time, and half dead even then. Jacques was right, though. Louis didn't need an army. Most of the battle was in his head, tangled up with his past so tight it left the poor bastard in knots. The trouble was, Etienne knew how to pull all the strings to cause maximum pain, and he did not think Louis could stand that again.

If Etienne lived, he would follow Louis to the ends of the earth, for Louis was his obsession and making Louis suffer his favourite sick delight. So, if Louis came here, so would Etienne, and Wolf would not leave the dirty work to Louis as he had so many years ago. He owed Louis for so much—for his life, and this, at last, would be a way of making things right.

He would kill Etienne Boucher once and for all, and this time, he'd make sure the miserable bastard stayed dead.

Pre-Order your copy here: To Dare the Darkness

The Peculiar Ladies who started it all…

Girls Who Dare – The exciting series from Emma V Leech, the multi-award-winning, Amazon Top 10 romance writer behind the Rogues & Gentlemen series.

Inside every wallflower is the beating heart of a lioness, a passionate individual willing to risk all for their dream, if only they can find the courage to begin. When these overlooked girls make a pact to change their lives, anything can happen.

Twelve girls – Twelve dares in a hat. Twelves stories of passion. Who will dare to risk it all?

To Dare a Duke

Girls Who Dare Book 1

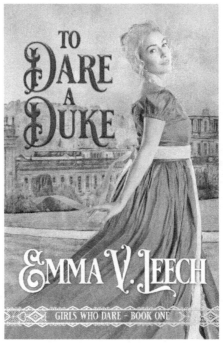

Dreams of true love and happy ever afters

Dreams of love are all well and good, but all Prunella Chuffington-Smythe wants is to publish her novel. Marriage at the price of her independence is something she will not consider. Having tasted success writing under a false name in The Lady's Weekly Review, her alter ego is attaining notoriety and fame and Prue rather likes it.

A Duty that must be endured

Robert Adolphus, The Duke of Bedwin, is in no hurry to marry, he's done it once and repeating that disaster is the last thing he desires. Yet, an heir is a necessary evil for a duke and one he cannot shirk. A dark reputation precedes him though, his first wife may have died young, but the scandals the beautiful, vivacious and spiteful creature supplied the ton have not. A wife must be found. A wife who is neither beautiful or vivacious but sweet and dull, and certain to stay out of trouble.

Dared to do something drastic

The sudden interest of a certain dastardly duke is as bewildering as it is unwelcome. She'll not throw her ambitions aside to marry a scoundrel just as her plans for self-sufficiency and freedom are coming to fruition. Surely showing the man she's not actually the meek little wallflower he is looking for should be enough to put paid to his intentions? When Prue is dared by her friends to do something drastic, it seems the perfect opportunity to kill two birds.

However, Prue cannot help being intrigued by the rogue who has inspired so many of her romances. Ordinarily, he plays the part of handsome rake, set on destroying her plucky heroine. But is he really the villain of the piece this time, or could he be the hero?

Finding out will be dangerous, but it just might inspire her greatest story yet.

To Dare a Duke

Also check out Emma's regency romance series, Rogues & Gentlemen. Available now!

The Rogue
Rogues & Gentlemen Book 1

The notorious Rogue that began it all.

Set in Cornwall, 1815. Wild, untamed and isolated.

Lawlessness is the order of the day and smuggling is rife.

Henrietta always felt most at home in the wilds of the outdoors but even she had no idea how the mysterious and untamed would sweep her away in a moment.

Bewitched by his wicked blue eyes

Henrietta Morton knows to look the other way when the free trading 'gentlemen' are at work.
Yet when a notorious pirate bursts into her local village shop, she

can avert her eyes no more. Bewitched by his wicked blue eyes, a moment of insanity follows as Henrietta hides the handsome fugitive from the Militia.

Her reward is a kiss, lingering and unforgettable.

In his haste to flee, the handsome pirate drops a letter, a letter that lays bare a tale of betrayal. When Henrietta's father gives her hand in marriage to a wealthy and villainous nobleman in return for the payment of his debts, she becomes desperate.

Blackmailing a pirate may be her only hope for freedom.

**** **Warning**: This book contains the most notorious rogue of all of Cornwall and, on occasion, is highly likely to include some mild sweating or descriptive sex scenes. ****

Free to read on *Kindle Unlimited*: The Rogue

Interested in a Regency Romance with a twist?

A Dog in a Doublet
The Regency Romance Mysteries Book 2

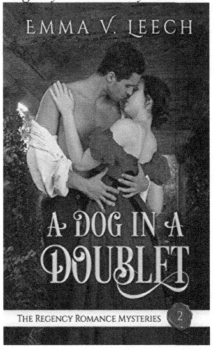

A man with a past

Harry Browning was a motherless guttersnipe, and the morning he came across the elderly Alexander Preston, The Viscount Stamford, clinging to a sheer rock face he did not believe in fate. But the fates have plans for Harry whether he believes or not, and he's not entirely sure he likes them.

As a reward for his bravery, and in an unusual moment of charity, miserly Lord Stamford takes him on. He is taught to read, to manage the vast and crumbling estate, and to behave like a gentleman, but Harry knows that is something he will never truly be.

Already running from a dark past, his future is becoming increasingly complex as he finds himself caught in a tangled web of jealousy and revenge.

A feisty young maiden

Temptation, in the form of the lovely Miss Clarinda Bow, is a constant threat to his peace of mind, enticing him to be something he isn't. But when the old man dies, his will makes a surprising demand, and the fates might just give Harry the chance to have everything he ever desired, including Clara, if only he dares.

And as those close to the Preston family begin to die, Harry may not have any choice

A Dog in a Doublet

Lose yourself in Emma's paranormal world with The French Vampire Legend series.....

The Key to Erebus
The French Vampire Legend Book 1

The truth can kill you.

Taken away as a small child, from a life where vampires, the Fae, and other mythical creatures are real and treacherous, the beautiful young witch, Jéhenne Corbeaux is totally unprepared when she returns to rural France to live with her eccentric Grandmother.

Thrown headlong into a world she knows nothing about she seeks to learn the truth about herself, uncovering secrets more shocking than anything she could ever have imagined and finding that she is by no means powerless to protect the ones she loves.

Despite her Gran's dire warnings, she is inexorably drawn to the dark and terrifying figure of Corvus, an ancient vampire and master of the vast Albinus family.

Jéhenne is about to find her answers and discover that, not only is Corvus far more dangerous than she could ever imagine, but that he holds much more than the key to her heart …

Now available at your favourite retailer

The Key to Erebus

Check out Emma's exciting fantasy series with hailed by Kirkus Reviews as "An enchanting fantasy with a likable heroine, romantic intrigue, and clever narrative flourishes."

The Dark Prince
The French Fae Legend Book 1

Two Fae Princes
One Human Woman
And a world ready to tear them all apart

Laen Braed is Prince of the Dark fae, with a temper and reputation to match his black eyes, and a heart that despises the human race. When he is sent back through the forbidden gates between realms to retrieve an ancient fae artifact, he returns home with far more than he bargained for.

Corin Albrecht, the most powerful Elven Prince ever born. His golden eyes are rumoured to be a gift from the gods, and destiny is calling him. With a love for the human world that runs deep, his friendship with Laen is being torn apart by his prejudices.

Océane DeBeauvoir is an artist and bookbinder who has always relied on her lively imagination to get her through an unhappy and uneventful life. A jewelled dagger put on display at a nearby museum hits the headlines with speculation of another race, the Fae. But the discovery also inspires Océane to create an extraordinary piece of art that cannot be confined to the pages of a book.

With two powerful men vying for her attention and their friendship stretched to the breaking point, the only question that remains...who is truly The Dark Prince.

The man of your dreams is coming...or is it your nightmares he visits? Find out in Book One of The French Fae Legend.

Available now to read at your favorite retailer

The Dark Prince

Want more Emma?

If you enjoyed this book, please support this indie author and take a moment to leave a few words in a review. *Thank you!*

To be kept informed of special offers and free deals (which I do regularly) follow me on *https://www.bookbub.com/authors/emma-v-leech*

To find out more and to get news and sneak peeks of the first chapter of upcoming works, go to my website and sign up for the newsletter.
http://www.emmavleech.com/

Come and join the fans in my Facebook group for news, info and exciting discussion...

Emma's Book Club

Or Follow me here...

http://viewauthor.at/EmmaVLeechAmazon
Facebook
Instagram
Emma's Twitter page
TikTok

Can't get your fill of Historical Romance? Do you crave stories with passion and red hot chemistry?

If the answer is yes, have I got the group for you!

Come join myself and other awesome authors in our Facebook group

Historical Harlots

Be the first to know about exclusive giveaways, chat with amazing HistRom authors, lots of raunchy shenanigans and more!

Historical Harlots Facebook Group

Made in United States
North Haven, CT
11 February 2023

32422210R00178